CW01621383

The Duke's Perfect Match

By

MJ Walker

Copyright © 2025 All rights reserved

Chapter 1

Alice Weatherby lay outstretched on the sofa in the drawing room of Longhall House, dressed in a plain cotton dress. She stared out through the window, listening to the grandfather clock go *tock-tock-tock* in the corner. Rain pattered against the window. Her older sister, Lucinda, sat with her embroidery, humming a soft tune.

"What a dreary day," Alice mumbled.

"I wouldn't say that," Lucinda answered. "There are plenty of things you can do to brighten your day. Like—"

"Paint? Or play the pianoforte? I can't paint to save my life, and my playing is horrid."

"That's what practice is for. You haven't done enough of it. How do you expect to catch the interest of a gentleman if you're not adequately accomplished and don't have at least a modicum of education?"

Oh, this again…

"When I first met Mr Evans," Lucinda continued, "I was no more special to him than any other woman seeking his attention. But as our acquaintance deepened into friendship, he saw what a future with me would be like and realised we were a good match."

I'm glad for you, sister, even if the man is an utter bore.

Alice sprang to her feet, the sudden movement earning her a suspicious glance from Lucinda. She walked around the table to Lucinda's sofa, running her fingers over the backrest.

"I'm not saying I have more to offer than anyone else, but surely it can't be so bleak that we are all the same in the eyes of men? That we can only set ourselves apart by our abilities at the piano or with a brush?"

"Have you been reading poetry again?" Lucinda asked as Alice placed her hands on her shoulders, leaning her head against hers.

"Maybe I have, sweet sister. It makes the grey of the day a bit lighter. I'm talking about love. Surely there must be a place for it in our time as well?"

"Nonsense," Lucinda said, shrugging Alice away. "What you're talking about isn't love but attraction. You cannot build a future on attraction alone. Attraction will fade, and what use will that pretty face of yours be then? There must be something more to fall back on, like a shared outlook on life."

"If you say so, sister."

Alice walked over to the window. She could feel the chill through the glass, the rain warping the misty world outside.

"What news is there about Mr Evans's rectory?" Alice asked.

"There are still some minor details to sort before the rectory will go to Mr Evans."

"How nice," Alice said, barely containing a sigh. "Then we can enjoy his sermons every Sunday to come."

"That we can. Speaking of which, we're having Mr Evans over for dinner, and it wouldn't hurt you to open the good book and read a passage or two."

"Or what? Is he going to catechise me again?"

"He might," Lucinda answered with a shrug.

"Maybe I should catechise him in Lord Byron's works, or those of Shakespeare? He might be surprised to find he still has some blood left in his body," Alice muttered.

"Hmm?" Lucinda said, looking up from her embroidery.

"Nothing, sister."

"And another thing, Mr Evans is bringing his younger brother, Ben." Lucinda looked at Alice over her handiwork, as if to say: *You'd better dress up and behave your best.*

Another Mr Evans? As if one wasn't bad enough.

"Twice the fun, then," Alice said. "I'm going out."

"Out? It's pouring outside."

"Nothing more than a drizzle."

As she walked down the footpath to the pond, she had to admit it was doing a bit more than just drizzle. Rain dripped from the hood of her grey wool cloak, and she knew Perdita would give her that tired look when she returned home with the hem of her dress dirty again. She didn't care. She just couldn't stay in the house with that clock going *tock-tock-tock*, feeling like her world stood still while everywhere else it spun full tilt. The only new thing in her life would be the younger Mr Evans, and she doubted he would spin her world in any positive way. If he was anything like the older Mr Evans, he surely would not. But then again, brothers could be as different as night and day, couldn't they?

The younger Mr Evans wouldn't be the first man of appropriate age and birth her mother seated beside her for dinner. She wasn't spoiled for choice but had found all her potential suitors severely lacking.

There was Mr Greenwood, who had read not the Bible to her but poetry, in a flat, lifeless monotone. Later, she found out that Lucinda had told him Alice liked poetry, and while he didn't, he had at least made the effort to read to her.

Then there was Mr Sanders, a thin reed of a man, who had taken things one step further by writing his own poetry, which, truth be told, was not an improvement—at all.

And, of course, there had been Major Pemberton, who, after sitting with her once, had grasped her hand to his chest, saying he had to relocate with his regiment to Kent, but that his love for her was eternal and—would she wait for him? Well, she couldn't wait for him to leave, but that was about it. She felt bad about that later, when she learned that Major Pemberton had been killed in the Battle of Vimeiro.

She didn't demand a man who would spin her world, really; just a normal, kind man who could appreciate her, even if her playing on the pianoforte was horrid. Surely a man like that had to exist somewhere in Walston or nearby?

The air was crisp and raw, moisture wetting her face. She had no idea why she wanted to go to the pond, except that anywhere seemed better than the drawing room at Longhall House, where her sister complacently stabbed a piece of cloth with her needle while the clock went *tock-tock-tock*.

There was nothing down at the pond, its surface an iron grey. On sunny days, she would sit in the pavilion, watching insects dotting the surface and the carp snapping after them. She could sit there for hours with a book, occasionally looking up at the pond. Today, it was the rain that dotted the surface.

Alice sat down in the pavilion, wrapping her wool cloak tighter. It wasn't just a feeling that her world stood still while the rest of the world did not—it was actually so, because it was April, and in London, the season had started. She missed it the previous year because her father had been all the way down to India and Ceylon on business. She was nineteen now and still a secret to the fine gentlemen of London. She was running the apparent risk of remaining a secret for yet another year because, even though her father was back in England, he had spent much of his time in London.

"Something political," her mother had said. That could mean a million things, but Alice wasn't so naive as to miss the fact that her father was trying for Parliament.

Say the name *Weatherby* in the fine halls of London, and the answer would come back like the echo of an owl: *Who-who-who?*

Her grandfather, knighted as a young man, had squandered the family fortune, leaving her father to inherit nothing but debts and the pain of seeing his lands belonging to more successful men. He was not a knight either, just a plain Mr, like the blacksmith or the fruitmonger in Walston.

Her father, though, possessed the fortitude her grandfather had lacked, and after twenty years of doing business in the colonies, earning his money through trade, he had bought back all of his lost land—and then some.

Some said he had done it by paying well; others whispered that he had been less of a gentleman about it—that he had paid local hoodlums to harass those who refused to sell.

Alice hadn't known about the rumours until, one day many years ago, she overheard two ladies in the butcher's shop saying that Mr Weatherby might be wealthy in land and property but poor in reputation. She had run all the way home that day, tears stinging her eyes.

How did the lords and gentlemen of London view her father? Was he poor in reputation there as well? She thought not, for most probably, he wasn't known at all. If he was known for anything, it was for having money. But a man with money could buy influence in the capital—or so her older brother, George, had told her.

He was in London as well, with Papa. Everyone was in London except her! And Lucinda, of course. And Wilma, who was too young to be genuinely upset about it.

Later that day, at the table in the dining room, Alice sat with her back to the crackling hearth, feeling the heat licking at her and making her cold body shiver. Perdita had collected her wet clothes with a slight shake of her head and carried them off to be washed. Her wet clothes were gone, but the cold in her body remained. Her mother sat at the end of the table with Lucinda and Mr Evans closest to her. She was still a beautiful woman, even if her face was a bit fuller these days and there were strands of grey in her chestnut hair.

For as long as Alice could remember, everyone had told her she looked like her mother. As a young girl, she hadn't been flattered—few young girls were when compared to their mothers—but now she didn't mind the comparison. They had the same chestnut hair and dark eyes, and lips that one of her mother's suitors (and they had been plenty) had said came directly from a play written by Shakespeare himself.

If Mrs Weatherby was all shapes pleasing to the eye, it was like being stabbed in the eye to look at Mr Evans. He was tall and scrawny, with a nose like a bulging sail. He had a pale, yellowish complexion, and a thick mat of brown hair. It wasn't his looks that had drawn her sister to him, Alice presumed, but rather his commanding presence. His dark eyes could have been his one redeeming quality, but they carried a constant stern and judgmental look.

Across the table, his younger brother, Ben Evans, sat. It was true that brothers could sometimes be as different as night and day, but sometimes they were not, and in this case, Alice wasn't sure if that was a good thing or not.

The younger Mr Evans was his own person but aspired to be everything his older brother was. He was a shorter, plumper version, and looked a bit healthier. His eyes tried very hard to carry the same gravitas as his older brothers, but the firmness of character he sought to convey became, at best, a fleeting impression.

Beside him, Wilma sat, leaning her head in the palm of her hand, soft blonde curls spilling over, while chasing a pea around her plate with her fork.

"It's a truth well known that a man is most at peace in his home with a good wife by his side. I have never felt the urge to leave Walston. Everything one could possibly need is right here in our little town," the elder Mr Evans said.

Lucinda nodded with a serious twist to her mouth.

"And as long as I'm close to God, every place is home to me."

Mrs Weatherby clapped her hands together, looking at Mr Evans as though she had never, ever heard such wisdom uttered before.

"Well, isn't that just true, Mr Evans!"

The corners of Mr Evans's mouth tightened as he tried to hide a smile, cutting his steak with his elbows raised.

"I'm of the same opinion," the younger Mr Evans said, dabbing the corner of his mouth with his linen napkin and glancing at Alice. "But even if God is the foundation of my life, I do feel that the love of a good woman is as important as the Lord's grace."

"That's a point hard to dispute," Mrs Weatherby said with a pleasant smile, raising her glass to him.

He raised his glass in return and nodded with the same restrained smile as his brother. Then he turned to Alice.

"And what about you, Miss Weatherby?"

"What about me?"

"What in life makes you happy?"

"I… many things."

"She loves playing the pianoforte," Wilma said with a mischievous smile.

"Is that right? I would love to hear your playing, Miss Weatherby," Ben Evans said.

"Oh, you really would not, I assure you."

"Modesty," Ben Evans said, smacking his lips. "It can be a virtue, as long as it's not of the false kind."

"I assure you again, it is not."

"She's just *maaarvelous*, Mr Evans. There's no greater grace in this house than hearing Alice play. I assure you," Wilma said with a giggle, which earned her a stern look of reproach from Mrs Weatherby. The younger Mr Evans finally saw things for what they were.

"I'm sure your playing is perfectly fine, Miss Weatherby, and I assure you, there's no need to blush for me. I—"

"Oh, please, your worries are misdirected, Mr Evans. I was out walking before dinner. It was cold and windy."

"Walking?" Ben Evans asked, slack-jawed. "But it's pouring outside."

"I told her," Lucinda interjected. "But according to Alice, it's only a drizzle."

"You need to take better care of yourself," Ben Evans said. "You women are fragile things, not meant to be exposed to cold weather and strong winds."

There was a murmur of agreement around the table.

"Please, again, do not worry about me, Mr Evans. I admire your devotion to the Lord, but being strong in spirit isn't enough for a happy life. Both body and soul need to be strong, and my walks help me with the former."

The younger Mr Evans listened with disinterested eyes, scratching his plump cheek.

"And my walks also help me keep that slender profile that men so much prefer, because I suppose even a servant of the Lord isn't immune to what moves other men?"

"Alice!" her mother barked. "That is enough!"

She turned to Ben Evans, shaking her head slightly.

"I'm sorry, Mr Evans. She's a bit headstrong, but in essence, she really is a pleasant girl. I assure you."

"Of course, she is," Alice said and took a sip of wine.

Later, when Alice and Mrs Weatherby watched the Evanses' carriage disappear into the mist, her mother gave a heaving sigh.

"Alice, Alice, Alice. What am I to do with you?"

"What do you mean, Mama?"

"You need to see your situation for what it is. No prince or lord is going to come through the door and sweep you away. We're in Walston. The number of suitable matches available is limited. This was the fifth suitor you've sent from the table. If you keep this up, you'll end up a spinster, living here at your brother's mercy. Is that how you envisioned your future?"

"It is not."

"I'm not saying that Mr Evans is the best match for you, but you need to at least give those seeking your attention a chance."

"But if Papa only allowed me to attend some of the assemblies at Bath, or at least Luton, then it would be quite different."

"It would," Mrs Weatherby agreed. "But you know your father—he always has a plan of some sort brewing. I'm sure he will not let your beauty go to waste."

"But he wouldn't mind me wasting it on Ben Evans?"

"I'm sure he would like you to make the best match possible."

And with that, not much more was said. The same held true for the rest of the evening. After Mrs Weatherby and Wilma had retired for the night, Lucinda and Alice sat in the drawing room with their embroidery, listening to the clock go *tock-tock-tock*.

"It really wasn't a fine thing you did to Mr Evans, embarrassing him like that," Lucinda finally said, pursing her lips. "He's a nice man with good prospects, and he thinks very highly of you."

"I know, and I'm sorry, sister. But he embarrassed me too by assuming I was blushing for him."

"That is…" Lucinda put her embroidery down in her lap. "…a thing only you could say. But for what it's worth, Mr Evans is a man worthy of your blush. If not him, who are you waiting for? What do you expect out of Walston?"

"You're starting to sound like Mama."

"And Lord knows, for good reason."

After that, nothing more was said. They worked in silence, listening to the clock go *tock-tock-tock*.

Then there was the sound of a carriage stopping outside. For a dreadful second, Alice thought it was Ben Evans returning. When she went to the window, she saw that it was not. It was her father's big black carriage. The coachman jumped down, holding a lantern high. Two footmen hurried forth with an umbrella.

"Mama!" Wilma screamed from upstairs. "Papa is coming!"

Alice and Lucinda exchanged a glance. What on earth was this all about? Their father wasn't one to come unannounced, and certainly not at this hour.

There was a rumbling on the stairs as the rest of the family hurried down. Mrs Weatherby went straight to the window.

"What now could this be?" she mumbled with some trepidation.

Their father stepped out of the carriage, his big, cumbersome body somehow moving with a distinct lightness.

The door flung open. Mr Weatherby threw his hat across the room and opened his arms as though he wanted to embrace the whole world.

"It is done, my lovely ladies! I will take a seat in Parliament, and we'll be relocating to London as soon as possible!"

"Oh! Oh! Oh!" Mrs Weatherby squealed, pressing her fingertips to her mouth.

Alice and Wilma looked at each other before bursting into joyous laughter, hugging each other. All the women in the Weatherby family were celebrating—except Lucinda.

Chapter 2

Thomas Overton was out in the stable, brushing his horse, Thunder. He had lived so long in his father's shadow that he hadn't yet gotten used to being the fourth Duke of Hexham. Even after his father's death, Thomas was still living in his shadow. The third Duke of Hexham had died a hero in the Battle of Salamanca, fighting against Napoleon's generals. Thomas's mother—the Dowager Duchess, Anne Overton—had already ordered a bronze statue of him to be erected at Piccadilly Circus or, at the very least, St James's Park.

Never give them a chance to forget our name, Thomas.

When his father was shot through the heart and tumbled off his horse on the plains outside Arapiles, Thomas had been twenty-one. He was twenty-three now, but the two years that had passed hadn't turned him into the duke his father and mother had hoped for. He wasn't even married and had no plans to be anytime soon.

He brushed the horse with long, firm strokes. Thunder flared his nostrils and breathed out in a lip-flopping sigh. Thomas had been out riding the whole morning, and Thunder's legs and abdomen were spattered with mud. The stable boy was perfectly capable of brushing Thunder clean, but Thomas preferred to do it himself. It helped keep his mind off other things.

He heard footsteps behind him.

"I guessed I would find you in here."

He turned to his mother. She was, as always, regal in appearance, her greying hair arranged in an elaborate coiffure. Her sharp eyes regarded him with disapproval. She wore a coat tailored to emphasise her slender waist. Her presence in the stable was unsettling; whatever had brought her here must have been important enough to warrant venturing into such surroundings.

"I cannot understand why you insist on doing that dirty work yourself."

"I find pleasure in it," Thomas said, turning back to the horse. "Not everything in life must reach the height of refinement. Working with your hands can, in moderation, uplift the spirit."

"Shall I tell you what I would find uplifting?"

He, sighed.

"I am sure you will tell me, regardless of my response."

"That much is true. I am sick and tired of seeing you frolicking about as though life is some grand adventure created solely for your pleasure. As the Duke of Hexham, you have responsibilities and obligations—such as getting our pitiful finances in order. There was glory in your father's war, yes, but he paid dearly for it, and I am not merely speaking of his blood."

"I am working on it, Mother."

"Are you? Our estates in the north are failing, yet you are not there to determine why. When was the last time you sat down with Mr Landon to hear his suggestions for saving this estate—our ancestral home? It is crumbling to pieces while you ride back and forth in the woods for your own amusement."

"And all this time," he said through gritted teeth, "while Father waged war on the Continent, you prided yourself on managing Somerfield's finances. But now it is my fault we are struggling?"

"Oh, please," she said, her tone heavy with disdain. "You know full well I can manage the day-to-day, but it is your responsibility to ensure there is something to actually manage. I cannot cut pieces of a pie that does not exist."

He threw the brush into the bucket, startling Thunder, who sidestepped nervously, the whites of his eyes showing.

"It does not help to lose your temper, my dear. You know I am right. So, what are you going to do about it?"

"It is not easy, Mother. The repairs Mr Landon wants to carry out cost money. The investments he proposes for improving the yield of our fields—they cost money. And it is money we simply do not have. Not until the Crown reimburses us for Father's expenses."

She sighed deeply.

"That is not something we could ever count on. But it is not so complicated, my dear, and it ties neatly into your other important obligation—that of securing the family line. Marry a wealthy girl, and both our problems will be solved."

He nodded and muttered a curse under his breath, stroking Thunder's neck.

"What was that?"

"I will."

"That you will. The season has started. London is swarming with debutantes. Start acting like the duke you are. Hand the reins to the stable boy and head to London at your earliest convenience. They are expecting you."

"Oh, are they?" He turned to his mother. "As a lord, I do as I please. No one but God and the Prince has authority over me."

She stepped closer. Although she was a tall woman, she still had to look up at him.

"I am telling you to go—as your mother. Are you refusing me?"

"Refusing you what?" he replied, his voice sharper than he intended.

"The peace of mind of seeing you settled with a nice girl. The sound of children playing, and my son at ease with himself."

Oh, how he hated this. He much preferred her anger. Disappointment would follow next, and that was the worst of all. She was, in reality, the third part of the holy trinity that had influence over him: God, Prince, and Mother—and not necessarily in that order.

"I know there have been… struggles in your life, but only lesser men let things like that dictate their lives. As a lord, you're *more* and must behave as such. So many are dependent on your actions. Can I count on you doing what needs to be done?"

He thought about the struggles his mother referred to. Immediately, there was a stab in his heart, and the past came rolling back. They didn't talk about Leana anymore. If she was mentioned, it was only in passing, as now, when she was reduced to the *struggle*.

"You can."

"Splendid! You're leaving early tomorrow and will meet the Fairchilds in Hyde Park at noon for a walk with Emma Fairchild."

It had all been settled in advance, then? He should have known.

"The Fairchilds, you say?"

"Yes, Lady Emma is very keen on you, as you might have noticed. And since she is regarded as a great beauty, I can't see why you should oppose to the match."

"And does the fact that Emmet Fairchild is one of the wealthiest men in England increase her beauty in any way?"

"It's an added benefit, I will admit. Now, get going."

The stable boy was summoned, and Thomas walked up to Somerfield Hall with a heavy step. The sun warmed the grass. A soft wind rustled the trees. The sky was blue with only a few strands of high, white cloud. He could appreciate none of it.

To him, Somerfield, with its smooth sandstone façade and twenty-four chimneys, wasn't just a grand house; it was the only place that truly felt like home. Surrounded by fields and rolling hills dotted with dense oak forests, the countryside was a place for living, while London was a place for business. And now, he was going to London purely on business.

He had to play his part to be able to return to Somerfield with his prize: a woman wealthy enough to save his estates and capable of producing an heir to enjoy them.

The next day, he was sitting in his carriage before the sun had risen above Oak Tree Hill. He leaned on his cane, gently swaying as he looked out.

The countryside rolled past.

Soon, he would be swallowed by the hustle and bustle of London.

Once, he had loved the city—loved the balls, the glitter, and the glamour. But after Leana, he could find no pleasure in it. He had met her for the first time in the village of Lowry, where the Overton's had one of their country houses. His father had still been alive then and would charge enemy lines for another two months before taking that fatal bullet to the heart. Thomas had met the mayor of Lowry, Mr Denham, during one of his walks. The mayor had introduced his wife and daughter, and… Thomas's world had stopped.

Leana Denham was tall and slender, with dark eyes and brown hair arranged with a single pin, allowing one strand to caress her neck.

If only he could remember her as she had been then—the look in her eyes. So much had been said between them in that moment, without a single word spoken. She had been proud—prouder than her common birth allowed. But rather than detract from her, it had enhanced the essence of who she was.

That was how he wanted to remember her: tall, proud, unbroken.

He chased the memories away.

The coachman stopped at an inn outside Royston, and while he ate his lunch on the coach box, Thomas endured a bland soup and a plate of stringy meat inside the inn before they continued south.

The shadows had grown long when he finally arrived at the outskirts of London. Due to the congested streets, it was dark by the time they reached Bleaker House on St James Street, its flickering lights guiding their way. The house, three storeys high, rested behind a wrought-iron gate and a stone wall. The gate stood open, and the carriage rolled into the courtyard.

Mr Morley, the butler of Bleaker House, had lined up the servants and kitchen staff on the cobblestones to greet him. Thomas was ashamed that he didn't know their names, but at least he stopped to thank them for their welcome. A gust of air swept the yard, causing a grey tuft of hair on Mr Morley's head to lift like the wing of a seagull. He quickly flattened it and made a small bow.

"Your Grace, the house is prepared, and a bath has been drawn in your private rooms."

"Excellent, Morley," Thomas said as three footmen began unloading the carriage.

Later, in the brass tub, with his head resting on the swell of the rim, he gazed through the window at the moon visible through the foliage of the back garden. He thought of Lady Emma, the woman his mother had chosen for him, but the thought of her stirred nothing within him. He wished he could feel some excitement for the morrow, but he couldn't. He was an empty well.

If one had experienced true love, how could one ever settle for less?

The memory of Leana returned. She wouldn't leave him alone this evening.

It hadn't taken long for them to find each other, and once they had, they had never wanted to be parted. She had been his first, and he had promised her she would be his last. Those nights they had shared had felt otherworldly. No one could be that happy without attracting the wrath of God—and he had.

Leana had fallen pregnant. She told him on the edge of her bed, her dark hair obscuring her face as she gently wept. He had stroked the hair away, kissed the tears from her cheeks, and told her that a child was not a cause for grief but for joy. Taking her hands in his, he had asked her to marry him.

His mother had balked at the idea, shooting up from the sofa and pacing the room, screaming that her son had lost his mind. Then she had returned, her eyes as hard as steel, and slapped him across the face.

"Forget this nonsense," she hissed. "You will, in time, be the fourth Duke of Hexham, and I will be *damned* if I see you drag our name through the dirt by marrying a little harlot who has turned your head."

"But, Mother—"

"Enough! I have told you several times that a good name is something money can never buy. Generations have built upon ours, and your father continues to build it now by fighting Napoleon. We are merely custodians of this name for future generations, and you, in an act of unrivalled selfishness, want to sabotage that?"

"Even kings have married commoners, and their names have been no worse for it."

"That's because they are *kings*! Don't you understand that beneath the highest step, there is constant strife? You will send us tumbling down the stairs."

She had taken another brisk walk through the room before returning to him.

"I will not allow it. If you act against my will, I'll see to it that your father takes proper action."

"What action?"

"Disownment."

Thomas had laughed in disbelief.

"I'm his only son. His only child."

"He has a cousin in Reading who would love to carry the family name on with dignity as the fourth duke instead of you."

He had given up then. Talking to his mother had been like trying to hold a raging bull on a rope, and he had let the rope go. When she noticed, her voice softened.

"Have you been… intimate with her?"

His silence was answer enough.

"Is she—"

"Yes."

His mother sighed.

"I understand. Tomorrow, you will return to London. I will stay here to sort things out. You will never meet this girl again, and we shall never speak of her."

"Sort it? How?"

"That is not for you to think about. You will leave before luncheon tomorrow."

He still didn't know how his mother had "sorted" Leana, but later he had learned that she had married a miller in Putney. A mayor's daughter marrying a miller? Her fall from grace must have been hard indeed. He had done that to her, wounded her in the most awful of ways. Even though he wasn't worthy of remembering her, he couldn't get her out of his mind.

He didn't sleep well, and when his valet, Mr Gray, withdrew the curtains with a sharp swish, it felt as though he hadn't slept at all.

"What hour is it, Mr Gray?" he mumbled, rubbing his eyes.

"Just past eight, my lord."

Mr Gray was, despite his name, still a relatively young man with black hair combed back from his forehead.

"Wonderful."

He was used to sleeping until at least ten, but it was still his mother's regime that ruled Bleaker House. He lay silently on his back while Mr Gray arranged his clothes for the day.

"The Fairchilds are expecting you at the Round Pond in Hyde Park at noon for a light picnic."

Mr Gray brushed the sleeve of a dark blue tailcoat hanging on a rack. He used a brush that looked like a miniature version of the one Thomas used to groom Thunder.

"I've prepared this newly tailored jacket for the occasion, if it's to your liking?"

"It is, Mr Gray. It looks very smart."

He ate his breakfast alone in the drawing room, reading a newspaper that had been ironed and brought in on a silver plate. War, destruction, and despair dominated the headlines. At least it seemed that Nappy was finally on his heels and that Lord Wellington had gained the upper hand.

Sipping his steaming tea, he glanced down the length of the table toward the fireplace. Above it, a larger-than-life portrait of his great-grandfather loomed, the man's stern gaze fixed on him. Painted in sombre tones, the portrait depicted his ancestor astride a black warhorse, dressed in a vivid red coat. His great-grandfather had spent much of his life at war, ultimately meeting his end overseas while attempting to retake Charleston from the American rebels.

There was something uncomfortably familiar in the condemning look that stared back at him—a resemblance to his father's sharp expression. Unlike his predecessors, his grandfather had not died for Britain and his portrait was relegated to a rarely visited room on the second floor. It was testament to the Overton family's peculiar tendency: their warrior blood skipped every other generation.

Thomas took another sip of tea. Was it now his duty to commission a stern-looking portrait of his father on horseback?

Probably.

That's what any dutiful son would do. But then again, his father could very well settle for the bronze bust his mother had arranged. For a moment, Thomas toyed with the idea of switching the portraits—banishing his stern great-grandfather to the upper floor and inviting the less martial grandfather down to the warmth of the fireplace.

But no. He would be haunted by the ghosts of both his father and great-grandfather, and, worse still, by his very much alive mother, who was far more frightening than the other two combined.

He spent the rest of the morning writing letters. There was a string of balls he was expected to attend, and he needed his friends there to make them bearable. He had no reason to doubt they would attend, but he had to ensure his presence in the city was known. It would be a humiliation to step into a ballroom entirely unannounced.

Mr Morley entered to announce a visitor. Before the butler even spoke the name, Thomas set his pen down with a smile. There was only one friend who would think it appropriate to pay a visit before noon.

"Viscount Merringer, Your Grace," Mr Morley said, pulling open the double doors.

Like the curtain rising in a theatre, the doors revealed John Merringer, a dandy if ever there was one, resting his hands on a walking cane. He was tall, with fair hair combed back from his forehead, blue eyes, and cheeks slightly hollowed, as though he sucked them in, anticipating a clever quip. He tapped his cane once before approaching Thomas with a wolfish grin.

Thomas laughed and spread his arms. They embraced, and then John clasped his shoulders and gave him a light shake.

"Brother! Not a day too soon you show your face in our humble little town once more. London has missed you, but not as much as the ladies, who are growing increasingly despondent over your absence from yet another ball."

"I assume you've kept them occupied in my stead?"

"Quite right, but a viscount doesn't shine quite as brightly as a duke. The curse of the less fortunate, I suppose."

"Must be. How did you know I was back in London?"

"My servants know yours, and apparently, there's been quite the commotion all week preparing the house for your arrival. I told my butler to alert me when your carriage was spotted. And, alas, here I am!"

Thomas reflected briefly on the revelation that the house had been prepared a week in advance, while he himself had only been informed of his departure two days prior. His mother was shrewd, as always.

"Impressive. We should send you to the front to gather intelligence on Nappy—you'd do a marvellous job."

"I'm certain I would, but I have more pressing matters here in London."

"Such as?"

"Balls and amusement, of course. What else?"

"Oh, naturally."

"So, brother, why are you back in town?"

"To walk with Lady Emma Fairchild in Hyde Park."

"Emma Fairchild, you say!"

John clapped his hands together and rubbed them like an eager child.

"A long journey for a short walk, but Emma Fairchild is certainly worth it. Pray, will the Fairchilds bring both their daughters?"

"From what I understand, only Lady Emma. Her elder sister, Beatrice, has already accepted an offer from Seamus Wainwright."

"How unfortunate—for the Fairchilds, I mean. As an earl, I'm sure Emmet had hoped to secure a more advantageous match than Seamus Wainwright, don't you think? Still, their expectations have always rested more heavily on Emma than on Beatrice. A grand prize she is. I wouldn't mind a walk with that kitten myself. But I presume you have intentions with her?"

"You presume wrong, John. My mother has far more intentions than I do."

"Mothers! The scourge of the earth and the saviours of lost sons. My mother wants me to marry as well—marry *properly*—but that has become something of a problem since I've developed a bit of a… reputation."

"Oh, what wicked tongues. Surely it's undeserved?"

"Well, of course it is, dear brother," John said with a laugh. "I'm as well-combed and decent as they come!"

"That is what I've heard as well."

"Then it must be true! I'm the victim of conspiracy and jealousy! No one can look this good and come away completely unscathed."

Mr Morley stopped at the threshold and made a bow that was little more than a tilt of the head.

"The carriage is prepared, Your Grace."

"Very well, Morley. I'll be out shortly."

Thomas turned to John. "I need to go, but we'll speak again soon."

"Amazing," John said after the butler left the room.

"What is?"

"You're actually starting to sound like the duke your father always wished you to be. It's true, then, as they say—no one can escape their destiny."

"Please, I don't feel like talking about my father. He served the kingdom, died a hero with the Union Jack clutched to his chest. This we already know."

"It's a story worth retelling. I'm sure Lady Emma will be eager to hear it on your walk."

"Please, John. I regard you as my brother, but even you have your limits."

"I'm sorry. I humbly retreat towards the door to avoid stepping on Your Grace's sore toes again."

"Oh, please," Thomas said, unable to contain his laughter. "Shall we meet this afternoon?"

"Of course. I'll be at Blacky's. He's hosting a reception tonight and would love it if you came."

"It's settled then."

His carriage crept along St James's Street and came to a halt at Piccadilly. The sun shone down on the rooftops, giving the cream-coloured façades a silky white sheen. Young women strolled the streets in muslin dresses, twirling umbrellas over their shoulders. Gentlemen stopped to tilt their heads and lift their hats. It was an ongoing ritual—the courtship, the charade, the theatre. A constant chase for happiness, money, and influence. Everyone was trapped in the same tedious play.

Passing Green Park and Buckingham Palace, the carriage continued up Kensington Road. Thomas disembarked, instructing the coachman to return to Bleaker House as he planned to walk back.

There were a fair number of people out walking, but from a distance, he could already guess where the Fairchilds were. To them, a picnic clearly meant something quite different from what it did to most others. On the flat expanse surrounding the Round Pond, a linen sunroof stood out. As he drew closer, he saw no fewer than five servants unpacking food from wicker baskets and carefully tightening the ropes of the sunroof. Beneath it, in sturdy fold-out chairs, sat Lord and Lady Carnbury, with Lady Emma on a blanket at their feet.

She looked like a sculpture in her white dress, carefully arranged. Passers-by tilted their heads and lifted their hats in their direction, but none of the Fairchilds paid them any heed. Their attention was entirely focused on Thomas.

He stopped before them, and they rose as one. Emmet Fairchild, the third Earl of Carnbury, gave him a slow nod.

"Your Grace," he said solemnly.

"Lord Carnbury," Thomas replied, returning the nod.

Emma gave him a secretive smile and the same slow nod as her father, echoed by Lady Carnbury.

Lord Carnbury was a thin, razor-sharp man with serious eyes and blue veins at his temples. His wife—a tall, high-strung woman with a half-pursed mouth—had likely once been the most prominent person in every room. Now, she looked positively uneasy before Thomas.

Emma stood as tall as her mother, but with a more confident posture and chin slightly raised. While Lady Carnbury's face had hardened with age, Emma was still a vision of beauty. Her hair was a perfect blonde, her eyes a cold blue, and her figure everything a man might wish for.

"So very good to see you again, Your Grace. I don't believe we've met since your father's passing?" Lord Carnbury said.

"I believe that is true. I would have met with you sooner, but our country estates have taken up much of my time."

"I understand, dear boy. If I may offer a suggestion—as one peer to another, though a somewhat more seasoned one—I propose we dispense with titles. It would make conversation so much more comfortable, wouldn't you agree?"

Thomas, with his hands clasped behind his back, made a slight bow.

"I would very much prefer that, Emmet."

"Capital! Now sit down with us."

He and his wife settled back into their chairs, while Thomas took a seat on the blanket beside Emma. He didn't like sitting at Emmet's feet as though he were the lesser man, but pointing it out would seem petty. He turned his attention to Emma instead.

"It's very nice to see you too, Emma. You were only sixteen the last time we met?"

"A full woman she has become," her mother interjected.

"Mama, please," Emma said before turning back to Thomas. "Yes, I believe I was. You look exactly as I remember you."

"I'm glad to hear that, but you certainly don't. Your mother is right—you've grown from a girl into a woman."

Lady Carnbury made a pleased murmur. The servants served tea and biscuits, and the conversation paused while they worked. When they retreated to the back of the sunroof, Emmet spoke again.

"We did wonder if you would show up this year, Thomas. The season is already in full swing, and it's a cruel thing to deny the young ladies of London your presence. Speaking of which, my

Emma was recently presented to the Prince Regent—to much praise and attention."

"To no one's surprise," Thomas said with a pleasant smile, glancing at Emma.

Lady Carnbury murmured in satisfaction while Emma lowered her eyes with a display of faux shyness.

"I'm glad you're back in London, Thomas. I hope we can reacquaint ourselves," she said.

"I hope so too."

They hadn't truly been acquainted before. They had attended the same balls and parties, but at the time, Thomas had been consumed by his dark grief, unable to see any woman but Leana. He saw Emma now.

Could he do more than just *see* her? Could he possibly love her?

His mother wanted him to marry her. The Fairchilds wanted him to marry her. And Emma herself certainly wanted it.

By the Lord, what was wrong with him? Emma was a gem of beauty, yet when he looked at her, he felt nothing. He tried to picture her naked—or rather himself relieving her of her dress and corset, feeling her body against his.

Nothing.

Something was truly wrong with him. He had come here hoping to be struck by her, hoping she could be the one to ease the pain of losing Leana.

Could she be?

He didn't know. Didn't there need to be something—*anything*—to begin with? An oyster couldn't create a pearl without the first grain of sand.

They talked about the weather, a new play set to open at the Theatre Royal, and then Emmet asked casually:

"So, how are your finances, Thomas? I understand your father left them in something of a disarray?"

The small talk was over. The business negotiation had begun.

"He did," Thomas said, setting his cup down on the platter. "The Crown called for his services, and far be it from him to refuse—even though he had to finance his cavalry unit himself. The Crown has assured our family that the financial part of the effort will be settled once the war is won."

"But the war isn't yet won."

"No, and until it is, our loan to the Crown will persist."

"A loan, you call it?"

"I do. I don't have it in writing, but I'm confident that the Crown will repay the family of a loyal servant who gave his life for King and country."

"Oh, I wouldn't be so sure, my dear boy. The Crown can be an old purse-clutching wench when it needs to be."

"Papa!" Emma said, her cheeks afire. "That's no way to speak to someone who has lost his father in the war!"

"Probably not," Emmet replied, unmoved by Emma's outburst. "And it's not for daughters to speak out of turn either. There will be many demands when Nappy is finally defeated, and in a post-war economy, those with written contracts will stand first in line."

"I presume you're right, Emmet, but I'm in no hurry. My estates provide me with a steady income while I wait for the Crown to do right by my family," Thomas lied.

"Very well. I'm glad to hear it," Emmet said, smacking his lips.

"Thomas, will you walk with me?" Emma interjected, almost as though trying to prevent her father from speaking further.

They walked slowly along the gravel path that circled the pond, under the watchful eyes of the Fairchilds in their bastion of leisure.

"I must apologise for Papa. He can be so… crass at times."

"I wouldn't say he's crass. He's frank, and I can appreciate that," Thomas said.

"Yes, I'm the same," she said quickly. "I can't stand false flattery or insincerity."

They walked in silence for a moment.

"It's nice to be able to talk without supervision, don't you think?"

"I do."

"One can speak more freely, and I intend to do so now. I've had many suitors since you left London, but I've turned them all down. Do you know why, Thomas?"

He gave her a sidelong glance.

"No?"

"Because, since that night at Gloucester House, I've had eyes for no one but you."

Gloucester House? His mind raced. What had happened at Gloucester House? He couldn't remember. After Leana, there had been nights when he had been less of a gentleman and had drunk too much. Had that night at Gloucester House been one of them?

"I see," he said.

"You said that a good woman was such a rare thing, and if one ever found one, he should fight to the death for her."

Oh, that night…

"I've flattered myself into thinking that I knew for whom those words were spoken. I was perhaps a little less certain when you disappeared for two years, but I presume losing one's father affects both the practical and emotional sides of life?"

"One could say that."

They walked in silence until Emma said:

"Lady Longleat is hosting her annual ball—not this Friday, but the next. It would be nice, I think, if we arrived together?"

"A very fine thing indeed," Thomas replied.

Chapter 3

Alice walked up the stairs to the second floor of their rented house at the north end of Victoria Road. Her spirits flared once more—she was in London!

From downstairs, she could hear the strained sounds of men carrying heavy luggage and her mother directing them. Further down the corridor, she heard Wilma singing and the distinct thumping of her feet as she danced around her room. Their father was out on business but was due to arrive later with George. Alice looked forward to seeing her brother again—it had been three months since they last met—but for now, her whole essence was occupied with the house.

From the entrance doors, a marble floor stretched to broad stairs of dark hardwood, draped in a dense emerald carpet. The corridor leading from the hall to the drawing room was also dark hardwood, polished to a gleaming shine. The drawing room, with its tall windows and deep cornices, housed a pianoforte in perfect tune—a feature of no use to her but at least useful for Wilma, who still harboured ambitions of mastering the instrument.

Upstairs, on the second floor, sunlight fell in through the windows at slanted angles. The library, with its plush chairs and antique carpets, smelled of warm wood and old pages.

She walked down the long shelves, her fingers brushing the spines of books. If life in London ever became dull—which she highly doubted—at least she would have enough to read.

She had already been corresponding with her Mary, who had lived in London all her life. Mary, her cousin on her mother's side, belonged to a family wealthy enough to be admitted to high society. Mary had promised to be Alice's guide in this world of intelligent and witty men—so far removed from the likes of the Evanses.

What wonderful prospects!

Her lady's maid, Lovisa, had already unpacked her bags when Alice entered her room. As the eldest daughter in the house, Alice had had first choice of rooms and selected one with a view of Hyde Park. From her window, she could see carriages trundling along Kensington Road and people moving about in the park's lush greenery.

Lucinda had remained in Walston as mistress of the house, and Alice could imagine Mr Evans settling in comfortably, soon coming to regard Longhall House as his own. Lucinda hadn't been happy to see them leave, and when she hugged Alice goodbye, it had been with a firm clasp and words of caution: to be careful, as London was nothing like Walston. The pitfalls for a beautiful country girl were many and deep.

Before long, the butler, Mr Davis, announced, "Miss Mary de Vries."

Alice turned on her heels and rushed downstairs, holding up her dress.

Mary shrieked and splayed her fingers when she saw Alice. Her eyes were perfectly round, and her face was an open display of delight. They hugged and laughed.

"Dearest cousin, how lovely to see you again!" Mary said. "It's wonderful to have you in town for more than a few weeks. There's so much I look forward to showing you."

They usually met only when the de Vrieses and the Weatherbys celebrated Christmas and Easter together, or when the Weatherbys visited London for two weeks every summer. Even though they didn't meet often, they regarded each other as sisters. They didn't look like sisters, though. Alice was a head taller than Mary—though she wasn't considered especially tall herself. While Alice had dark eyes and chestnut hair, Mary had green eyes, milky white skin, and red hair, betraying her father's Irish roots.

"It is! And I'm looking forward to everything you have to show me. But first—our walk, I presume?"

"I have an even better idea—and exciting news. Prepare the carriage instead."

The carriage was soon brought round, and Mary and Alice rattled east along Kensington Road.

"Listen closely. There's an assembly at a gentleman's house this evening. I'm invited, and I don't think anyone would object to me bringing you along as well."

"Can one simply show up like that? Uninvited?"

"There are two kinds of assemblies, Alice. The formal ones and the informal ones. This is just a gentleman opening his doors to friends and their friends. No one will object, but we'll need to bring Mama as a chaperone."

"Yes, of course." Alice's head spun at the thought of going to a party so soon.

"But what shall I wear? I presume the fashion of high society is very different from what I'm used to in the country?"

"Oh, very much so. But what do you think we're doing today, dear sister? We'll find you something that will catch the attention of the gentlemen. I already have the perfect thing in mind."

Suddenly, the notion of attracting the attention of gentlemen didn't feel as appealing to Alice as it had before. They would see her for what she was—a country girl—within moments. She would have preferred to spend some time acclimating to their world before drawing any attention, but she was quite sure Mary wouldn't allow that.

They stopped at Bond Street, in front of a large white building with a broad set of stairs leading to a colonnade.

"What is this place?"

"The Western Exchange. If we can't find you something to dazzle the gentlemen here, we never will."

The Western Exchange was an enormous hall adorned with Corinthian pillars and lavish gold accents. A fountain stood as the centrepiece, and light poured down from the glass ceiling. The sounds of the crowd reverberated strangely in the vast space.

"What a marvel," Alice said. "It must be ten times the size of Walston Church."

"I wouldn't be surprised if it is. Come with me—I want to show you something."

Mary grabbed her hand and led her through the bustling crowd to a shop at the far end of the hall.

"Look at that dress, Alice! Wouldn't that be perfect for you?"

In the shop window, a wooden mannequin was draped in a dress of silver satin embroidered with beads.

"It's lovely, but—"

"I saw it a week ago. Someone ordered it but couldn't pay, so now it's on display. If it fit me, I'd buy it without thinking twice—but it doesn't. I bet you're slender enough to wear it."

"But how much does it cost?"

"Look, this isn't the kind of place where they display the prices, but I bet the tailor just wants to get rid of it by now. Besides, your Papa has the money, and he wants you to marry properly. I don't think he'll object to you looking your best."

Alice didn't think so either, and when Mary grabbed her arm and steered her towards the entrance, Alice let her.

The tailor was a thin man in glasses and an apron, with tufts of black hair protruding behind his ears. They discussed the dress in the window, and after taking Alice's measurements, he said he only needed to take it in slightly at the waist to make it fit Miss Weatherby perfectly.

"Oh, goody!" Mary said, clapping her hands.

"You can send someone to collect it at six o'clock," the tailor said as he went to the window to remove the dress from display.

Alice and Mary continued their walk through the Western Exchange, stopping at every shop window. Mary talked incessantly. She was always full of energy, but today she was positively brimming. Much of her chatter revolved around preparing Alice for the evening and the inspection of gentlemen's gazes. However, Alice suspected Mary had her own intentions of catching an eye or two. When she asked, Mary smiled.

"Papa wants me to marry Mr Orson, his business partner, but I don't like him very much. He's far too serious about everything. I think if he ever laughed, something inside him might burst."

"Oh."

"Oh, indeed. But there's this other gentleman, Mr Carmichael. I really like him, and I think he likes me too. He makes his money through intercontinental shipping and is as handsome as they come. And he's tall! You know I like that."

"I know."

"But I'm not the only one looking his way, and since he's a gentleman, he gives every girl her fair share of attention. It's impossible to know if he favours one over the others. It's bloody frustrating! I should punish him by not talking to him at all tonight. Yes, that's what I'll do."

"And see all those other girls flock around him, fluttering their eyelashes? I think not. I know you too well, dear cousin."

Mary burst out laughing.

"Yes, you do!"

"And you wouldn't want to find yourself in a position where the grave and serious Mr Orson is your only option," Alice said, mimicking Mr Orson's severe tone.

Mary laughed even harder, her light, bouncing laughter filling Alice's heart with happiness.

The night promised to be a good one—Alice could already feel it.

They arrived at the assembly in the de Vrieses' carriage. Mrs de Vries, with her auburn hair, was a full-figured woman who looked ready to burst out of her expensive satin dress, though she often claimed she still had the same measurements as when she married. For the last thirty minutes, she had interrogated Alice about her family, particularly her mother, and repeatedly apologised for not yet visiting them in person. The sisters always seemed to have some minor grievance with each other—something said or unsaid during their last meeting—but all was quickly forgotten when they met again. Alice assured her that everyone was well, especially her mother, and that they were all thrilled to be in London.

"Of *course* you are," Mrs de Vries said, patting Alice's knee with a pleased smile. "Tell my sister she can expect my visit before the week is out."

The assembly was hosted by Lady Blackwell, wife of Viscount Horatio Blackwell, the next Earl of Northumberland. When they stepped out onto the cobbled yard in front of the tall building on Pemberton Row, Alice felt a pang of nervousness. Her dress had been ready as promised, but she wasn't yet comfortable in it. Made of silver satin, it whispered and slithered as she moved. It was *bright*, so much more ostentatious than her usual dresses of cotton or muslin.

"We'll be presented to the room first and then introduced to the Viscount and Lady Blackwell," Mary whispered as they approached the footmen at the door. "If they speak to us, we reply, but we don't prolong the conversation with questions."

Alice nodded. Mrs de Vries fanned her neck, which had turned slightly red.

At the door, the butler took their names before leading them into a high-ceilinged hall with a black-and-white chequered floor. Alice could hear voices and piano music behind the closed double doors to the left. The butler pushed them open, letting the music spill into the hall, and stepped into the room.

All eyes turned to them.

"Mrs Mary de Vries, Miss Mary de Vries, and Miss Alice Weatherby," the butler announced in a clear, steady voice.

The room was filled with extravagant women in extravagant dresses and men with perfectly arranged hair, some of whom raised their glasses slightly towards them. They were led to the Viscount, who stood by the window, talking to one of the elaborately dressed ladies.

He didn't look anything like Alice had imagined. Stout and rough-featured, he resembled a farmhand more than a nobleman. When he turned his small eyes towards them, his smile was crooked but genuine, with a surprising warmth.

They curtsied, holding out their dresses and doing their best imitations of swans.

"Oh, no need for that in my private quarters," he said. "We're a bit more informal here. If we meet at the theatre, though, I'll insist on those curtseys."

He broke into a harsh laugh that sounded hostile but wasn't.

What an odd and charming man.

"And you shall have them, Lord Blackwell," Mary said.

"You most certainly shall," Mrs de Vries added emphatically.

He nodded in affirmation before turning back to his lady companion, who regarded Mary and Alice as though they were lesser creatures—which, in her world, they undoubtedly were.

"That went well, I think," Alice said as they walked away.

"It did, but it seems Lady Blackwell has already retired for the night—probably another of her headaches."

"Poor creature," Mrs de Vries said. "Missing her own party."

"Yes, poor creature indeed," Mary murmured, her voice distant and her eyes scanning the room.

Alice guessed she was searching for Mr Carmichael—a man of wit, charm, and height. Mrs de Vries spotted some friends by the wall and excused herself. Mary didn't seem to notice. Instead, she jolted and touched Alice's arm lightly.

"Do you see those men over there? Don't stare."

Alice glanced over. Three men stood near the fireplace. Two of them were deep in conversation: a fair-haired man gesturing animatedly as he explained something to the other, who nodded with eager interest. But it was the third man who caught Alice's eye. The tallest of the three, he stood silently, exuding boredom as he listened. His dark hair, cut short and neat rather than styled in the soft curls of current fashion, accentuated his strong, angular features. Broad-shouldered and radiating pride, he carried himself with a conceit that suggested he considered himself above even this illustrious gathering.

Her gaze shifted to the nodding man. Somehow, she knew he was Mr Carmichael, though nothing in his appearance set him apart from the other two. His finely tailored clothing and confident posture could have allowed him to blend seamlessly. Yet, there was a subtle difference. The other two men carried themselves with a natural ease, the relaxed confidence of those born to privilege.

"That's Mr Carmichael over there," Mary said. "Talking to Viscount John Merringer."

"And the man standing next to the Viscount?"

Mary gave her an amused look.

"So, he caught your eye, did he? Well, the Duke of Hexham usually does. But he's said to be a cold and distant man—not agreeable at all."

"You've never spoken to him?"

"Oh, goodness no. People like us aren't meant to talk to the likes of him. He's a duke, you know. If, for some reason, he wishes our attention, he will introduce himself to us."

"What a narrow, boring world that must be."

"What do you mean?"

"If he only ever associates with his peers and never experiences the joy of a chance meeting… that sounds like a life of poverty to me."

"Poverty!" Mary blurted. "He's a duke! He's richer than you can ever fathom!"

"Yes, but I was saying that—"

"What on earth is Mr Carmichael doing, speaking to a duke and a viscount?" Mary mumbled.

"It looks like he's speaking to just one of them," Alice said, which was true, as the Duke of Hexham was staring at the chandelier, not even trying to hide his disdain for the company.

Mr Carmichael was living proof that beauty was in the eye of the beholder. He was a rather plain-looking man with dark blonde hair and—Alice noted when he turned his head to look at them—friendly eyes. He smiled broadly when he saw Mary and waved for them to come over.

"Oh, he's waving us over," Mary said, her voice trembling slightly.

Lord Merringer tilted his head towards them, and even the duke managed a sideways glance before returning to inspect the chandelier.

Mary and Alice made their way to the fireplace.

They curtsied to the duke.

"Your Grace."

And then to John Merringer.

"My lord."

Lord Merringer, in a charming breach of convention, took Mary's hand and kissed the top of her gloved fingers.

"Enchanté."

He then gave Alice the same treatment, looking her deep in the eyes as he straightened.

"Enchanté."

Alice blushed and inclined her head in response. The duke, forced to acknowledge their presence, gave a sharp nod for both Alice and Mary to share.

What an insufferable man!

"Your Grace, my lord. May I present Miss Mary de Vries, eldest daughter of William de Vries. And…"

Mr Carmichael hesitated, his expression panicked, as though he thought he should know Alice's name.

"Alice Weatherby," she said. "Cousin to Miss de Vries. I only arrived in London the other day, so you are excused, Mr Carmichael, for not knowing my name."

"But now that we do know it, it will never be forgotten," Lord Merringer said with dramatic flair, making both Alice and Mary laugh.

How different he is from his dour friend! Light-hearted and pleasant, just as a gentleman should be. Alice corrected her earlier opinion: The Duke of Hexham was a man who would gain nothing but discomfort from a chance meeting and clearly had no desire to expand his world.

"We were talking about shipbuilding," Mr Carmichael explained." Lord Merringer has a great interest in ships of all kinds, from trading vessels to ships of war."

"I certainly do. A cousin of mine was the commander of HMS *Culloden* but was killed in the raid on Batavia. He and I shared a deep interest in ships and even visited the Chatham Dockyards to oversee the building of the *Culloden*."

"That's magnificent," Mary said.

A brief silence followed. Alice couldn't help but pity Mary; the reason they had been called over was now obvious. It had nothing to do with any warm feelings Mr Carmichael might have held for her cousin and everything to do with her father's ownership of a shipbuilding company.

"I like ships as well," Mary tried.

Mr Carmichael gave her an awkward smile.

"I'll help you out, Miss de Vries," the duke said abruptly. "Your friend, Mr Carmichael, thinks that because your father owns a shipyard, you'll know all about blocks and pulleys, and perhaps even have some amusing anecdotes about famous ships. My guess is that you do not. My guess is that you're more interested in frocks and gowns than ships. And since your father only builds midrange trading vessels, any amusing anecdotes would be hard to come by. Am I right?"

Mary blinked.

"Yes."

Mr Carmichael cleared his throat, his ears turning red. Alice's heart began to pound. Duke or no duke, she wouldn't stand for anyone speaking to her cousin like that.

"We're all very thankful that you finally decided to grace us with your presence, Your Grace. But if needless cruelty is your only contribution to the conversation, I think we'd all much prefer if you simply kept your peace."

The duke stared at her.

"It's alright, Alice. I didn't mind," Mary said in a small voice.

"Y-Your Grace," Mr Carmichael stuttered, the redness from his ears spreading across his cheeks. "I beg your pardon, I—"

The duke raised a hand to silence him.

"No, I was in the wrong. I beg your pardon, Miss de Vries. My words were undeserved."

Mary gave a quick nod.

"I didn't mind, really…"

The duke bowed first to Mary, then to Alice, before excusing himself. Lord Merringer gave Alice a wolfish grin and whispered as he passed:

"Well done, Miss Weatherby."

Once they were out of earshot, Mr Carmichael turned to Alice.

"Well, that was a fine display of utter rudeness, Miss Weatherby! Don't they teach manners in the country?"

"They do, Mr Carmichael," Alice said coldly. "I'm sad to see the same can't be said of the city."

Mary grabbed Alice's arm and pulled her to a window where they had spoken to Lord Blackwell. Mary covered her face with her hands, her shoulders shaking. Was she crying? When she lowered her hands, Alice realised she was trying to suppress laughter.

"Thank you, dear cousin! I never thought you'd dare to stand up to a duke on my behalf, but I'm so glad you did. The truth is, his words *did* hurt me, and I'm glad he got some of your sharp tongue in return."

"I didn't plan to, but the way he spoke…"

"You set him straight."

"I didn't, unfortunately. The contempt he showed wasn't a momentary lapse of manners—it's who he is at his core. And at his core, the Duke of Hexham has proven he's not a good man."

"I won't argue, Alice, but I can't share your disappointment in the duke when I have my own disappointment to grieve—Mr Carmichael."

"Oh, believe me, I'm not disappointed in the duke. I didn't know him, so there was nothing to be disappointed in. If anything, I share your disappointment in Mr Carmichael."

"Doesn't he know me at all? Dragging me over there to talk about boats, of all things, when I couldn't care less about them! He embarrassed me—and acted like the embarrassment was his alone."

"He didn't show himself in a favourable light."

"But he really isn't *like* that. I understand him, in a way. He had the attention of a lord who could be useful for his business and wanted to keep it. There's no harm in that, is there?"

"If he throws you into the fire to do it, I'd say there is. But it's not for me to judge Mr Carmichael—that's for you to decide."

Soon after, Mr Carmichael joined them at the window.

"I beg both of you pardon," he said, lowering his head. "I spoke out of affection and didn't mean what I said."

"Apology accepted," Alice said, glancing at Mary, who nodded, her shoulders still tense.

"I'm sorry for putting you in that position, Miss de Vries. I don't know what I was thinking. Would you take a walk with me in the garden? It's supervised, so it won't endanger your reputation."

"I'd be glad to, Mr Carmichael."

Mary smiled at Alice over her shoulder and gave an apologetic shrug as Mr Carmichael led her away, leaving Alice alone in a room full of strangers.

A servant approached her with tall glasses on a silver tray. She took one and sipped—a chilled drink, sweet and bitter at once.

At the other end of the room, she noticed the Duke of Hexham and Viscount Merringer talking. Were they talking about her? Perhaps. She didn't care. Pretending not to see them, she only hoped they would return the courtesy.

Thomas was still shaken—and angry. That girl had made a fool of him, something he wouldn't soon forget. At the same time, he deserved her scolding and ought to remember that as well.

This had been a day of unrelenting misery, from the meeting with the Fairchilds to this wretched party he hadn't even wanted to attend. John, clearly bored as well, had spun some tall tale about a cousin being the commander of HMS *Culloden* to amuse himself. Mr Carmichael, of course, had swallowed it whole and thought it a splendid idea to present them to a shipbuilder's daughter.

Wonderful.

The plump red-haired girl and her cousin came over, and John performed his usual ridiculous French routine. The dark-haired cousin blushed and cast down her eyes—and by God!—she looked exactly like Emma Fairchild when she played out her own routine of faux shyness.

The theatre again.

Oh, how tired he was of it.

There was no escaping it.

Then Mr Carmichael, in his infinite wisdom, had decided to push his woman friend out onto thin ice, and there she had stumbled around in their shared silence, searching for words. Thomas had seen it as a service to her to end the charade then and there. But when he spoke, he had unleashed all the frustrations that had been building throughout the day, and he hadn't held back.

And then the tables had turned—with a verbal slap that still made his ears ring.

The shy girl hadn't been shy at all. Despite her controlled words, he had seen a magnificent fury spark in her eyes.

Didn't she know this play? Didn't she know that to catch the interest of a duke, she was supposed to play the part of the subservient admirer? Offending him in public? That wasn't in any script he'd ever heard of.

But it hadn't been an act. He had misjudged her completely, and she had not hesitated to make him aware of it. Then he had looked at the red-haired girl, her face shrunk in upon itself from the words he'd pelted at her. The shame had hit him as hard as the girl's scolding.

After apologising, he hadn't felt he could stand there amidst them, the creator of an uncomfortable silence, so he had excused himself. To most, it must have looked like he had fled the field—chastised by a common country girl.

John came over to his side, chuckling.

"Well, that came as a surprise," he said.

"Indeed," Thomas replied, glancing across the floor where the girl stood with a glass in hand, looking a little alone and abandoned. What was her name again? Weatherington? No, Weatherby—that was it.

"But she was right," John continued. "You didn't act the gentleman with that poor girl."

"I know, and I apologised, didn't I? With that, I hope the matter is settled?"

"Oh, for sure," John said, plucking two glasses from a passing tray and handing one to Thomas.

"She's a pretty little thing, though, wouldn't you say?" John asked, nodding towards Alice.

"Indeed. But what of it? Aren't we used to seeing pretty girls at every party we attend? Pretty girls with better temperaments and softer tongues?"

"Well," John smiled, looking across the floor to Alice. "I wouldn't mind experiencing her soft tongue, I tell you that, brother."

"Behave. Your reputation doesn't need that."

"True. It's a good thing I can always rely on you to talk me straight. If only I could do the same for you."

Thomas gave him a look.

"What do you mean?"

"How was your walk with the exquisite Emma Fairchild? Are you giving her a single thought, standing here brooding and sulking? Any man in town would go down on one knee before her with only half the hope she's given you. And what do you do? Nothing."

"We will attend Lady Longleat's ball together next Friday. Will that be enough to soothe your worried mind?"

"It's a start, at least."

Chapter 4

Alice was in her room, gazing out at Hyde Park with a smile. The night before had been magical, save for her encounter with the Duke of Hexham. Standing alone by the window had not worked to her disadvantage, as a young gentleman named William Stockton had soon approached her. He bowed and asked if he might do her the honour of keeping her company. His family, one of the founders of the East India Company, was among the richest in London. When spontaneous dancing broke out later in the evening, they had danced two dances, laughing and smiling. Nearby, Mr Carmichael and Mary had also danced, just as cheerful.

Alice's initial harsh assessment of Mr Carmichael's character hadn't entirely been eradicated, but it had softened considerably.

Throughout the evening, she had noticed the duke standing by the wall, sipping from his glass, occasionally shooting her a glance across the room. He must have disliked her greatly, given how much attention he paid her. She had done her best to pretend he wasn't even in the room, and she thought she had succeeded quite well.

After her dances with Mr Stockton, he partnered with another girl, while Alice was led to the floor by another gentleman. Her feet had been sore by the end of the night, but her heart was alight. Later, Mary and Mr Carmichael performed a duet by the pianoforte, earning applause from the gathered crowd. Mary had sung beautifully, though Alice suspected her courage had been bolstered by three glasses of wine.

Just when Alice thought the evening couldn't get better, Viscount Merringer approached their group and invited them all to the Longleat Ball the following Friday. Mr Carmichael and Mary had exchanged stupefied looks. When Alice inquired, they explained that the Longleat Ball was one of the most prestigious events of the season. The guest list was carefully curated, but distinguished lords could bring whomever they pleased.

They had been invited.

Alice hoped for similar luck for Mr Stockton; she wouldn't mind dancing with him again.

From downstairs, she heard a commotion—Wilma hollering and the sound of footsteps rumbling down the stairs.

She stepped out into the corridor and walked to the staircase. From the landing, she saw George standing on the marble floor of the hall, hugging Wilma. He looked up at Alice, his thick brown hair neatly trimmed and his dark coat in the latest fashion, complete with an elegant cravat. He smiled, and his often-serious face came alive.

Alice let out a cry of joy and hurried down the steps to join her sister in George's embrace.

"George!" she exclaimed. "We haven't seen you in more than three months!"

"Sisters," he laughed. "Any more of your love and you'll smother me to death."

"But we *miiissed* you," Wilma said, jumping up and down, still holding George tightly.

They settled in the drawing room, and George looked around.

"It's a fine house Father has found. For the moment, I'm living down at Grosvenor Square—it's closer to the office."

"Is everything going well, then?" Alice asked.

When their father secured his seat in Parliament, he had to distance himself from the business side of things. Not only could it clash with his political decisions, but associating with trade and commerce wasn't advantageous when building ties with the lords and gentlemen of Parliament. The responsibility now fell to George.

"I'd say so. Father thinks I've a good head for business, but that remains to be proven, as a father's praise is the worst indicator of true talent."

Alice laughed.

"That is true. I suppose you'll stay for dinner?"

"That I will. So, how has London treated you so far?"

"It's been great, brother," Wilma blurted. "We walked the whole of Bond Street with Miriam yesterday and saw the most exquisite hats and dresses! Then we stopped for tea at Gunter's Tea Room. They had more than twenty kinds of biscuits and over a hundred different types of tea."

"That's impressive," George said. "And you, Alice? Have you been indulging in tea and biscuits as well?"

"We didn't eat all twenty kinds!" Wilma protested. "We'd look like *this* if we had."

She puffed her cheeks and crossed her eyes. They laughed politely.

"I haven't, but I attended a party at Lord Blackwell's house yesterday. It was most charming."

"Blackwell's? I've been here for months trying to make connections, and you just waltz right into Blackwell House?"

"I did, with some help from Cousin Mary, of course."

"Ah, Cousin Mary. Perhaps I need to ask her to introduce me to some important people. Did you meet anyone interesting?"

"As a matter of fact, I did. A Mr Stockton. We danced twice and had a lot to talk about."

"Stockton? As in East *India* Stockton?"

Alice nodded.

"I'd very much like to exchange a word or two with him. His family has monopolised trade routes that would greatly benefit ours."

"I'll see if he's at the Longleat Ball. If he is, I'll hear his opinion on the matter."

George blinked.

"The Longleat Ball? Are you going to the Longleat Ball?"

"I shall. Both Cousin Mary and Mr Carmichael have been invited as personal friends of Lord Merringer."

"*Viscount* Merringer?"

Alice nodded.

"Hmm, I see."

"See what, brother?"

"He's the sort of man who can ruin a woman's reputation simply by association. You must be careful with him. Do not walk anywhere with him unsupervised. Why did he invite you as his personal friend? You can't possibly know him from before."

"I do not, and I don't like your tone. We were introduced to him and the Duke of Hexam. I had to protest the way the duke spoke to Cousin Mary, and… it seemed to amuse Lord Merringer."

"The way you protested… What does that mean? Please don't tell me you offended him."

"Well," Alice said with a shrug. "He looked far less amused than Lord Merringer. That much I can say."

George put a hand over his eyes and shook his head.

"Alice, Alice, Alice. You've been in London for mere days and already managed to offend one of the most respected men in the country? How is that even possible?"

"I'm sorry, brother, but if you'd heard how he spoke to Mary, you'd side with me on this matter."

"I would not. He's a duke, and he speaks as he sees fit. His father died at Salamanca, leading a cavalry charge. His family has spilt their blood for Britain for generations. He's not a man to offend lightly."

"In that case," Alice said, without much conviction, "it won't happen again."

"Oh, but it will," George said, stroking her cheek with the back of his fingers. "That's what makes you my beloved sister. But please offend someone less important next time?"

They laughed. Wilma, wanting to join in, declared she could offend people too.

"Just point to the person you want offended, and I'll see it's done."

"I'm sure you will, sister."

"You said 'beloved sister' to Alice," Wilma said in a sulky tone. "Am I less beloved to you?"

"Of course not. You are both my most beloved sisters."

With that, Wilma dramatically draped herself around his neck.

The evening was joyous, as the entire Weatherby family was gathered around one table. Mr Weatherby sat at the head, carving the roast while asking his daughters about their day. Alice's announcement of attending the Longleat Ball made him pause.

"Are you going with any special gentleman?"

"No, Father. I'll be going with Cousin Mary as friends of Lord Merringer."

Her father and George exchanged a glance.

"I've already told her, Father."

"Told her what? Alice going to the Longleat Ball is capital! The people there are exactly the kind she should associate with."

"Yes, but—"

"I know, George. But have faith in your sister. She has the Weatherby wits and will do nothing without thinking twice. Isn't that right, Alice?"

"It is, Papa. I've no interest in the gentleman in question and, having learned of his reputation, even less so."

"There you go," Mr Weatherby said, tilting his head at George. "She's no fool, this one."

After dinner, her father and brother went to the library to discuss business, while the women sat in the drawing room. Alice continued working on her embroidery, Wilma pretended to read a book, impatiently huffing through her nose. Alice's mind drifted to the coming Friday and the grand ball at Lady Longleat's. She thought of Mr Stockton; it didn't seem likely he would have been invited. She didn't much care for what she'd heard about Lord

Merringer but presumed she would have to dance at least one dance with him, if asked, since she would be attending the ball as his guest.

Sitting with the same embroidery—a bouquet of amaryllis and chrysanthemum—that she had worked on in Walston, Alice couldn't help wondering what her past self would think if she could see her now. Would she have believed that she would be in London, in a position to grace a lord with just one dance at one of the biggest balls of the year?

How quickly life changed.

Things hadn't changed a bit in London, just as Thomas had dreaded. When he kicked off his boots and leaned back in his favourite chair, listening to the servants preparing his bath, he felt utterly exhausted. He had just returned from a private gathering arranged by Baron Moles, where every young woman in the room had approached him, eager to tell him how grand it was to have him back in town.

Lady Ann Pommels had curtsied with a look full of promise. So had Lady Lisa Balmore and Miss Hastings.

He had exchanged brief pleasantries with Lady Ann about the weather. With Lady Balmore, he had discussed poetry, and she had agreed with everything he said, offering not a single opinion of her own. The same was true of Miss Hastings, who had little to say that wasn't rehearsed. When he'd broken away from her conversation about hosting the perfect dinner party to ask if she preferred life in

London or her family's estate in Devonshire, she had fallen silent before meekly replying that one could arrange good parties in the country as well.

And so it had gone.

Lady Lisa had carefully probed about the Longleat Ball, and Thomas had mentioned his plan to attend with Lady Emma. Disappointment had coloured her face. She might have been able to compete with Lady Ann and Miss Hastings, but Lady Emma was an opponent no girl wanted to challenge. By the end of the evening, the room had seemed to agree that he was as good as engaged to Lady Emma. Though it wasn't entirely true, at least he had been left alone.

But there would be other nights like this.

Perhaps he should simply go down on one knee before Lady Emma and get it over with?

Perhaps.

His valet, Mr Gray, entered the room and inquired if everything was in order. Thomas nodded and then asked:

"Mr Gray, are you a married man?"

"I will be soon, Your Grace."

"Congratulations. Who is the lucky girl?"

"It's Miss Planchard, Your Grace—one of the maids here at Bleaker House."

"Oh, I see… She's a very nice girl. Congratulations again," Thomas said, hoping Mr Gray wouldn't realise he had no idea who the girl in question was. "May I ask you a more… personal question, Mr Gray?"

"Certainly, Your Grace."

"How did your… affection evolve? Was it instant?"

"It was not, Your Grace. At first, I simply found her pleasing to the eye, though I did enjoy her light spirits and quick laughter. But I believe it's only when you truly know a person that love can grow. It was when I noticed the little things about Miss Planchard—the way she always counts the keys on her ring to find the one for the downstairs pantry, even though she knows it's the third from the left, or the way she sings *The Soldier and the Sailor* while polishing windows—that my feelings deepened. The smiles and laughs we present to the world are façades. What's behind the façade is what matters."

Thomas nodded slowly.

"I believe you're right, Mr Gray."

Of course, he couldn't expect to fall in love with Lady Emma after only a few meetings. On reflection, the very notion was absurd. He needed to know her, to see behind her façade. When he did, perhaps feelings would begin to grow. He didn't know her, and she didn't know him. They were two empty façades, looking at one another without revealing a single crack of humanity.

At the ball next Friday, he resolved to speak to her as a friend, not as a man forced towards the altar.

Chapter 5

Alice went out before breakfast the following day. She loved everything about London, but at times she missed the peace and quiet of the country. The early mornings in London were the closest she could come to that tranquillity.

A horse clopped down the street, pulling a cart, its head bobbing slowly. The sound of its hooves against the cobblestones didn't displease her any more than birdsong in the woods back home would.

Hyde Park was shrouded in milky mist and stepping into it felt like entering another world. She had expected to be alone, but as she followed the gravel path, she heard voices ahead—boys hollering and hooting with excited cries. Her curiosity urged her to edge closer, but caution held her back. She was here unsupervised, after all.

She continued along the path, determined not to let some random commotion ruin her morning walk. She would simply keep a good distance from the noise.

As the fog began to lift, she spotted a gathering further away on the field. Men from all walks of life stood in two lines, facing each other. Workers in caps and rough breeches stood shoulder to shoulder with gentlemen in jackets and high hats. They hooted and shook their fists in the air.

What on earth was going on?

Were they angry and about to clash?

No—she could sense, even from a distance, that the crowd was excited rather than agitated.

Further up the field, flanked by spectators, two riders tore down at full speed, hunched low over their horses, their tailcoats flapping in the wind. This was Rotten Row, she realized, notorious for its races where daring riders pushed their prized horses to the limits of their abilities.

The winner, riding a red bay, stood in his stirrups and waved his hat in triumph.

Alice stopped.

The man celebrating his victory was none other than Mr Stockton, the gentleman she had danced with at Blackwell House. He turned his horse and rode back to the crowd, dismounting near a stout man with a pipe protruding from the corner of his mouth.

"One can only be grateful that they conduct their business in the early hours," said a voice close by.

Alice jumped. An elderly couple stood beside her, arm in arm, gazing over the field. She hadn't noticed their approach. The man, with a white beard and an old-fashioned hat, had spoken. He wore a black jacket, and his wife was dressed in the voluminous style common for ladies of her age.

"I presume it is," Alice replied.

"Gambling…" the man said with a shake of his head. "Today it's seen as harmless entertainment, but it's a device of the devil."

"Indeed," his wife agreed.

They watched as Mr Stockton received a handful of banknotes from the stocky man with the pipe.

"Is it less of an evil if one bets on oneself? Confidence in one's abilities—that's surely the mark of a gentleman?"

The man turned to her for the first time.

"A lesser evil, perhaps, but it's still an evil from the same root," he said. Then his stern expression softened, and he tipped his hat to her. "I must apologise, Miss, for discussing such unpleasant matters before we've even been properly introduced."

They introduced themselves as Mr and Mrs Peters, regular walkers in the park at this hour. Alice gave her name, and they were delighted to learn her father was a member of Parliament.

"The Peters estate is in the north, near the Scottish border," Mr Peters said. "We've left its care in capable hands, but Parliament needs more country gentlemen. Too many city men, and the politics will reflect it."

Then he gave Alice a fleeting glance.

"As a young woman from the country, you might not know that this park, even though it's on the better side of town, can harbour unpleasantness. It isn't proper for a young lady of good birth to walk here alone. If you'd like, you can join us. We're walking around the Serpentine and back."

Alice said she would love to, though it wasn't entirely true. She had been looking forward to walking alone with her thoughts. But to insist on going alone after being warned, especially with a rambunctious group of men nearby, might risk her reputation.

So, she walked with them.

The Peters were pleasant, chatting easily about small matters. They didn't seem to expect much response, so Alice nodded at appropriate intervals as her mind wandered.

Then she saw a figure on horseback ahead. It was Mr Stockton.

"I must confess," she said hurriedly, "that the man we spoke of earlier is an acquaintance of mine."

Mr Peters didn't reply. Alice's hasty confession needed no explanation when the rider approached. Mr Stockton reined his horse with a smile and tipped his hat. He had a square, strong face, and his hair—brown with a hint of rust—caught the light. His eyes seemed to shift between green and blue; today, they were unmistakably green.

"Miss Weatherby. What a most joyous surprise."

"Likewise, Mr Stockton."

She introduced the Peters, and after the exchange of nods and pleasantries, Mr Stockton asked if he might join them.

"Please do," Mr Peters said, though his wife turned her head away and remained silent.

Mr Stockton dismounted and led his horse beside him. The Peters, whatever they thought of him, courteously slowed their steps to allow Alice and Mr Stockton to walk ahead, out of earshot.

"I must admit," Mr Stockton said, "I didn't expect to see you here at this early hour."

"Likewise, Mr Stockton. But I see it was worth your time."

"It was." He patted his horse's neck. "This beauty cost me a small fortune, but she's worth every penny. And, as you noticed, she does bring some of that money back, along with the exhilaration of a close race. Yes, I am a gentleman—do not doubt that, Miss Weatherby—but even gentlemen must have their fun, don't you think?"

"I'm in no position to judge, but I do believe people should be allowed to do what makes them happy, so long as it doesn't intrude on the happiness of others."

He gave her a wry smile.

"That's a rehearsed answer, Miss Weatherby, and an expected one. But if one cannot, from time to time, live fully in the moment, one shrivels up and dies. To gallop down an open field, the wind whipping my face and my heart pounding—that is life to me."

"I see."

"What is life to you, Miss Weatherby?"

"This is rather an odd morning conversation."

"Do you object to it?"

She couldn't hide a smile—she didn't object to the conversation. She had presumed he would talk about the weather, exchange the usual pleasantries, and then swing back up onto his horse with a tilt of his hat. How much more interesting this was!

"As a woman, I'm not allowed to seek pleasure in the same way men do. I don't know if I'd find amusement in barrelling down an open field, as you put it, but perhaps I would. I find great amusement in books, chiefly because they broaden my horizons, since I'm not permitted to travel alone. Much of my future happiness, then, depends on finding a man who enjoys travel and might even let me ride a fast horse."

She blushed as the words left her lips. She hadn't planned to say so much, but now that she had, it was an open invitation for him to continue offering his company. And why not? He was good company; there was no reason to object.

"Husbands like that are hard to come by, I've heard."

Oh, well—she might as well continue down this path now.

"I've heard that too."

"I'll let you know if one shows up."

"Please do."

They shared a laugh that was like everything else about him—easy and light-hearted.

"I'll be going to the Longleat Ball this Friday," she said. "Might I expect to meet you there?"

He raised his eyebrows.

"The Longleat Ball? I'm afraid not. My family doesn't have the reputation required to gain access to a ball like that," he said, his voice carrying a tone that was part statement, part question: *and neither does yours.*

She could not answer the implied question. For some reason, she was embarrassed to admit she had been invited by Lord Merringer.

Mr Stockton, however, was not one to dwell on discomfort. He brightened and informed her that he would attend a ball the Friday after the Longleat Ball, hosted by Mrs Sophie.

"I'm not acquainted with Mrs Sophie, so I wouldn't expect an invitation, but I'm sure we'll meet again on some occasion."

"Maybe," he said with a smile, then swung back up onto his horse. "I'll keep an eye out for you, Miss Weatherby. Perhaps I'll even find that rare creature you described—the one who would care for your future happiness."

"Please do," she said, blushing again.

He tipped his head.

"Until next time, Miss Weatherby," he said and spurred his horse forward.

He disappeared down the path at a speed Alice doubted was generally approved of. She had assumed rightly, for the Peters were at her side again, shaking their heads.

"It's not that I want to meddle, Miss Weatherby," Mrs Peters said, "but I'd recommend staying away from that particular gentleman. I don't think he's fully grown up yet."

"I believe you're right," Alice replied, looking after the galloping horse with a poorly concealed smile, thinking:

If so, I hope he never will be.

Thomas stood on the second floor of Bleaker House, at the library window. He pushed the curtain aside with the back of his hand and looked down at his mother's arriving carriage. This evening would test his endurance. His mother had come to take command of Bleaker House and to act as hostess for tonight's dinner party.

The Fairchilds were invited, of course, along with other esteemed families with unmarried daughters. Thomas knew his mother well enough to understand her strategy: signal to the Fairchilds that while they were the favoured alliance, there were plenty of other options. In plain terms: *How high a dowry can you afford? What's it worth to have your daughter named Duchess of Hexham?*

He was fully aware of his family's need for money, but if his mother could have had the decency to stay at Somerfield, the arrangement might have felt less like an open market.

The staff gathered in the yard to greet her, as they had greeted him, but neither he nor the staff doubted who truly commanded the house.

The Dowager Duchess of Hexham stepped out of the carriage, steadied by Morley's white-gloved hand. She passed the line of bowing servants without so much as a nod of recognition.

Thomas descended the stairs to meet her in the vast hall of Bleaker House. She was pulling her white crocheted gloves from her fingers as she entered. She gave him a stern smile and a brief peck on the cheek.

"You look well," she said.

"Likewise."

"Enough pleasantries. We've a lot to do before the guests arrive."

They certainly did, but Thomas had no intention of involving himself. His father had been a successful commander, and his mother was very much his equal, commanding her army of maids and servants. She relished it far more than he ever could. He retreated to the library, leaving her to her work.

Settling into his favourite chair—a deep red velvet one with a high backrest angled towards the window—he picked up a book. But today, he couldn't focus. His gaze drifted to the street below, where people bustled about, each a miniature universe in themselves.

So much hope and so many expectations on display.

What wouldn't he give to be one of them again? He had nothing to hope for. No expectations. His life had been staked out long before he was born, leading him to this moment where he was expected to choose a wife of his mother's liking.

What chance did he and Lady Emma have when she left him cold at the very start of their courtship?

Then there was Lady Sara Fitzwater and Miss Everett, both of whom would dine with them tonight. Fine young women, all of them, yet they left him equally unmoved.

The problem wasn't them. It was him.

Before the guests arrived, he needed to temper his selfishness and learn to appreciate the fact that three beautiful women would sit at his table tonight, hoping to become his wife.

A man could wish for less, certainly.

And yet, he found himself wishing for more.

When the rattling of carriages began in the yard, Thomas stood by his mother's side in the downstairs drawing room. Morley soon swung open the gilded double doors and announced:

"Lord Walter Fitzwater, the Earl of Donley, the Countess of Donley, and their daughter, Lady Sara Fitzwater."

The Earl of Donley was significantly older than his wife, with tufts of white hair around his ears and a large reddish nose. Exceptionally tall, his stature made the contrast with his wife—short and slightly plump—almost comical. She had a snub nose, and her brown hair was tied in a tight bun. Their daughter, Lady Sara, seemed to have inherited the average height from her parents, standing at a perfectly normal length. She had fair hair with a hint of red, milky white skin, and a freckled nose. Half a smile of anticipation played on her lips as she curtsied before him.

Once all had greeted each other in the appropriate manner, Morley appeared again.

"Lord de Montague, Lady de Montague, and the Honourable Liza Everett!"

Another round of greetings commenced, this one just as ceremonious. Liza Everett was every bit as beautiful as Lady Sara Fitzwater, though she was her complete opposite, with raven-black hair and dark eyes.

When the Fairchilds were announced, Emma offered Liza and Sara a polite yet dismissive smile. The Dowager Duchess appeared surprised to see Morley return yet again, this time announcing:

"Lord Merringer!"

The Dowager Duchess turned to Thomas, who gave her a small smile and a half-shrug. Her neck reddened, but she maintained a composed expression, greeting John as though he had been invited like the other guests. In truth, John had been invited—not by her, but by Thomas. If Thomas was to endure the evening, he needed at least one ally by his side.

John's presence had the added benefit of shifting some of the attention away from Thomas as the main prize of the evening. Now, there were two eligible bachelors at the table, a detail The Dowager Duchess seemed less than pleased about.

"I believe you know my friend, Lord Merringer," Thomas said to Emmet, who stood closest to him.

"I believe I've heard the name," Emmet said without much warmth.

"It's an honour to speak with you in person, Lord Carnbury," John said, bowing deeply.

"Granted it is," Emmet replied.

After John had been properly introduced, the Dowager Duchess moved toward the double doors leading into the dining room.

"Well, to the table, then."

Thomas took his place at the head of the table, with his mother to his right and Lady Carnbury ready to take the seat on his left. She paused, offering a light laugh.

"Oh, I know this is a breach of etiquette, but I really think you will find my daughter far better company than me, Duke. I hope you won't frown upon me giving my seat to her?"

"Your company is a loss, I assure you, Lady Carnbury, but I believe your daughter will be just compensation," Thomas replied, ignoring the noticeable rumble of discontent from further down the table.

"But of course," Lord Montague interjected, his tone light. "Why keep the young ones apart, dividing them with so many accumulated years and dust?"

For a moment, Thomas expected the baron to demand his own daughter, Liza, be moved closer to the head of the table. Fortunately, the baron settled for his comment.

"That was my thought exactly," Lady Carnbury said, nodding in agreement. She moved further down the table to take a seat opposite John Merringer.

Emma sat to Thomas's left, casting her eyes down as she folded her hands neatly in her lap.

"I hope you didn't take offence. Mama can be a bit wilful about conventions sometimes."

"Not at all," Thomas replied, fully aware that every ear at the table was attuned to their conversation—and would remain so for the rest of the evening.

The servants brought in the first course—a cold spring soup. The group ate in restrained silence until Lady Montague broke it by praising the velvet green curtains in the room. The Dowager Duchess absorbed the compliments, elaborating on the fabric, the shop where she had purchased it, and the seamstress who had sewn them. When she finished, silence fell again.

"I, for one, am very glad to see Bleaker House has a master once more," Emma said. "It's disheartening to see such a grand house standing empty and silent. I told Thomas as much during our walk in Hyde Park yesterday."

Lord and Lady Fitzwater exchanged a glance, Emma's casual use of his first name a subtle jab at their ambition.

Lady Fitzwater leaned towards Thomas, raising her snub nose.

"I assure you, Duke, if walking appeals to you, we have great estates in the west with oak trees as far as the eye can see—perfect for walking."

"Indeed," Lady Sara added. "I've walked in those forests all my life. They have an almost magical quality. I'd love to show them to you at your convenience."

"A gracious offer, indeed," Thomas said, raising his glass to her. "I'll take it under consideration."

"Oh, you certainly should, Duke," Lord de Montague said, raising his own glass. "Young people like you benefit greatly from the physical exercise of walking. I, like any true Englishman, cherish the great forests of the west, and Lord Fitzwater's estate is renowned for its beauty. A jewel of England, even if it's technically in Wales. I'm not bothered by the squalls of rain and storms from the Atlantic. Refreshing for body and soul, I say! But if I had to choose, I'd take the south—Cornwall has been home to my estate for generations."

"Oh, isn't that the truth, Papa," Sara said, drawing a deep, smiling breath as if she were envisioning the beauty of Cornwall at that very moment. "Oak forests are splendid, but I must admit, I prefer the southern seafront. On a clear day, one can even see France."

Everyone agreed the southern seafront was indeed beautiful, though it had little to compare with the splendour of the places where they themselves had estates.

"All parts of our proud country have their merits," the Dowager Duchess said. "But unfortunately, Hyde Park is the closest thing we have to the rural beauty you are all accustomed to. I'm sure my son could find time for more walks during his stay if anyone could bring themselves to walk in such meagre surroundings?"

All the young women quickly assured her they could.

"Just to have it out there," John said, "I'm a rather avid walker myself."

This garnered polite laughter, but the attention swiftly returned to Thomas. He found himself slightly amused by the display unfolding. After all, John was a viscount. Lady Sara and Miss Everett had no reason to overlook him the way they did—though John's reputation might have played a role.

The courses continued, and by the time the chocolate terrine was brought in for dessert, the conversation had shifted to the war. They discussed the French defeat at Toulouse and whether it might truly mark the end of the conflict.

"I daresay," Lord de Montague declared, "your father's sacrifice makes us all proud. He has showered the Overton name with new glory, adding to a history that already holds so much of it."

Everyone around the table nodded solemnly in agreement.

Lord Carnbury let out a hum of satisfaction as he tasted the chocolate terrine.

"This chocolate terrine is magnificent. Send my compliments to the cook," he said, then paused and looked up at Thomas. "He's not French, is he?"

"He's not," Thomas replied.

Lord Carnbury burst out laughing.

"Wouldn't mind if he were, cooking like this!"

The table erupted into laughter. Emma rolled her eyes.

After dinner, the women retreated to the drawing room while the men poured their brandy and leaned back in their chairs.

"The eye of the storm," Lord Carnbury sighed.

Lord de Montague let out a short laugh.

"Yes, the blessed silence."

"Indeed," John said, sipping his brandy.

From the drawing room, not a single word could be heard. Thomas imagined the young ladies sitting on separate sofas with their mothers, quietly observing the details of the room and simply waiting for this part of the evening to pass.

"I heard you're taking Lady Emma to the Longleat Ball," Lord Fitzwater said, glancing at Thomas.

"That depends on what you mean by *taking*," Thomas replied. "We've agreed to make an entrance together."

"I know what I mean by it," Lord de Montague said with a smirk.

"Please, can't we leave this to the women?" Thomas said, his impatience seeping through.

"Oh, yes, of course," Lord de Montague said, taking a large gulp of brandy.

Lord Carnbury held his glass with both hands, leaned back a little further, and smiled softly.

Thomas wished the evening would end. He'd have one day of rest before attending the Longleat Ball. His plan was already clear: he would arrive with Emma, making everyone at the ball draw the same conclusion as Lord de Montague, that the deal was already sealed. He would dance with Emma more than any other girl, and by Saturday, he would visit the Fairchilds to formalise matters.

When the men and women reunited in the drawing room, John seized the chance to speak privately with Thomas.

"What a horrendous dinner party, dear friend. The young women, lovely as they are, have eyes only for you. What's a poor viscount to do to earn a laugh or a smile in this dreary gathering?"

"Just be your own charming self," Thomas said, noting Emma making her way towards him.

The other ladies remained seated, watching her approach with discontented eyes.

"Thomas," she said, "what a lovely evening this has been. I've made so many new acquaintances. I rarely meet girls like Liza and Sara in my own circles, but they're very nice girls. Perhaps a bit plain to the eye and unimaginative in conversation, but well-mannered, at least."

"Yes, they seem like very nice girls indeed," Thomas replied.

John gave a surprised laugh.

"I can't comment much on their conversation, Emma, but plain to the eye? I beg to differ. Do you find them plain, Thomas?"

"Since we're not previously acquainted, I believe that is *Lady Emma* to you," Emma interjected sharply. "And I really don't think your opinion of the girls in question is the important one."

"I know I'm just a humble observer," John said, grinning mischievously, "but what beauty I've observed tonight! What do you say, Thomas? What of the dark eyes of the lovely Miss Everett or the depth of Lady Sara's? Aren't they a thing to behold?"

Thomas suppressed a smile as Emma's jaw tightened, the muscles visibly working.

"Yes, perhaps *plain* was a little harsh," she admitted. "I didn't mean to put myself forward in any way."

"Of course, you didn't," Thomas said. "It's never wrong to state one's opinion, as long as it's an honest one."

"Yes, that is my thinking as well," Emma quickly added, seizing the opportunity. "I simply can't stand dishonest people."

"Agreed," John interjected. "They're the worst."

Emma turned her unblinking gaze on him, her smile frosty.

"Your opinion, Lord Merringer, has been duly noted."

"John, perhaps you could go and entertain some of the other young women?" Thomas suggested, allowing a hint of amusement to colour his tone. "They look a bit abandoned over there."

"Yes, please do," Emma said. "I'm sure they'll find your charm utterly irresistible."

John smiled, tipped an imaginary hat, and made his way to the sofas.

"I must apologise for John," Thomas said, venturing a smile of his own. "He rarely considers the consequences of his words."

"I don't understand why you keep his company," Emma replied, her brow arching slightly. "You are aware of his reputation?"

"I am."

She nodded, clearly tempted to press the issue further, but to her credit, she refrained. Instead, her features softened into a pleasant smile.

"I think we ought to plan our entrance at the ball. Don't you agree? We need to make a proper impression. I'm considering wearing a..."

Thomas nodded and hummed in what he hoped were the appropriate places, but his mind had already begun to wander.

Chapter 6

Mary had been quite right, Alice realised—her father did not hesitate to spend generously on fine dresses once the gates to the fabled aristocratic ball at Longleat House had opened for her. In Alice, he placed all his hopes for a future where his lands, trades, and seat in Parliament would no longer be the sum of his legacy. A future where he could return to Walston, not as a mere baronet's heir, but as a revered figure rather than a scorned one.

He hadn't spoken of this openly, of course, but Alice knew him well enough to understand. It was why she now, accompanied by her mother, stepped out of the carriage in front of Longleat House—a building grand enough to rival any country estate.

Lit torches lined the path from the gates to the broad staircase that led to the pillared entrance. The double doors stood ajar, spilling silvery strains of music into the warm evening. A house servant steadied Alice as she descended from the carriage. With her mother by her side, she climbed the stairs and entered the grand hall.

The space was larger than many homes, its walls lined with portraits of stern-faced men astride horses. A grand fireplace of white marble dominated one wall. Alice barely had time to admire it before they were ushered through a broad corridor to towering double doors. Two servants with military precision swung them open, revealing the ballroom.

"What a splendid room," Mrs Weatherby gasped.

Alice said nothing, her mouth slightly agape. Longleat House wasn't merely a house—it was a palace. The ceiling soared high enough for birds to fly freely, and immense chandeliers, the size of carriages, cast a soft, magical light over the scene.

Alice's imagination raced. Surely, she wasn't still in London. This was some enchanted realm where anything was possible. The creamy white and gold walls gleamed, and the marble floor bore the Longleat family crest inlaid with gold.

Young women sat on benches along one wall or mingled with their chaperones and gentlemen. There was a constant exchange of bows and curtsies, punctuated by glances toward the floor—silent pleas from the seated girls to be asked to dance.

"You must sit down now, dear," Mrs Weatherby urged, her eyes darting nervously about. "Make a fine figure for the men, and perhaps you'll be asked to dance."

Alice turned to her mother, her own nervousness matching hers.

"I will, in time. But we must wait for Mary. I can't sit alone without anyone to talk to. Please, Mama, stay with me a little longer."

Mrs Weatherby opened her mouth to respond but froze, her gaze fixed on the dance floor.

Alice followed her line of sight and saw Lord Merringer striding toward them, a pleasant smile on his face.

"Do be careful with him," her mother muttered as he approached.

"Mrs Weatherby," Lord Merringer greeted with a bow. "A pleasure to meet you. Your daughter and I are newly acquainted, and I must say I'm delighted to see her here tonight."

"Why are you glad, Lord Merringer? Aren't there enough pretty girls here to please your eye?" Mrs Weatherby asked bluntly.

Oh, Mama, please, Alice thought in despair. Don't be rude.

"I can see where Miss Weatherby gets her frankness," Lord Merringer replied, his smile unbroken. "To answer your question, Mrs Weatherby, your daughter is a breath of fresh air in a stale room. For that reason alone, I'm glad to see her. But I assure you, I regard her as a dear friend only. That said, my words carry weight in a room like this, and I'd be happy to introduce her to appropriate speaking partners, should you wish it."

Mrs Weatherby softened, nodding graciously.

"In that case, I'm very grateful for your friendship with my daughter. And if you feel inclined to make introductions, I wouldn't object."

"I'd be glad to," he said, turning to Alice. "In exchange for the first dance, Miss Weatherby."

"Of course," Mrs Weatherby agreed, tilting her head.

Alice echoed the gesture, and Lord Merringer bowed before returning to his friends. She watched him go but had little time to dwell on his offer, as Mary's voice called her name.

Mary approached with a radiant smile. "What a marvellous room!" she exclaimed, her gaze sweeping the space.

The cousins immediately began chatting, marvelling at their good fortune to be there together. They retreated to the punch room, their chaperones in tow.

"So," Mary asked, her eyes sparkling. "Have any gentlemen caught your eye yet? Or you theirs?"

"We've just arrived. I don't know anyone here except Lord Merringer, and he's asked me for the first dance."

"Oh," Mary replied, raising her eyebrows. "Then let's hope he asks for a second."

Alice huffed a quiet laugh. "Mama wouldn't allow it, and I doubt it's a concern. He only asked out of courtesy."

Just then, the doors opened again, and an awed murmur swept the room. The Duke of Hexham entered with a woman of breathtaking beauty on his arm. Her porcelain skin and elaborately styled platinum hair gave her the air of a princess. Her confident smile made it clear she knew it too.

Beside her, the duke looked as bored and aloof as ever. Alice pitied him. If he couldn't enjoy himself at a grand occasion like this, in such company, when could he? What an empty life he must lead.

Their eyes met briefly, his gaze hardening before he looked past her. Alice smiled faintly. If the lords and ladies of this room couldn't stir him, a mere daughter of a mister certainly wouldn't. But she was determined not to let him dampen her spirits.

The music began, and Lord Merringer approached to claim his promised dance. Alice took his hand, and he led her to the floor.

As they joined the line of dancers, he smiled. "I'd wager this is your first time dancing in a room like this, Miss Weatherby?"

"It is. But even if the surroundings change, the dancing remains the same."

"Well, I'd hope that one's partner is also worth considering," John said, offering her a grin.

"It is," Alice replied, smiling as the dance commenced.

Emma had achieved the reaction she wanted, Thomas thought grimly. All eyes had been on them as they made their entrance. Amongst the gathered faces, so familiar and predictable, one had disrupted the scene—a face that stood out like a candle flickering in the dark.

His reaction had preceded his thoughts, and for a moment, he couldn't place it. A pretty face, certainly—dark eyes and a serious mouth poised as if to smile in defiance. Then recognition struck.

The girl from Blackwell's reception.

The memory sent an uncomfortable twist through him, and he looked away. What on earth was she doing at an assembly like this? Surely Lady Longleat, the esteemed patroness of the ball, hadn't extended an invitation to her.

As the music began and he saw John striding toward her, the puzzle clicked into place. Of course. The girl's audacity at Blackwell's had amused John enough to bring her here, likely as another of his stunts. It was exactly the sort of mischief John delighted in—stirring the pot purely for his own entertainment.

Thomas watched as John offered her his hand, and she accepted with a smile that lit up her entire face. He felt a pang of envy. To her, this evening was something magical, an experience she would remember for the rest of her life. Her canvas was still blank, full of possibilities, while his own was a muddled, overworked mess.

Emma gave his arm a tug. "What are you thinking about, Thomas?"

"Oh, just painting and such," he said, sighing.

They were soon drawn into conversation with acquaintances, but Thomas's gaze kept straying to the line of dancers. Miss Weatherby—yes, that was her name—didn't belong here. She might think she did, but her radiant joy betrayed her. While the other girls held the practiced indifference expected of them, she tilted her head back and laughed aloud. John, meanwhile, appeared to be thoroughly enjoying himself.

How simple and carefree John's life seemed, Thomas thought with another pang of envy.

When the dance ended, John bowed to Miss Weatherby and—oh, for God's sake—led her toward him and Emma. She was still smiling, her cheeks flushed, but her expression faltered when she realised where she was being taken. Her smile disappeared entirely as she curtsied stiffly, addressing Thomas with a curt, "Your Grace."

An odd feeling it was, to be able to extinguish a woman's smile with one's presence alone.

"There's no need for that, Miss Weatherby," he muttered. "I believe we're previously acquainted."

Her lips curled into a faint smile, one he couldn't quite interpret.

"Previously acquainted?" Emma's tone sharpened as she glanced between them.

"We met briefly at the Blackwell reception," Thomas explained.

"Oh, I see," Emma replied with a thin smile. "Lord Blackwell is known for his… diverse tastes. And Lord Merringer, of course, is no stranger to variety."

"That is how the world works, Emma," John interjected cheerfully. "Some are givers, and some are takers. I, for one, am a giver!"

"That is debatable," Emma said.

"He gave me the honour of the first dance, so his words hold true thus far," Alice said.

Emma regarded Alice with thinly veiled surprise, as if she hadn't expected her to speak at all.

"Well, I'm glad for you, Miss Weatherby," Emma replied, her words laced with condescension. "We were all terribly concerned that you might not be shown the proper honours."

"What a selfless act of altruism!" John exclaimed. "Always thinking of others, Emma. If the world is full of givers and takers, you're a saint among us—giving until there's nothing left but a hollow shell."

Emma's eyes narrowed. "What?"

Thomas noted the exchange of glances between Alice and John, the unspoken camaraderie in their secret smiles. Suddenly, the divide opened like a gorge between them. On one side, light-hearted humour, an embrace of life, the ponding heart, on the other—stone-faced, high-strung conservatives.

A flash of anger jolted him.

He hadn't chosen this side. As with so many moments in his life, he seemed to have been corralled to this point without ever realising it. Was this who he was now? Lips pressed tight with a serious face?

Yes.

In this environment, he could hardly be anything else. He couldn't be the man he was out on Somerfield, the one who relieved the stable boy with a pat on the shoulder and an easy smile. He couldn't be the man who rode into town, tipped his hat to the townsfolk, and, for a fleeting moment, felt as though he truly belonged. He couldn't be the man who shared a secret smile, a hasty glance of mutual understanding, with a beautiful girl.

In his world, everything was already carved in stone, and whichever way he turned, he collided with immovable objects.

John turned to Alice with a bow. "Miss Weatherby, would you do me the honour of the second dance as well?"

Alice hesitated, clearly aware of the implications. Dancing two consecutive dances with John Merringer would be noticed here—and discussed far beyond. With John's reputation, the gossip would hardly be kind.

Before she could respond, Thomas found himself speaking. "Why don't you spare the poor girl your frivolous conversation, John, and let me have the second dance instead?"

Emma stiffened beside him. Alice blinked, clearly stunned, then nodded sharply before retreating to the bench where her friend waited.

John watched her go, his smile undiminished.

"I thought you'd outgrown your habit of rescuing strays, Thomas," he said with a laugh. "Well, I'll leave you to your gallantry. I'm off to the card room."

Once John was gone, Emma turned on Thomas, her voice low and icy.

"The effect of making an entrance together is somewhat diminished when you give away your first dance to a random girl."

"She isn't random, and it wasn't about the dance. I didn't want to see her reputation ruined two weeks after arriving in London. She doesn't know what kind of man John is."

"But you do, and yet you call him your friend?"

"He makes me laugh," Thomas said. "A man needs that in his life, Emma."

"Of course. But perhaps I can hope for your *second* dance then? If you aren't otherwise engaged?"

"That you can," Thomas replied, glancing across the floor where Alice was talking to her friend with something looking like shock in her face.

Understandable.

He'd surprised himself too. But now that the deed was done, did he regret it? No. He had stepped over the divide, and for that, he felt no remorse.

"What are you going to do?" Mary asked.

"What can I do? I've already agreed to dance with him."

"I suppose you must, then. But why he asked you, I still can't understand."

"Oh, I have an idea," Alice said, "and if it's true, it puts him in a more agreeable light—though it still baffles me."

"What reason could that be?"

"He asked shortly after Lord Merringer requested a second dance, sparing me from what might have been an unwise choice. If what you say about Lord Merringer's reputation is true, then the duke might have saved me from a precarious situation."

Mary frowned.

"That doesn't sound like the Duke of Hexham. But then again, we don't know him at all, do we? Perhaps he just wanted to make Lady Emma jealous?"

They glanced across the room to where Lady Emma stood, her back stiff and her cheeks stained with dots of red.

"If so," Alice said, unable to suppress a giggle, "it seems to have worked."

When the orchestra struck up for the second dance, Mr Carmichael appeared, bringing a light to Mary's face. He came directly over and requested her hand, while Alice watched the Duke of Hexham approach with the expression of a man walking to his execution.

This ought to be festive, she thought with a wry mental sigh.

He bowed, extending his hand. She took it, and he led her to the dance floor. They took their place in the line, and he regarded her with disinterested eyes.

"I must thank you for your sense of decency, Your Grace," Alice said as they prepared to begin, "for sparing me that second dance with Lord Merringer. If that was your reason?"

"It was," he replied. "Consider it penance for our last meeting."

"You've already made penance for that, but I do appreciate the thought. If you expect me to apologize, though, I won't. I spoke out of conviction, and I still stand by my words."

"And so you should," he said, his tone betraying no emotion.

The dance began. Alice noticed Emma further up the line, dancing with a man who looked every bit the proper lord. Yet Emma's focus wasn't on her partner but firmly on the duke and Alice.

Understandable, Alice thought. But uncomfortable.

It should have been more so for Thomas, yet he seemed entirely unaffected. He seemed to go through the motions of, not only the dance, but the evening as a whole. Alice had a suspicion it didn't stop there. Was this how he lived his life, floating from ball to ball with the same lacklustre effort of achieving a single memorable moment?

If that was the case, she pitied him.

"What a grand evening for you, Your Grace," Alice ventured. "Your entrance with Lady Emma was quite the spectacle."

"I'm glad you appreciated it."

"I did. Though Lady Emma seemed to enjoy it far more than you did, Your Grace."

"That's in her nature, to delight in the admiration of others."

"And it's not in yours?"

"No, it's not."

"If I may ask, Your Grace, what *do* you enjoy?"

He turned to her with a confused, slightly irritated look.

"What prompts a question like that?"

"Well," she said, unfazed, "it's every gentleman's duty to converse with his dancing partner, is it not? And since you promised to rescue me from Lord Merringer's trivial conversation, I hoped for profound observations. But as you don't seem inclined to provide them, I assumed you might, like many men, enjoy speaking about yourself."

"Miss Weatherby, may I remind you that I'm not here primarily to amuse you but to safeguard you from Lord Merringer's intentions?"

"You are right. I'm both sorry and grateful. Let us then share the next fifteen minutes in silence."

And so they did, passing each other back and forth through the line of dancers.

Eventually, Thomas broke the silence.

"I apologize for speaking harshly, Miss Weatherby. Perhaps I read more into your question than was there. To answer you—what I enjoy most is an early morning in the country, when the mist lies in the grass and I ride alone through the fields, with nothing but the birds and the sky above me."

Alice smiled.

"That's a fine picture you've painted. I love the country as well, but London claims all my attention for now."

"She's a demanding mistress."

Alice glanced at Emma further down the line, her cheeks still flushed with indignation.

"And so, it seems, is Lady Emma."

Thomas caught her glance and allowed a brief, sardonic smile.

"Yes, she is."

"Then I imagine it won't be long before you return to your fields and open skies? Your business here looks nearly concluded, judging by Lady Emma's determined watchfulness."

"Are you always this forward in your observations?"

"Usually, yes."

"In that case, yes. We are a good match, and both families favour the union."

"That's wonderful. I'm happy for you both and I', sure you will be very happy."

They would not. She saw that clearly. Was it, perhaps, just as clear to the Duke? If so, she could understand his dour demeanour. The thought of Ben Evans surfaced—his broad face and borrowed views. The fate awaiting the Duke of Hexham... he deserved her sympathy more than her aversion.

"I believe it is you who has turned distant now, Miss Weatherby," he said.

Alice shook her head, as if to banish an unwelcome memory. "Forgive me. I was merely lost in thought."

"Pleasant ones?"

"Not particularly," she replied, a faint smile returning.

"Looking at you, one would think you hadn't a care in the world."

"Don't we all? My cares, I imagine, are quite different from those of a duke, though" she said. "But it seems we've exchanged roles entirely, Your Grace. You're usually not so forthcoming with *your* thoughts and reflections."

"Perhaps you don't know me as well as you think."

"I know you well enough."

"No, you don't," he said abruptly, his tone hardening.

The music ended. He bowed stiffly and left without another word. Alice watched the duke's retreating figure for a moment, slightly taken aback by the abrupt ending to their dance. She shook her head and returned to Mary and Mr Carmichael, who were waiting by the wall.

"Well?" Mary demanded the moment Alice joined them. "How was he? What did you talk about?"

Alice hesitated before replying. "He's not a malicious man, as we first thought, but I wouldn't call him pleasant either. Very private, and to be honest, somewhat dull. I hate to sound so harsh, but not even an earthquake could shake that man out of his inertia."

Mr Carmichael chuckled, glancing across the floor to where he stood, glass in hand, listening to a bald man with a bushy moustache who gestured enthusiastically.

"Remarkable. He's a man who has everything and yet seems unable to find contentment in anything. If I had his fortune and luck in life, I'd be more like Lord Merringer—savouring every moment."

"Yes," Mary said with a thoughtful nod. "For a man like the duke to truly understand joy, he would need to first experience loss like the rest of us."

Mr Carmichael grinned. "I'd be happy to relieve him of his fortune if it would make him happier."

The three of them laughed at that, the tension from earlier conversations fading into a moment of shared amusement.

Chapter 7

"She's quite exquisite, don't you think?" John asked from where he sprawled across the sofa in Thomas's drawing-room. "One of those rare creatures full of both life *and* light."

"Is there a difference?" Thomas asked, leaning over his desk as he wrote a letter.

"There most certainly is. Her red-haired friend, for instance, is full of life—eyes wide, marvelling at everything. But it's only those with light who are truly special."

"You're speaking in riddles, my friend."

"I am not. Tell me you can look at her, completely unmoved, and I'll call you a liar."

"Then call me a liar. I'm indifferent to her."

"As you are to poor Lady Emma. You're indifferent to life, my friend! I've taken it upon myself to open your eyes to all this world has to offer men like us."

"I'm perfectly aware, thank you."

"Of course, you are. But still, the first truly uncharacteristic thing you've done in years was asking Miss Weatherby to dance—right in front of Emma. Oh, what a delightful moment! The look on her face will stay with me forever. Yet, here you are, claiming indifference to the girl?"

"I merely sought to save her from your bad influence."

"I see," John said, grinning. "But you can't always be there to save her. You see, I'm far from indifferent. In fact, I'm quite taken. And since she's of no interest to you, I've decided I shall have her before her twentieth birthday."

Thomas stopped writing and turned to the window.

"Have her? Meaning?"

"Exactly what you think, dear brother. I have a reputation to uphold."

"I see," Thomas said, his tone colder as he returned to his letter. "And you'll do this knowing full well it will destroy her chances of future happiness?"

"I'll be delicate about it. You know I will."

"Yes, because your reputation is built on delicacy," Thomas replied.

After John had left, Thomas called for Morley. "Deliver this to Lady Emma at Belcham House," he instructed, handing over the letter.

Once alone, he leaned back in his chair, staring out at the garden below. The letter he'd sent requested that Emma accompanies him on a walk next Tuesday. Her parents would come along, and before the walk, he intended to ask her father for permission to marry her. He'd propose at the pavilion by the Round Pond, the kind of public spectacle Emma relished. By sealing this chapter of his life, he hoped to move forward with clarity.

But Emma wasn't on his mind at that moment. Instead, it was John and his reckless vow to ruin Miss Weatherby's future. Could Thomas consider himself a gentleman if he stood by and allowed it to happen? Granted, Miss Weatherby was a recent acquaintance, and her well-being was of no particular importance to him. Yet, he couldn't ignore the shadows of his past.

He had done this before. Leana, like Miss Weatherby, had not been a woman of prominence. His selfishness had nearly ruined her life. Though she'd managed to marry—a miller, no less—it didn't absolve him of his actions.

Would Miss Weatherby be so fortunate? Or should he simply stay out of it? From their brief dance, he'd gathered she was sharp and fully aware of John's reputation. Surely, she wouldn't fall for his charms. But if she did, perhaps she wasn't worth saving after all.

Still, uncertainty gnawed at him. He called for Morley again.

"Summon Mr Anderson," he said. "You know the man I mean?"

Morley gave a slight bow. "I do, Your Grace. He'll be here within the hour."

Morley had over-promised. Mr Anderson, clad in a cheap jacket and clutching a worn bowler hat, didn't appear until after dinner.

"Your Grace," Anderson said, making a stiff bow.

"Mr Anderson, thank you for coming on such short notice."

"For Your Grace? Always."

Thomas had first employed Anderson to uncover Leana's fate after their ill-fated affair. The man had proven resourceful, returning with news of her modest marriage and new life.

"I require your expertise once more," Thomas began.

"I see," Anderson replied with another bow.

"Miss Alice Weatherby. She arrived in London two weeks ago. Her cousin is Mary de Vries, but I know little else about her family."

"And what would Your Grace like to know?"

"Everything. Is there anything noteworthy about her family? Any black marks in her history?"

"I see. And when do you require these details?"

"As soon as possible."

Anderson gave a nod, tapping his hat against his palm. "It will be done, Your Grace."

When Anderson had left, Thomas returned to his place by the window, hands clasped behind his back. Below, the streets bustled with people, each one a universe of dreams and ambitions of their own.

He reflected on his own absurdity. Did he really need evidence of Miss Weatherby's virtue to justify saving her from John's clutches? Wouldn't it be nobler to intervene without hesitation? Yet, the decision to dance with her at the ball had already set things in motion, disrupting Emma's carefully managed world. To abandon her now would render that act hollow.

The sun had just risen over the rooftops, the sky a soft blue streaked with thin, high clouds. Alice walked with her mother and Mary toward Hyde Park, listening as Mary spoke without pause about Mr Carmichael—his height, his gentle eyes, his soft-looking hair, and his brilliant intellect. And he read books!

Alice couldn't help but laugh.

"You have indeed secured the finest man in all of England, dear cousin. And since I can see his feelings are the same, I can fully rejoice in your happiness."

"You think they are?"

"I know they are. He couldn't pretend indifference if he tried."

Mary sighed, fanning herself with her hand.

Mrs Weatherby glanced at Alice.

"And you, my dear? Did you meet any agreeable gentleman at the ball?"

"I think Papa has too high hopes for me. There isn't a gentleman for me to marry at a place like that. They're lords from the most prominent families in Britain—they belong to another world. I'm grateful for a glimpse into it, but I harbour no illusions about belonging there. Still, it was wonderful, wasn't it?"

"Indeed, it was," Mrs Weatherby agreed. "And Lord Merringer? What do you make of him?"

"Don't worry about him, Mama. Surely, you don't think me so foolish as to throw myself at any gentleman who shows me attention?"

"I certainly do not."

They walked in companionable silence for a while, even Mary momentarily running out of words. Then Alice said:

"I hope you're not still upset with me for not encouraging the younger Mr Evans?"

Mrs Weatherby covered her mouth as she laughed.

"That poor man! I received a letter from Lucinda yesterday—he's still asking when you'll return to Longhall. Truthfully, I hope he waits forever."

"I'm glad to hear it," Alice said, smiling.

"It may sound strange, but things have changed, haven't they? Even if you're not part of the world of lords and ladies, your world has certainly grown, hasn't it?"

"It has."

"And with these changed circumstances, I can admit you would have thrown yourself away on Mr Evans. But how was I to know your father would finally come to his senses and bring you to London to find a man worthy of you?"

"I think you have the lords of Parliament to thank for that."

"Which I do! I thank them, and the lord in the sky as well!"

As they neared Rotten Row, Alice spotted Mr Stockton further up the path, walking toward them. When he saw her, his face lit up. He stopped and bowed, and Alice introduced him.

"Stockton as in East India Company Stockton?" Mrs Weatherby asked.

"The same," he replied with a warm smile.

"How lovely. I've heard your name for years, as my husband has business in the colonies. He's retired now, leaving matters to our son since he's taken his seat in Parliament. It's a pleasure to finally meet you."

"It's most likely my father's face you've sought, Mrs Weatherby, as he oversees the family business. But I often work at his side, learning the trade."

"As a good son should. Will you walk with us?"

"I would be delighted, Mrs Weatherby," he said with another bow.

They continued together, though Alice found herself separated from Mr Stockton, who walked alongside her mother, answering her questions with ease. When the path forked, and Mr Stockton needed to take another route, Mrs Weatherby invited him to dinner the following evening, which he gladly accepted. He tipped his hat to Alice, then Mary and Mrs Weatherby, before strolling off.

"I like him," Mrs Weatherby said as they resumed their walk. "A nice young man."

"Indeed, he is," Alice replied. And he was. His good nature and easy manners made him pleasant company, though that was all he was to Alice—for now. Her mother, however, already had them halfway down the aisle.

"It would be favourable for George to have a brother-in-law like Mr Stockton. Most favourable indeed!"

"He seems very nice," Mary added. "And tall. Though not as tall as Mr Carmichael."

When Wednesday evening arrived, Alice dressed in one of her favourite gowns and, with her lady's maid, Lovisa, made an extra effort to arrange her hair. Mrs Weatherby made a pleased hum as Alice descended the stairs to the drawing room.

"Yes, most pleasing," she murmured, more to herself than anyone else. "The gentlemen will be here within the hour."

Alongside Mr Stockton, her father, brother, and Mr Carmichael were also expected to join the dinner, as well as her cousin Mary. Wilma, too impatient to sit still, fidgeted on the sofa.

"I bet Mr Stockton is really good looking. As good looking as he is rich, at least!"

"Wilma!" Mrs Weatherby snapped. "No such talk in front of Mr Stockton."

"I'm not stupid, Mama," Wilma retorted, her voice wounded.

"Promise me you'll think before speaking in front of him."

Wilma sighed and rolled her eyes. "I promise."

"Yes, his family is rich," Mrs Weatherby continued. "And so is ours. That makes it an even match. So don't you give him any reason to have second thoughts about the family he might marry into."

"I said I promised!"

"Yes, but that doesn't mean you fully understand the consequences of bad manners. I trust you do now?"

"I do, Mama."

"May I in turn ask you, Mama," Alice said lightly, "to be a little less eager to plot out my entire future with Mr Stockton? You haven't even asked if I like him."

"Of *course* you like him," Mrs Weatherby replied in a tone that made it clear there would be no further discussion on the matter.

Before the gentlemen arrived, Mary came in, jittery with excitement. Mr Stockton was the first of the men to appear. The moment Davies, the butler, took his coat and hat, he fixed his full attention on Alice, smiling as though they hadn't seen each other in weeks. Mrs Weatherby swooped in, effusive with declarations of how pleased she was he could attend on such short notice.

Wilma, suddenly shy, peeked at him from behind the sofa. When her mother urged her forward, she performed a deep curtsey, which made Mr Stockton smile warmly, as if he already regarded her as a little sister. Then he turned to Alice, bowing formally but adding a mischievous smile just for her.

"Miss Weatherby."

"Mr Stockton," Alice replied, matching his smile.

Not long after, Mr Weatherby strode in, accompanied by George, his booming voice filling the room.

"Ah! Mr Stockton, I presume!"

"The same," Mr Stockton said, shaking his hand and then George's.

Mrs Weatherby rang the butler's bell. "Davies, would you please bring the refreshments?"

Davies returned shortly with a tray of punch. While they sipped their drinks, the last guest, Mr Carmichael, arrived. Alice noticed the way his eyes sought out Mary as soon as he entered, and the nervous smile he gave her before greeting Mr Weatherby for the first time. Once introductions were made, Mr Carmichael quickly drifted toward Mary, clearly at ease in her company.

Alice left them to their conversation and wandered the room, fully aware that Mr Stockton's gaze followed her every move.

When dinner was announced, Mrs Weatherby escorted Mr Stockton to the far end of the table, seating him with Mr Carmichael and George. At the head of the table sat Mr Weatherby, Alice, and Wilma. The table, though far from the grandest in London, was large enough to keep Alice and Mr Stockton at a considerable distance, leaving no chance for private conversation.

Mrs Weatherby kept Mr Stockton engaged, smiling and gesturing with a restrained elegance, occasionally nodding down the table toward Alice.

"A gentleman of good fortune he is," Mr Weatherby said, slicing into his roast. "And even if money isn't something this family lacks, a suitable match it is."

"I'm glad you approve, Father. It seems I'm the only one who hasn't been asked my opinion on the matter."

"So, if I were to ask now?"

"I feel like Mother liked him at first glance—a luxury for a future mother-in-law, but not necessarily for a future wife. I don't know him well enough yet, but I certainly don't *dislike* him."

"Well, that's a promising start."

Alice tried to suppress her laughter but failed. Mary tilted her head, curiosity lighting her eyes.

"What?"

"We've just established that my potential for loving Mr Stockton is in great vigour, solely because I didn't hate him at first sight."

"Oh," Mary said, perplexed.

"What are you discussing?" Mrs Weatherby asked, smiling from the other side of the table. "Please, do share. Laughter is best enjoyed together."

"Oh, it's nothing," Alice replied. "Just Father sharing his worldly wisdom."

"That ought to be a deep well to draw from," Mr Stockton said, raising his glass.

Mr Weatherby raised his in return, clearly amused. Alice realised Mr Stockton had charmed yet another supporter for his cause. And what was his cause? Though unstated, it was obvious: he was here to court her.

And she didn't mind. He was good-looking and agreeable, and as both her mother and father had already pointed out, a good match. His interest was certainly not for her family's money. To her family, he was a resounding yes; to Alice, he was at least a maybe.

After dinner, when the women retreated to the drawing room, Wilma pounced.

"He's so nice! And handsome! I love his face! And his eyes—blue like the sky on a summer's day. I need to write that down; it sounds poetic, doesn't it? I've always known I was a poet at heart. Are you going to marry him, Alice? Please say you will."

"It's too early to tell, Wilma. I don't know him well enough yet."

"What's there to know? He made Mother laugh, he has nice teeth, and he's tall."

"Not as tall as Mr Carmichael, though," Mary interjected.

"Leave your sister be, Wilma," Mrs Weatherby said gently. "She needs to catch her breath."

They drank coffee as the conversation gradually shifted to Mary and Mr Carmichael. Though no one asked outright, Mary volunteered the information anyway.

"He's meeting with my father tomorrow. Mother wasn't supposed to tell me, but she did. I won't be able to sleep tonight—I just can't wait for tomorrow."

"Maybe he's seeking business advice," Wilma teased, "or asking for a loan."

Mary pressed her lips together, clearly unsettled by the notion.

Alice reassured her. "It's nothing like that. But my sister is right—you should temper your expectations, just in case."

"Oh, the lot of you!" Mary groaned, collapsing into the sofa dramatically. "Now I won't sleep at all."

"Wasn't that already the case?" Wilma asked with a sly smile.

"Yes! But for far more pleasant reasons!"

When the men joined them in the drawing room, Alice noticed Mary casting an inquisitive glance at Mr Carmichael, as though searching for clues about what tomorrow might hold.

Mr Stockton made his way over and seated himself next to Alice.

"This has been a most pleasurable evening," he said, his tone warm.

"I'm glad to hear it. I hope my father and brother didn't bore you too much with their business talk."

"Their talk is my talk," he replied with an easy smile. "We had a productive exchange, but I must admit, I've been far more eager to speak with you. That hasn't been made easy this evening—until now."

"Well, here we are," Alice said. "What is it you'd like to say to me, Mr Stockton?"

He hesitated for a moment, his expression turning mischievous. "What I *would* like to say is how much I admire your spirit, the light in your eyes, and the sound of your laughter. But that would be far too forward after such a short acquaintance. So instead, I shall comment on the room—the high windows and the truly impressive fireplace."

Alice couldn't help but giggle, her cheeks warming.

"So, the room is to your liking then?"

"It most certainly is," he said, his gaze lingering on her. "It has all the qualities one could ever want from a room of this kind—and then some. If a man could spend his life in a room like this, he would be a truly happy man."

To that she had no answer. During the evening their conversation didn't become quite as personal again, but when Alice walked around it, speaking to the other guests, she could once again feel Mr Stockton following her with his eyes.

Chapter 8

Thomas paced the second floor of Bleaker House, hands clasped behind his back, his gaze fixed on the intricate patterns of the carpet. As expected, Emma had returned his letter promptly, stating she would be delighted to take a walk with him. The pretence of his letter had been painfully obvious—no one sent a letter just to request a walk. When he sent it, he had been resolute about getting the proposal over with. But as the night wore on, his conviction faltered, and by morning, it had turned into full-blown remorse.

If one hesitated before jumping into the fire, perhaps it was wise to pause and examine the reasons for plunging headfirst into the flames. His sleepless night had replayed Emma's venomous remark to Alice:

That was what we all were worrying about—that you hadn't been shown the proper honours.

Alice hadn't exchanged a single word with Emma prior to that moment, so where had such bitterness come from? Was this the kind of woman he wanted to spend the rest of his life with—someone capable of such petty spite?

In two hours, he would need to be in Hyde Park to meet the Fairchilds, and they would expect him to drop to one knee and ask the question Emma had likely been anticipating for months. But he wasn't ready.

Could he cancel? There was still time to send a letter.

But—good Lord—what would that change?

The expectations of the Fairchilds would only be deferred, and in a few days, he'd find himself in the same situation. No, he had to deal with it now, though he had no idea how.

He left the house early, intending to walk slowly to Hyde Park, hoping the fresh air might provide some clarity. The question loomed in his mind: how could he avoid the inevitable without creating irreparable discord? A man like John might weasel his way out of such a predicament with ease, but Thomas lacked those particular skills.

He strolled along the street, oblivious to his surroundings, tipping his hat automatically when others greeted him. His mind churned with possibilities until something stopped him—a tug at his thoughts. Turning, he saw two familiar figures he had barely noticed as he passed: Mrs Weatherby and Miss Weatherby.

When they realised he had paused and turned, they stopped as well. He tipped his hat again, still unsure why he had stopped for these two after ignoring so many others.

"Mrs Weatherby. Miss Weatherby," he said stiffly.

"Your Grace," Mrs Weatherby replied with a polite nod, echoed by Alice.

He groped for something to say, the first words that came to mind tumbling out awkwardly.

"Out walking, I see?"

The statement hung in the air, obvious and unnecessary. His voice was tight, hurried. Surely, they must wonder why he had stopped at all.

"Yes," Mrs Weatherby replied, but her tone held little more than polite acknowledgment.

"Good," Thomas muttered, fumbling to continue. "It's a nice day for it."

A rare feeling of helplessness washed over him. His words were failing him entirely. He wasn't himself—his thoughts were already in Hyde Park, anticipating stern looks from Emmet Fairchild and the stifled sobs of Emma. He needed to escape this encounter before he made a complete fool of himself.

"Good day, ladies," he said abruptly, his lips tight and voice strained. He touched the rim of his hat and walked away, shutting his eyes in frustration as he went.

What on earth had come over him? He had never before lost his composure in such a manner. It didn't bode well for the far more challenging task ahead—facing the Fairchilds, where he would need not just control over his words but mastery of them. The only solace he found was that this disaster had occurred in front of people of lesser importance.

Arriving at Hyde Park, he spotted the Fairchilds waving and smiling. There was no turning back now.

"Thomas, my dear boy!" Emmet greeted him heartily. "You've certainly chosen a fine day for a walk. A fine day indeed!"

You may find it a little less fine by the time we're done, Thomas thought grimly but managed to return the man's smile.

Emma and her mother were full of pleasantries, and soon the group began their walk. The ladies took the lead while Thomas and Emmet brought up the rear.

"It's a great benefit to have such a large park for walks and recreation in the middle of the city," Emmet remarked.

Thomas recognised the subtle prompt. Emmet wasn't one for idle chit-chat; he expected Thomas to lead the conversation. The comment, however, sparked an idea—a means of delay, if not escape.

"During the dinner party at Bleaker House, I never shared my own thoughts on the best place for walking," Thomas began. "For me, it's Hertfordshire. I don't believe my father ever invited you to Somerfield?"

Emmet glanced sideways at him. "I believe that's correct."

"I'd like to correct that oversight. I'd be honoured if you and your family would visit Somerfield to see the estate and its grounds."

Emmet's expression turned thoughtful, his silence weighing heavily on Thomas.

"It's well known that the Somerfield estate is one of the finest in Britain," Emmet finally said. "But... are you suggesting we leave in the middle of the season?"

If Thomas said yes, it would signal the same commitment as a proposal. However, suggesting a visit after the season would expose his invitation as a stalling tactic.

"It's unconventional, I admit," Thomas said carefully. "But sometimes a breather from all the balls and parties is much needed."

He felt the absurdity of his words even as he spoke them. Inviting the Fairchilds to Somerfield was a greater cruelty—letting them envision Emma as mistress of the estate—than simply admitting his doubts now. But he had already taken this step, and he couldn't go back on it now.

"Yes," Emmet said, a rare smile softening his otherwise severe expression. "That would be most satisfactory."

Then he called for his wife and daughter. Their eager anticipation… it only deepened Thomas's guilt. Truly, he was the lowest of men.

The reaction was as expected: first, a fleeting plunge into disappointment, but then, they interpreted the invitation in the most favourable light. Their acceptance was swift and enthusiastic.

Five days later, Mr Anderson returned to Bleaker House. Thomas led him to the drawing room, remaining standing as he leaned against the mantelpiece.

Mr Anderson carefully placed his hat on the table and smoothed his moustache with his thumb and forefinger.

"Her father is the son of a baronet," Mr Anderson began, "but the son isn't anything like the father."

"That doesn't sound promising," Thomas remarked.

"On the contrary," Mr Anderson said. "The father squandered the family name and fortune, but the son has worked tirelessly to restore both. He's wealthy. Very wealthy. Owns extensive land, but much of his fortune comes from trade in the colonies."

"And why is he in London?"

"He's recently secured a seat in Parliament. Naturally, he's also here to marry off his daughters."

Ah, Thomas thought. People married for either money or reputation, and since the Weatherby's clearly didn't lack money, it had to be the later. He needed to applaud Miss Weatherby's art of cunning and strategy, then, to get herself into the most prominent balls of the aristocracy. Skilful navigation indeed, yet he couldn't deny a nagging sense of disappointment.

"She has an elder brother, George, who has ostensibly taken over the family business, though the father remains firmly in control. As for Miss Weatherby, she has never been engaged, and there's nothing in her history to stain her honour."

"I see," Thomas murmured.

"And then there's the youngest sibling, Wilma," Mr Anderson continued. "Too young to be of concern, but she's wild at heart. The father will have his hands full when it's her turn to debut."

Thomas nodded. "There's always one in every family. Thank you for your report, Mr Anderson. Speak to Morley; he'll see to your payment."

Mr Anderson stood, bowing deeply. "Your Grace."

Once alone, Thomas turned to the window, gazing down at the bustling street below.

Had he taken too much of an interest in Miss Weatherby's future? No, he decided. It was the decent thing to do—for her and, in a way, for himself. He owed it to Leana too.

During the days that had passed since his meeting with Miss Weatherby and her mother, he had not been able to let go of the incident. The way he had reduced himself to a stuttering fool. Well, he hadn't actually stuttered, but he might as well have. What would they be thinking of him now? They couldn't possibly know that his odd behaviour had nothing to do with them.

Well, maybe he could make some amends since the Monroe Ball was tonight, and John, with an eager grin, had told him he had ensured that an invitation was sent to Miss Weatherby.

The thought of simply telling John to stay away from Miss Weatherby, to avoid ruining her future, had occurred to him, but he knew John too well. To tell him something was forbidden was to him what a jar of honey was to bees. He was spoiled rotten, a man of no morals, and perhaps, as Emma had said, unworthy of Thomas's friendship. But in a world where everyone was so darn obsessed with appearances, so eager to flatter or be flattered, John was a completely different breed. Thomas simply couldn't do without him in London. That didn't mean he could stand by and watch as John brought down a good woman. Mr Anderson's report had confirmed what he had already suspected—that Alice Weatherby was indeed a woman worth saving. If John didn't stay away from her, Thomas would just have to tell her the kind of man John was and perhaps even introduce her to someone better suited to her, both in temperament and background.

When he stepped out of his carriage outside Lady Monroe's house, his mind was focused solely on speaking with Miss Weatherby as quickly as possible. Perhaps he couldn't erase the memory of their last meeting, but he could at least leave her with a better, more recent impression of him. As he walked up to the house, he became annoyed with himself. Why should it matter to him what a girl of her simple birth thought of him?

The house in front of him was a large stone building, blackened with age. The garden lay in darkness, but bushes and trees were sporadically lit by the light spilling from the building's tall windows.

The footman opened the door as he approached. Emma would be arriving a little later, so he would have to make his entrance alone, which he didn't particularly mind.

When he entered the ballroom, the music from the orchestra engulfed him. It was being played from a balcony on the second floor, out of sight and out of mind.

The setting was different from the Longleat Ball—dark wooden floors and gilded embellishments—but everything else was the same. The same faces, the same nods across the floor, and glasses raised to greet him. He scanned the room for Miss Weatherby but couldn't find her.

A servant approached him, and he took a glass of iced punch from the tray. A tap on his shoulder interrupted him, and before he turned, he already knew who it was. No one but John—even though they were lifelong friends—would dare address a duke so informally.

"Brother," Thomas greeted him with a broad smile. "I should've known you'd already be here."

"I'm always present, in one way or another."

"That's true. Any closer to fulfilling your mother's wish to see you properly married?"

John scanned the room and shook his head. "There's one last thing I need to do, as you already know, before I can grant my mother that wish. But I don't see the particular lady here tonight. Well, a lady she isn't, but you know what I mean."

"I know she'll never have the chance to be considered a lady once you're done with her. Is there nothing I can do to make you reconsider?"

"There isn't. My mind is quite set on the matter. I like her special glow, and what I like, I take. Hasn't that always been the way of the lord?"

"Perhaps in a darker, less enlightened era," Thomas replied, sipping his punch.

"My brother," John said, spreading his arms. "Don't be so serious and gloomy. This is the last time, I promise. Then I'll behave and make everyone happy by marrying some dull girl of acceptable background."

"I think you underestimate this girl. She won't be easily swayed by your tricks and promises."

"Oh, is that a challenge I hear?"

"It most certainly is not."

"And why, may I ask, are you so concerned with this particular girl? From what I see, you're mere acquaintances."

"You're mistaken," Thomas said, sipping his punch again. "I have no special regard for her. I only think it's time for you to grow up. That's all."

"Such harsh words for a man who, when it comes down to it, has a heart of gold."

"You're beginning to test my patience."

"Impossible. I've been told I'm quite charming. If there's any doubt, I'll choose to believe the former reality over your suggested one. Annoying? Ridiculous."

Just then, the doors opened. Emma entered with her mother, radiating confidence, her smile commanding the attention of the entire room.

"I don't know," John said, his voice low. "But I always feel like biting my knuckles when I look at Emma. Such beauty wasted on such a cold creature."

"That would be my future fiancée you're referring to," Thomas said, attempting to adopt some of Emma's coldness in his tone.

"Oh, pray not," John murmured as Emma approached, her smile reserved solely for Thomas.

"Thomas," she said, inclining her head gracefully.

"Lady Emma," John interjected, before Thomas had gotten a chance to reply, and made a deep bow. "And with the proper civility being displayed, I'll retreat to the punch room. Join me for a card game later, will you?" he said to Thomas before strolling off like he had no care in the world.

In that moment Thomas envied him copiously.

"What a dreadful man he is," Emma said, looking after him with an almost unnoticeable shake of her head. "One could even argue that his conduct makes him unworthy of the title lord. That does actually come with some obligations." Her face softened and she looked at Thomas with a smile. "In my mind a lord has to be dignified, sure of himself and what he wants, but never act in a way that could be deemed improper." She grabbed him gently by the arm, tucking it close to her body. "A lord should be precisely what you are, my dear Thomas."

"And a lady should be everything that you are, Lady Emma," he replied, because he had to, but the omission of a "dear Emma" made her straighten and let go of his arm, instead placing a strand of her platinum hair behind her ear and looking out over the room.

"I very much look forward to visiting Somerfield. I've heard only the best of things about it. Will you and Father set a date?"

"That we will," he said.

The doors opened again, and Thomas saw Miss Weatherby enter in the company of her mother and Miss de Vries. Miss de Vries was, as usual, gawking at the room, while Miss Weatherby looked at the people in it with a reserved look that he saw for what it was, nervousness masked. Yes, he thought, thinking about Mr Anderson's report. She had done well to get this far but her uncertainty was justified. She was clever enough to understand that the only reason she was here was because of John, and if she was half as clever as he thought she was, she understood the reason why. Her ambition to marry up and secure a title for herself was seriously inhibited by the presence of John. No one would look at her as long as she kept his interest, and if she lost it, the doors to balls like this would close before her.

Quite an interesting little conundrum there.

"Oh, it's that girl again. I can't understand what she's doing at an assembly like this. Is it John that keeps inviting her?"

"It is."

"I don't know if I should pity her or not. The attention of a lord is enough for a girl like her to ruin herself on hope alone." She gave Thomas a sideways glance. "She has just such a… *common* appeal, don't you think? Daughter of a tradesman. She could just as well be selling fruit down at the market."

Yes, maybe, Thomas thought. Her smile and easy manners would stop enough customers to make it worthwhile.

He jolted mentally. Where did that thought come from? He didn't know but needed to keep his mind in check. Obviously the Weatherby girl was more entrenched in his mind than he had previously thought, but at the same time he knew the reason for it, his dismaying behaviour the last time they met. When he had cleared out that blot of ink from his mind, he would be able to oust her completely.

"Thomas? Did you hear me?"

"Yes, selling fruit down at the market. I think she would be quite good at it."

"I do too," Emma said, encouraged by his response. "With her rural charisma she would be perfect for the job."

His and Alice's eyes met. She stopped briefly, giving him a slight nod but no change of her expression, before letting her gaze drift past him.

"Did she *nod* at you?" Emma said, exasperated.

"It certainly looked like it. We're, after all, previously acquainted."

Emma sighed.

"Yes, that is unfortunate, but it honours you that you didn't return that nod. Such an insolent manner of greeting one's superiors."

I didn't return the nod, he thought, *because she looked away before I had the time.*

Her cold recognition of his presence bothered him more than he liked, and not for the reasons that agitated Emma. He needed to talk to her but couldn't very well just tell Emma to wait while he crossed the room to do it. She needed to come to him, but she had no reason to do that. But maybe if…

He turned to Emma.

"Lady Emma, may I ask if you would oblige me with the first two dances?"

She blushed and fluttered her eyelids.

"You may, and I will."

"Capital. And now, would you care for something to drink?"

She did, and since no waiters were around, he offered to go fetch refreshments for them. As he walked into the punch room, he found people mingling around the punch bowl. He was maybe not a master of psychology, but he understood that if a person felt out of place and exposed, she would feel better holding a glass.

And he was right.

Miss Weatherby stood with her mother and the de Vries girl by the wall, all with fresh glasses of punch in their hands. He grabbed one for himself and Emma and, when leaving the room, he walked close enough to them that it would be impossible for him to not "notice" them.

Miss Weatherby tensed visibly when she saw him. So, this was what he had to overcome? Mrs Weatherby reacted in the same manner. He smiled and bowed to them.

"Mrs and Miss Weatherby. I'm glad to see you here tonight."

"Likewise," Mrs Weatherby said. "It's really such a grand place."

"It is," he said, stealing a glance at Miss Weatherby, who immediately cast down her eyes. "But rather than talking about the house, I would like to apologise for my odd behaviour last time we met."

Miss Weatherby looked up again.

"I was quite in a world of my own and assume I came across as a bit rude. That wasn't my intention."

Mrs Weatherby put her palm to her chest and laughed.

"You did nothing of the sort, Your Grace. You were quite the gentleman."

"Oh, but Mother, you shouldn't let him get away that easily," Miss Weatherby said, glancing at Thomas with half a smile. "Because if you do, he will never better his ways."

"Alice! That's not a way of speaking to a duke!" her mother blurted, cheeks colouring.

Thomas returned Miss Weatherby's cordial smile.

"And do my ways need… bettering?"

"They most certainly do, Your Grace. Some words of apology can never make amends for the atrocity of not chatting long enough about the weather and the wind during a random encounter with an acquaintance."

Her mother made a nervous laugh.

"You are correct, Miss Weatherby," Thomas said. "My ill doings cannot soon be forgotten. I can only hope that you, in time, will find it in your heart to forgive this slight of your person."

"Oh, I very much doubt that will be the case," she said. "But with such ample time to think, I might reconsider."

He couldn't help widening his smile and, for a brief second, he dared to ponder how life would be spent together with a woman with such a liberal way of speaking. It could not happen, of course, but the thought of it warmed him for a second. Mrs Weatherby was looking between them, as if not certain what was going on. Her face was still coloured, but the strained and anxious look on it had disappeared. She was not of her daughter's disposition, he could clearly tell.

"I hope you will, Miss Weatherby," he said and gave a slight bow.

He would like to stay longer in her company because he assumed that this was as much amusement as he would get out of the evening. He liked the playful tone of her voice while she hurled what, in other instances, would be insults, in his face. Was that a part of the light John had been talking about? He presumed it was.

She and her mother tilted their heads in return. When he turned to the doorway, he saw Emma standing there, watching them. He froze in place for half a second before gathering himself, raising the glasses slightly as if to say that the objective was completed. When he worked his way over to her, she accepted the glass with a strained smile.

"Miss Weatherby?"

"Yes, we ran into each other at the punch table. Courtesy demanded I share at least a few words with her."

"The smile on your face didn't make it look like much of an effort."

"It wasn't. She has some wit and charm."

"In a trivial, common way, I assume?"

"If you prefer."

They stood in silence, drinking punch. From behind, Thomas heard John in his most vivid and cheerful manner. He was addressing Miss Weatherby.

Thomas's grip on his glass tensed.

He tried to hear Miss Weatherby's reply but couldn't make it out.

Then the dance was about to start, and he led Lady Emma to the floor. She was smiling and nodding to everyone looking her way, but her hand in his was stiff and cold.

Chapter 9

The day after the ball at Monroe's, the Weatherby family was gathered at the breakfast table. Mrs Weatherby leaned closer to Alice.

"I saw you dance with that Lord Merringer again last night. I'm not sure I like it, Alice."

"So you've said, Mama, but without him, we wouldn't even be in those great halls."

"I know. But maybe you should ask yourself if you need to? I understand that it's a beautiful and wondrous world to take part in, but it's not our world. Lord Merringer and no man of his stature would ever look at a girl like you with serious intent."

"I thank you for your high opinion of me," Alice said, but with a smile and half a laugh. "But again, I'm not that gullible. It's a fairy tale world, I know, but after having lived in complete dullness the last couple of years, I think I'm in my right to indulge myself a little."

"Surely," Mrs Weatherby agreed. "But don't get blinded and dazzled by the high lords when a lovely man like Mr Stockton so clearly has shown his interest in you."

"Yes, such a lovely man and with such a lovely fortune!"

"Oh, hush you!" Mrs Weatherby said with a frown. "At least we know he won't marry you for money."

"Now you're there again, Mama, having me married away before the question has even been asked."

"He'll talk to your father soon enough, you'll see."

"What are you two talking about?" Wilma demanded.

"Nothing of importance, dear," Mrs Weatherby said, cutting her fish.

"You'll learn, little sister," George said. "That when women have attended a ball, they can talk about it for about as long as the ball itself lasted. So for me, there's no mystery at all about what they are talking."

"Oh, I long *so* for when I will be allowed to attend the balls," Wilma said dreamily. "I'll bet I'll be a huge success."

"No one is in doubt about that, Wilma," Mr Weatherby said while reading the paper. "Since your older sister is already married, you have only to wait for your second oldest to do the same."

"So why don't you," Wilma said, "just pick the one you prefer and be done with it!"

Mrs Weatherby chuckled.

"You are too much of a child to understand these matters and that, in return, makes you too much of a child to attend a ball."

"I'm not!" Wilma clenched her fork. "I can be every bit as grown up as Alice if needed."

"Sure you can, little sister," Alice said in her most soothing voice. "But this is just how these things work, and when I find the man I prefer, I will do as you wish, and just pick him."

"How long will that be?"

"That's quite enough," Mrs Weatherby said in her sharp voice.

Wilma silenced and started to shuffle her food around on the plate.

Mrs Weatherby leaned closer to Alice again. "I must as well say that his grace, despite his other peculiarities, behaved as one could expect from a gentleman last night."

"Yes," Alice agreed. "I think I need to cross him off my list of sworn enemies."

"I wouldn't go that far," Mrs Weatherby replied. "But my opinion of him has shifted slightly in his favour."

Alice giggled. It wasn't often, but sometimes she really felt like her mother's daughter, and this was one of those moments.

She had been a bit startled to meet the duke at the ball, not that he was there—that she had known in advance—but that he stopped and talked to her and her mother. Last they met, it had seemed a great burden for him to do so, but yesterday it had been almost a completely new man walking up to them. He had been polite and respectful, but not in a forced manner. It had actually felt like he was happy to talk to them. But, she hadn't been able to resist giving him a little stab with the needle, to see if she could deflate him.

She hadn't.

He had accepted her challenge and surprised her by actually having a sense of humour. How different wasn't he suddenly? And how different wasn't he compared to his boisterous friend, Lord Merringer, who seemed to crave all of her attention, all the time? When he excused himself to return to Lady Emma, she had realised that she wouldn't have minded talking to him some more, if anything else, just to see if his transformation was a permanent thing or if he would soon revert to his old, cold self.

"What are you two laughing about?" Wilma demanded.

After breakfast, Alice sat down on the sofa with a book and a cup of tea while Wilma played on the pianoforte, repeating some scales. Mrs Weatherby sat on the sofa by the window, knitting. The day was windy, and the sky grey. The elm trees outside shook and bristled in the stiff wind and rain—no more than moisture carried by the wind—streaked the windows. Inside, the hearth crackled and sent embers up the chimney. Alice was deep in her book, sipping tea, when she heard a carriage outside. Mrs Weatherby and Alice looked at each other while Wilma banged down on the keys and rushed to the window.

"A visitor at this time of day?" Mrs Weatherby said. "It must be either someone ill-brought-up or someone too high and mighty to care."

It proved to be the latter because Wilma reported back that the coachman was wearing a black and green livery; the colours of the Fairchilds.

"There's a tall woman with fair hair stepping out," Wilma continued. "Oh, she's gorgeous. You should *see* her!"

"Oh, that must be Lady Emma," Mrs Weatherby gasped. "What a remarkable honour." She started puffing up the pillows around her. "Just to think that you have attracted the friendship of such a person, Alice… Wilma, get away from the window! And when Lady Emma enters, you'll introduce yourself and then you don't speak unless spoken to. Is that understood?"

Wilma sat down on the sofa and nodded, her cheeks pale from the soon-to-come encounter with a woman who had been introduced to the Prince Regent himself. The only one in the room who wasn't excited by the visitor was Alice. She had a sinking feeling, because she had a very good idea of what had brought this visit on, and it wasn't friendship.

Mr Davies swung the doors open and introduced, without much surprise, Lady Emma Fairchild.

The Weatherbys stood up as one when she entered. Lady Emma nodded politely to Wilma, who made her best curtsey, holding out her dress and tilting her head.

"Tea, Lady Emma?"

"Thank you, Mrs Weatherby, but I'm not planning to stay long. I was hoping to maybe talk in private with Miss Weatherby."

"Oh, but of course, of course," Mrs Weatherby said, fluttering Wilma and herself out of the room.

Alice and Lady Emma sat down on opposing sofas.

"Miss Weatherby."

"Lady Emma. I wasn't expecting you—"

"No, Miss Weatherby, I'm not going to grace you with small talk and pleasantries, but I will grant you the favour of frank speech. I do not appreciate your conduct with my fiancé, Thomas Overton."

"Conduct? I don't understand. I've talked to his grace thrice during my stay in London. There has been nothing improper about it."

"That would certainly be the case for a casual observer, but I see how you try to snare him with your laughs and cheeky remarks. I'm here to tell you, since Thomas is too much of a gentleman to do it himself, that he has no interest in you and would prefer it if you just stopped bothering him."

"Bothering?" Alice had to calm herself before continuing. "Not once during the three times I've spoken to his grace have I been the one to initiate the conversation. If he wants rid of me, it's the easiest thing in the world for him to achieve. He only needs to not engage me in conversation next time we meet."

Lady Emma gaped.

"Such… *insolence!* To even suggest that a man like Thomas Overton…" She briefly turned her head away, and when she looked back, her cheeks were afire, and her eyes were hard with contempt. "I understand how women like you work, Miss Weatherby. You don't approach; you just *happen* to run into the man in question. Right? Like you stood in ambush at the punch table just the other night. What could he do but stop and give you the attention you can demand as a previous acquaintance? It's foul play, Miss Weatherby, and it has to stop, for your sake and his."

"For my sake? I believe you have misinterpreted this entirely. I have no interest whatsoever in his grace. If I never speak to him again, I would be no worse off, but there's another thing entirely when one like yourself demands it of me. You might be a lady and I the daughter of a tradesman, but that grants you no power over me, and you will see that it was a mistake coming to my home and speaking to me in such a manner."

"So, you will persist in this endeavour? Is that it?"

"I will persist in this 'endeavour' as I previously have—by doing nothing at all. And if that infuriates her ladyship, then so be it."

"I hoped that I could talk some sense into you. I see now that it was a fool's errand. You are just as simple as your common birth would suggest. Too stupid to realise that the idea of you with the Duke of Hexam is just a laughable prospect."

"And yet, here you are, in your own high and mighty presence, to explain the impossibility of it all," Alice said with a solemn smile. "Doesn't really seem worth the effort, wouldn't you say?"

Lady Emma gave her a smile in return, a cold and unpleasant one.

"You don't want to play this game with me, Miss Weatherby. One word from me and your reputation will be ruined forever."

Alice looked at Lady Emma in silence, slowly realising what she was saying.

"You say that there's been nothing improper in your conduct with the duke, but can you say the same for Lord Merringer?"

"Indeed I can."

"And if I say otherwise… Who do you think they will believe? You have your reputation to think of, but what reason would I have to lie? None. None whatsoever… What? Cat caught your tongue? No witty remark? Don't you know that people are talking already? 'What on earth,' they say, 'is it with that common girl and Lord Merringer? Why does she pop up at every party and ball he attends? What can a plain girl like her have to entice a lord?' There can be only one thing, they say. You see, little Miss Alice, Lord Merringer is known for tasting common girls with questionable morals. Nothing is decided about you and your morals—yet, but as I said, one word from me will decide your future forever. Do you understand?"

Alice gave a nod, feeling her insides like boiling, red-hot metal. Lady Emma was so far off the mark that it would have been comical in other circumstances, but the power her word held wasn't something Alice wanted to test. So, she did the only thing she could do and swallowed her pride.

"I understand."

"You will never again talk to him. If he enters a room, you leave through the other door. Are we agreed?"

"We are."

After Lady Emma had left, Mrs Weatherby and Wilma were brimming with curiosity to hear every word uttered by the esteemed lady. Alice was less than inclined to retell the conversation, or even the gist of it, and lied—saying that Lady Emma had stopped by out of politeness and that they weren't to be considered friends. To this, her mother reacted with a disappointed "oh" followed by a confirmation that friendships needed time to grow, just as love did, and that a stop out of politeness could soon be the coming together of sisters. *We'll see,* Alice had responded before putting on her pelisse and a shawl, almost fleeing from the house. Mary was to come by later, but Alice felt that she needed a moment alone to clear her thoughts.

She didn't walk towards Hyde Park that day but to Kensington Square Garden. The wind tugged at her clothing, and she had the streets to herself. She felt, in want of a better word, shattered—her thoughts like fragments of a broken vase.

She knew that Lady Emma didn't think much of her, but what had made her travel through town to knock on her door, sit down on her sofa and hurl insults at her?

And threaten her?

It didn't make sense.

Her fiancé Thomas Overton… *Fiancé*? Was he really? She had heard nothing about that, but on the other hand, did it matter? No, what did matter was that Lady Emma, for some reason, had come to think that Alice was out to steal Thomas from her. What had led her to that conclusion, Alice couldn't fathom. Thrice she had spoken to the man! Twice he had been downright rude and impolite. The last time he, for the first time, had acted like a gentleman. Was it that meeting alone that had thrown Lady Emma into a fit of jealousy? If so, Alice guessed she spent a lot of her time making house calls.

She tried to rethink her conversation with Thomas, the back and forth between them. She had enjoyed it; she had already admitted as much. And hadn't she got the feeling he did as well?

Yes, she had.

And if she had got that feeling, she could be darned sure Lady Emma had as well.

No mystery there, then.

Alice hated to be bullied into submission, but the threat from Lady Emma wasn't to be taken lightly. From here on, she had to break all contact with both the duke and Lord Merringer. She had no grievance over that, though. Her main interest wasn't in any of the high lords but in Mr Stockton, whom she was to meet again at the ball at Mrs Sophie's. He had implied that an invitation might find its way to her, and it had.

She very much looked forward to it.

She hadn't more than got back to the house and handed her wet pelisse to the maid before a rider in the Merringer livrée appeared at the courtyard. Alice was by the fire, warming her hands when Mr Davies announced the rider, and she got the opportunity to make good on her decision. The butler handed over an invitation to the Halcomb ball Mrs Sophie's that was to take place the coming Friday. Mrs Weatherby, who was back on the sofa by the window, knitting, lifted one of her eyebrows. When she heard Alice's answer to the footman, the other eyebrow rose as well.

"Send my thanks to Lord Merringer, and my apologies as well, since I'm otherwise engaged."

The footman took a bow and left, and when they were alone again, Mrs Weatherby said:

"Was it wise to decline an invitation like that?"

"Wasn't it you, Mama, that said I was just a visitor in the grand halls of the aristocracy and should focus my energy where it would better serve my future?"

"Yes, I did, but…"

"And since you are such an insightful woman, I decided to take you up on those words and decline Lord Merringer in favour of Mr Stockton and the ball at Mrs Sophie's. Who needs the grand halls of the aristocracy?"

Mrs Weatherby put down the knitting in her lap and sighed.

"Perhaps, but can't you do both? Your father is very much in favour of you attending those balls. You know what his highest wishes are?"

"For me to marry into a life of joy and happiness?"

Mrs Weatherby gave her a stern look.

"Yes, of course, but the world isn't as black and white as you want to make it, Alice. You can marry up and still be perfectly happy, as you can attend both the balls of the aristocracy and those of a… more modest nature."

"Ah, I see it clearly now, Mama. You want me to secure Mr Stockton, but if a better opportunity arises, I shall dump him overboard like a sack of old potatoes?"

"Oh, for the love of… Black and white, Alice. That's all I'm saying. Black and white. Nothing is ever as clear-cut as the youth of the world would prefer. There are scales of grey, my dear, and since you have recently become friends with such an impressive woman as Lady Emma, maybe you're starting to entrench yourself in their world? Maybe it can be your world as well? You know, there's nothing wrong with ambition."

"You too, Mama? But what if I don't want to be part of that world? Maybe Mr Stockton is everything I've ever wished for?"

"But… is he?"

"He could be… maybe. I don't know what I wish for. Maybe I just want to make my own choice and not be forced into marriage with the likes of Mr Evans. But such is human nature; when one has got what she wants, she wants more. I've never fantasised about my future husband, how he should look and be and all that, but if I should do that now, I wish for love. I wish for love and longing. Someone to respect and be respected by. Is that man Mr Stockton? I truly don't know. You see, Mama, this is a lottery. You don't know who someone is before you truly know them, and to truly get to know a person takes longer than our hasty courtships allow."

Mrs Weatherby snorted.

"Talking like an oracle of wisdom, yes? You are a mere 19 years old but talk like you've seen all of what the world has to offer? Experienced all its joys and disappointments? The world isn't going to grant you special treatment, Alice. If it's a lottery, you have to take part in it like everybody else and hope you pull the winning ticket."

"I'm not arguing that point, Mama, just saying I don't know if Mr Stockton is the man I'm hoping he is. Because that is all I can do, hope."

"Well, hope has worked marvels before, and if you're set on Mr Stockton, then Mr Stockton it shall be! Talk to your father about some new dresses. Let us dazzle Mr Stockton to show his true colours!"

Mary came to visit after luncheon and was in high spirits. Mr Carmichael hadn't yet talked to her father about the most important question, but he had at least invited her to watch the fireworks at Vauxhall Gardens that very night, and pray, wouldn't Alice come as well? She could maybe bring Mr Stockton. Alice found it to be a most agreeable idea. The weather had cleared, and she had for the longest time wanted to see the much-talked-about fireworks at Vauxhall Gardens, and maybe even the Cascade, a technological marvel in the form of an artificial waterfall, made of tin with the sound of thunder and storm.

"It's a splendid idea, dear cousin!"

When the soft summer evening came, the party set off for the Vauxhall Gardens on the south side of the Thames. Much luck had been involved in getting Mr Stockton to join them. He hadn't been at home when the Weatherbys' footman had knocked at his door, but he had appeared just as the carriages were about to roll out from the Weatherbys', smiling and bowing. Now Alice was sitting face-to-face with him in a carriage they shared with Mrs de Vries. They looked at each other, secret smiles at both ends, while Mrs de Vries talked for the whole company.

"You will marvel, Alice, at all the fantastic things you will see at the garden! Nothing of the sort is to be found outside London. This I'll promise you!"

"I'm really looking forward to it, aunt," Alice replied.

"Don't promise too much," Mr Stockton said. "The appreciation of anything has to do with expectations, wouldn't you agree, Miss Weatherby?"

"Indeed, I do."

"So you see, Mrs de Vries, this is precisely why I've taken great care to lower Miss Weatherby's expectations of me—ensuring I won't disappoint her later."

"Oh, you scoundrel," Mrs de Vries said, smiling and flapping a gloved hand in the air. "Surely you couldn't disappoint even if you tried."

"You don't know half of it! You weren't there the early morning when she spotted me on Rotten Row, horseracing. Her company looked at me most disregarding."

"Could the same be said of me, Mr Stockton?"

"A hesitant glance I saw, but maybe nothing more than that. I think I've redeemed myself since, which of course has the unfortunate effect that it will make it even harder for me to not disappoint you further."

"But you will try?"

"Oh yes, I will! It's in my nature," he said with a laugh.

When they neared the Vauxhall Gardens, a row of carriages lined the road up to the entrance. Far was it, apparently, from the esteemed guests to step out before their carriage was actually in front of the entrance gates. A great shame it must be to walk past carriages with their peers looking out on them, even if it would save them half an hour of their lives. When they finally arrived at the fabled wrought iron gates of the gardens, Mr Stockton exited the carriage first, to be able to help Alice and Mrs de Vries out, steadying them by the hand. From the carriage behind them, Mary, Mr Carmichael and Mrs Weatherby spilled out. The sisters immediately picked up their conversation from where they had left off. Mary and Mr Carmichael joined Alice and Mr Stockton.

"Just to think we would get an evening like this, after that horrible brush of bad weather earlier," Mary said.

Incredible it was. The night was silky, and the sky a deep blue but not yet black. The lights on the other side of the Thames had just flickered to life. From behind the high wall of dense hedges, she could hear music. When they passed through the gates, she saw a three-storey structure, well-lit, painted in lively colours and open at the front. In all the three storeys, musicians played their strings and brass, sending silvery tones through the warm evening. It was an evening of promises, Alice thought. Maybe even a magical one that would never be forgotten? She hoped for that, but was Mr Stockton the man to make it unforgettable? She hoped for that too.

"Isn't it lovely, Alice?" Mrs de Vries asked, and even if Alice agreed, Mrs de Vries wouldn't have allowed her to be of a different opinion.

"Indeed, it is."

They walked the gravel paths of the garden, the scent of roasted almonds wafting in the air, hearing music through the greenery, passing the Rotunda and the Chinese pavilion. Actors in colourful clothes walked the paths on high stilts and colourful paper lanterns floated like firebugs in the night. Workers in their finest clothes milled around with members of the nobility in their expensive dresses, tailcoats and high hats.

"When do the fireworks start?" Mary asked.

"I think you'll notice," Mr Stockton said.

"Yes, of course, I will, but I want to be up on the knoll when it starts, to see it so much better."

"We will all be at the knoll in good time. I'll see to that," Mr Stockton answered.

"Yes, we'll see to it," Mr Carmichael added.

"Isn't that..." Mrs de Vries started but never completed her sentence.

They looked the same way she did, and further up the walk, three gentlemen in high hats and tailcoats walked, looking bored. The one on the right Alice well recognised. Her heart skipped a beat and froze.

It was the duke.

Lady Emma wasn't anywhere to be seen, but that didn't mean there weren't other people there to see. She could only hope for the duke and his friends to pass her without noticing.

That didn't happen.

For a brief second, he just stared at her, as though he had expected pretty much anyone to be in the garden, except her. Then he gave a smile and a nod, turned to his friends, told them something, and started to walk towards her.

Those assembled around Alice stiffened and straightened. Mr Stockton's hand flew up to his cravat to make sure it was proper.

The duke stopped before them and bowed, a gesture that was returned with great emphasis by the men. Mrs de Vries curtsied while Alice and Mary, as previous acquaintances, tilted their heads.

"Your Grace, I'm very glad to make your acquaintance," Mr Stockton said, making a new bow just for the sake of it.

"Likewise," Thomas said and went through all the necessary pleasantries without ever letting his attention wander away from Alice.

"It's nice to see you again, Miss Weatherby," he said before turning to Mrs de Vries. "May I walk in your company for a while?"

"Oh, yes, certainly, Your Grace. We would be honoured."

When they started walking again, the duke had taken place by Alice's side. She gave him a sideways glance.

"I think your friends deserted you, Your Grace."

"They didn't. I told them to continue without me."

And why on earth's name did you do that? she thought but did not say. He had, at the Monroe Ball, more than made amends for their uncomfortable meeting the week previous. He had no reason at all for this continuing show of attention towards her.

"I must congratulate you on your engagement to Lady Emma. It's a most suitable match."

He frowned but didn't look at her.

"Engaged? To Lady Emma? From where have you gotten that notion?"

Alice looked forward as well, wishing she could take her words back because she felt she had ventured out on thin ice.

"Well, from the lady herself."

"Ahh," Thomas said as if that explained everything.

They walked in silence for a moment before he continued:

"I'm not, though. Engaged to Lady Emma. I don't presume it would be of a special interest to you, Miss Weatherby, but I'd rather not have untruths like that circulating."

"I perfectly understand."

She glanced at him again. He was dressed in a maroon tailcoat, perfectly polished black boots and a top hat. He really was a most handsome man. She hadn't given herself the chance to see that before, since all she had seen was his haughty arrogance.

This, she realised, was their first moment of actual privacy. Sure, Mrs de Vries walked beside them, but her constant talking to her sister about this and that created more of a protective shield towards the others than an intrusion on their privacy. But what did Mr Stockton think? She had invited him here, but now the duke had commanded her attention. But, she hadn't had much of a choice, had she? He was a duke, after all, and if he wanted to walk by her side, there wasn't much she could do about it.

At the other side of the company, Mary and Mr Carmichael seemed absorbed by a story Mr Stockton was telling, vividly moving his hands. Mr Stockton was perfectly all right then and, at least not yet felt the slight of having Alice's attention stolen from him.

"Your Grace," she began. "You have already shown me every bit of attention one could ask from a man of your stature. You have no further obligations towards me."

"Oh," he said, looking at her with half a smile. "Does my company bother you so?"

"It does not, but I'll admit it confuses me."

"Hmm, as usual, you're very direct in your statements."

"If you prefer, I could speak in riddles and metaphors?"

"Oh, please, would you? It would make me a great deal more comfortable."

He met her startled eyes with a smile and a chuckle.

"See, I can play this game as well."

"You most certainly can, Your Grace. If you're not careful, you run the risk of losing that air of pride surrounding your lordly person."

He made a quiet laugh.

"I'll take my chances."

"But you're still far off from being a full-on jester like your friend, Lord Merringer. Isn't he with you tonight?"

"He's otherwise engaged. I planned on coming with Lady Emma, but she has fallen ill and, since I'm not much for sitting alone, I decided to go with some friends."

"Nothing serious, I hope?"

"A common cold. She was out in the rough weather earlier today, but she'll be up and about in a couple of days."

She couldn't help noticing the lack of affection in his voice when talking about his, presumably, soon-to-be fiancée, but didn't know what to make of it, if anything. Some people just didn't have it in them to show affection, and she had a strong feeling that the duke could be one of those persons.

But what did she know?

If someone would've told her after that night at Blackwell House that she would be walking with his grace at Vauxhall Gardens, she would have said that it would never be, that she would rather go back to Walston than walk with such an odious man.

But the man walking beside her now was a completely different man—not only compared to what he had been, but different to his class. He talked to her like it was a perfectly natural thing to do, and even if she tried to provoke him, just a little to see if she could ruffle his feathers, he took it with a smile and a sly retort.

He was a strange man indeed. He and Lord Merringer both, but while she felt like she always had to be on her guard with Lord Merringer, she didn't feel that with the duke.

What she did feel was the constant nervousness that she would overstep her boundaries because she knew that it was ingrained in her person to try to ruffle feathers if one had too much pride, and often she did it without thinking first.

And it was now that the realisation came to her, that she cared for what the duke thought about her. She wasn't a part of his world, didn't have much prestige to lose in his eyes, but still she found that she cared.

"I hope she will be well soon."

"Yes," he answered in a distracted manner. "I've been rethinking our conversation when we danced. Do you remember?"

She did.

"You asked me what in life lifted my spirits. I told you that it was riding in the countryside with nothing except the birds and the sky above my head. That was true, in a way, but I have come to understand that it's more than that. That picture I was drawing up for you represents a feeling, but feelings are fleeting things. They do lift the spirit, but when they are gone you are back where you started, and the place you go back to is of course more important than those short bursts of happiness."

"I would agree wholeheartedly. But as a man of great fortune, surely you have a happy place to go back to?"

He looked at her with eyes surprisingly intense.

"And why is that a given?"

"Because," she started while sorting her thoughts. "Nothing in the world could ever be out of reach for you. If you are bored with London, you go to the countryside. If you're bored with the countryside, you go abroad. You can fill your life with whatever you want, so how could a life like that ever be empty?"

"I've never said it was empty, far from it, but what if what I can fill it with is dictated by others? It's all going back to that picture of the rider beneath a cloudless sky—the freedom. Without freedom, a life can never be full. Sometimes I think the happiest people alive are the workers down at the docks, that live day by day, not knowing what tomorrow will hold for them."

"That is very much a privileged outlook. I guess what the day mostly holds for them is the threat of starvation, constant angst of being able to put food on the table for one's family."

"Yes, maybe," he said, looking down at the path, and it seemed like he contemplated her words, rather than trying to come up with an argument to shoot them down. "I beg your pardon, Miss Weatherby. I didn't intend to ruin your evening with gloomy thoughts about life and everything in it. I'm not usually this severe in my opinions."

"There's nothing to be sorry for, Your Grace. So much of the talk I endure is nonsensical and out of politeness, so I thank you for this moment of respite."

He nodded to her, retreated back into formality and said that he had been holding her from her company long enough and that he should be on his way. She surprised herself by saying:

"If you must, Your Grace, but not for my sake. I have very much enjoyed your company."

He tilted his head.

"If so, I will stay in your company for a while longer, but it would be rude of me to further keep your attention all to myself."

When the party stopped at a junction, deciding which path led to the Cascade, the duke looked past the chatting sisters to Mr Stockton. That was all the encouragement the latter needed to step over to them. With him followed Mr Carmichael and Mary, and soon the duke was in the centre of everybody's attention.

Alice studied him in his interactions with her friends and family, expecting him to be a reluctant participant, but he was not. He was maybe not the most open person, dazzling his admirers with smiles and jokes, but he was attentive, and even if he didn't say more than he needed, what he said mattered and was well thought out.

When, for example, he said they needed to take the right path to get to the Cascade, no one felt the need to argue the point, and before five minutes had passed, they stood in front of the contraption that was as close to true magic as this world could muster.

"Oh, how could this be," Alice said in a breathless tone, her eyes wide with wonder.

Mrs de Vries' smile was broad and content. "Didn't I tell you it was the most magnificent thing?"

Even though Alice knew the waterfall in front of her was made of tin, carefully and deceptively illuminated while moved by skilled artists in the background, she couldn't believe the waterfall wasn't real. She could see the fast, downward flow of the water and hear the steady rumble of it hitting the surface below, where it misted.

"It's all mechanics," his grace said, once again by her side. "It's quite ingenious how they did it. I can explain it to you if you want me to."

"Oh, please don't," she said, putting her hand on his forearm instinctively. "Don't ruin the illusion for me."

The moment the words left her mouth, she realised what she had done and withdrew her hand as though she had burnt herself. What had she been thinking? Her face heated with embarrassment.

"Don't… react like that," he murmured, still looking at the fake waterfall, his expression suddenly tense. "I didn't particularly mind."

"Nonetheless," she whispered back, "I beg your pardon. I didn't mean to overstep. Sometimes I act before thinking. It won't happen again."

To that, he didn't reply.

Then, the first of the fireworks exploded in the sky. Mary gave a delighted shriek. Mr Carmichael, caught off guard, stumbled slightly before steadying himself and ordering everyone to move in the direction of the knoll.

"It's too late," Mary said with a mixture of exasperation and excitement. "We'll just watch it from here."

And so they did. Alice, however, found her attention divided. The fireworks were indeed breathtaking, bright bursts of crimson, gold, and silver illuminating the dark sky in fleeting, dazzling patterns. Yet, she couldn't help but glance sideways at the duke. His face, lit by the flares in the sky, held a rare softness. He seemed enraptured, not just by the display above but by some thought or feeling she couldn't quite discern.

And then it happened.

As the last cascade of light faded into the night, the duke turned his gaze to Alice. Their eyes met, and for a brief, infinite moment, the noise of the crowd, the laughter, the music—it all disappeared.

He opened his mouth to speak but then closed it again, a slight, thoughtful smile playing on his lips.

"Thank you, Miss Weatherby," he said at last, his voice low and warm.

"For what?" she asked.

"For allowing me to see tonight through your eyes."

She didn't know how to respond, so she simply smiled, and for a moment, the world felt weightless.

When the party began making its way back through the garden paths, Alice found herself walking alongside Mr Stockton again. He was charming and attentive, as always, and yet, her thoughts strayed to the man who had just walked away, his maroon tailcoat blending into the evening shadows.

It was a night she would not soon forget. But as she listened to Mr Stockton talk about plans for the next ball, she couldn't help but wonder what it was about the duke that seemed to linger, like the echo of the last firework fading into the night sky.

Chapter 10

"A most undesirable turn of events, dear brother," John said, his face pinched in discontent. "It seems young Miss Weatherby has turned down my invitation to the Halcomb ball."

Thomas looked at him and set down his glass of brandy on the table at White's gentleman's club. Was that a spark of joy he felt in his chest?

"Oh, really. How come?"

The windows were open to the street to vent some of the heat in this hot day. The sounds of horses' hooves, people talking, and a paperboy shouting from a street corner floated into the club.

"I'm asking myself that very same question," John said, snapping his fingers at a waiter, far removed from his usual cheerful self. "But, apparently, she prefers a more common man—a Mr Stockton, to be exact."

The spark of joy in Thomas's chest was immediately extinguished.

"I've been asking around, you see, and she's been seen a lot with this Mr Stockton. The very same voices tell me Mr Stockton is going out of his way to run into Miss Weatherby. He seems determined to get her for himself. I don't shy away from some honest competition but, really? The son of a trader against a lord? That's not an honest competition, but still, I'm losing. What good is this beautiful face, this slender figure, and this wealth of charm if I can't even knock a Mr Stockton off the playing board?"

"Who could tell? But maybe it's because the Mr Stockton in question doesn't regard Miss Weatherby as the main prize in a grand game. Maybe he's more than just good looks and charm?"

"What could possibly be more important than good looks and charm?"

"A future, maybe. I've said it before, and I'll say it again—you have underestimated this girl. Despite your status and wealth, you have nothing to offer her, unless you bring her to the altar, which you will never do. And this she knows. So, you're right, it isn't an honest competition. Mr Stockton had you beaten as soon as he presented himself as *Mr* Stockton."

"You know," John said, his gaze drifting away in the murky room of old dark wood, "maybe I *should* bring her to the altar. Maybe it's a girl like her that would make me happy. Her light and wit, paired with my charm? Our children would rule Britain within a generation."

Thomas picked up his glass and sipped.

"Most possibly," he agreed.

When he got home, he went up to the second floor. He had planned to round off the day with a good book and maybe another glass of brandy, but he knew it wouldn't be so.

Did one know when crossing the line dividing the sane from the insane?

Probably not.

It snuck up on you.

Thomas had, a few days ago, been struck with the awful realisation he had crossed that line.

The particular insanity that had infested him was of the sort that made his appetite disappear and words in a book float into obscurity.

He knew the name of his insanity but wouldn't for the life of him take it in his mouth.

He was an idiot, truly. He had already been here, trodden this path before, and knew that nothing good would ever come from it, and only an idiot repeated the same mistake twice, expecting a different outcome.

He had denounced Leana because of her birth. He had folded before his mother when he should have stayed strong and taken the fight. To feel what he now felt was betrayal of the worst kind—a betrayal of Leana. But could one really be accused of what one felt? One hadn't any control over such things.

Oh, the humanity...

If he traced his steps backwards to the point where the insanity had grabbed him full force, it had been the night at the Monroe Ball, in the punch room. All the signs had been there, but he had neglected them: his eagerness to get close to her, to repair her impression of him, to make her mother more approving of him. And, if he were to pinpoint the exact moment of the outbreak, it must have been when Miss Weatherby told her mother not to let him off so easily. There were a million things she could have said. A million other things more expected, but what she actually said was Miss Weatherby through and through. She had given him a sideways glance, and something in her dark eyes had made him capitulate to her; a playful spark, yes, but also a more serious undercurrent that swept him away. He had liked so much being in her company as a friend rather than a foe, and stepping away from her to Emma had been like leaving a warm hearth to step out into a blizzard.

He hadn't actually thought all these things during their brief conversation, of course. They had come to him afterwards, piece by piece, and if he were to be true to himself, her poison had probably started working far earlier; why else would he have been so eager to redeem himself in her eyes that he sought her out like he did, knowing that Emma would strongly disapprove?

So, if not the Monroe Ball, when?

Could it have been the very first night when he felt nothing but scorn for her after being chastised by her publicly? Well, all things considered, probably yes. But when it started was less important than how it ended.

When he had seen her at the Vauxhall Gardens, he had felt blessed. The woman who was constantly on his mind was there in the real world with him. To not approach her hadn't been an option. He saw her and had needed to go to her. It was as simple as that. He knew now that she was poisonous, that he couldn't trust himself with her, and that meant he needed to stay away from her. He should forget her, marry Emma, and continue his life as life was intended for him as a duke, to follow convention and unite two great families.

He paused his thoughts and stared at the bookshelf.

A jab of panic.

He probably couldn't even meet her now, even if he wanted to. Most of their rendezvous had been a product of her association with John, and now that she had broken that off, she had effectively broken it off with him as well.

They would never again have a random meeting unless he, like Mr Stockton, went out of his way to make them happen. He wouldn't do that. *Why* would he do that? Hadn't he made up his mind on the matter, that he would, at all costs, stay away from Miss Weatherby and let her poison wane? Yes. So why even think about how Mr Stockton went about his business with her? It wasn't any of his concern.

Oh, by the lord, what had he done to deserve this?

He sat in silence, brooding, staring down at the carpet.

Maybe this was the perfect time to invite the Fairchilds to Somerfield? Miss Weatherby was to attend the ball at Mrs Sophie's, and he couldn't very well turn up at a venue like that without questions being raised. And rather than sit in his library thinking about her dancing and laughing just some blocks away, he could start building his distance from her by physically leaving town. He needed only to rest his senses from her for a while, and the spell she had cast over him would break.

He started planning for the trip back to Somerfield, but his mind wandered.

He wasn't a romantic man, not easily moved, but an image had taken a powerful hold of him.

He was standing on a windswept field, eye to eye with Miss Weatherby. She was dressed in a plain cotton dress, her brown hair blown back from her face by the gusts. Her expression was one of silent anticipation, tinged with a trace of hesitation. He longed to extinguish that hesitation because she should never have to doubt him. Not ever.

In the vision, he reached out and gently brushed a strand of her hair from her cheek, curling it behind her ear, the cold of her skin lingering against the back of his fingers. His hand moved instinctively to her waist, pulling her closer as he kissed her, eagerly, almost desperately. She responded in kind, her arms wrapping around him as if she, too, could no longer bear the distance between them. Something deep within him broke, and suddenly, his world expanded.

It was as though the entire horizon opened before him, revealing possibilities he had never dared to imagine. With her, everything felt within reach; without her, all would fade into darkness. He could feel the wrenching pain in his chest at the thought of her turning and walking away, leaving nothing but emptiness and misery in her wake.

"Bloody hell!" he roared, leaping to his feet. The vision dissipated, leaving him standing in the centre of the room, breathless and unnerved. "Please… get out of my head… Stop torturing me," he murmured but Miss Weatherby had no such plans—not at all; she had made herself at home and wasn't planning on going anywhere, and wherever *he* went he realized—to Somerfield or otherwise—she would follow.

He froze in place, his thoughts shifting abruptly. If he couldn't have Miss Weatherby, he could at least ensure her future was with someone worthy. Someone who would treat her with the respect and love she deserved.

It seemed she was free of John Merringer's grasp, but what of Mr Stockton? What were his intentions? Could he truly provide her with the happiness she deserved? Thomas clenched his fists. If Mr Stockton proved unworthy, Thomas would see to it that she was protected from him.

And if Mr Stockton married her...

The thought sent a sharp pang through him. She would be forever out of reach, and perhaps then, the torment she caused him would finally cease. Or perhaps it would only worsen.

He could not take that chance.

"Summon Mr Anderson," he barked to the butler who entered the room, startled by the forcefulness in his master's voice.

"Yes, Your Grace," the butler replied with a deep bow before retreating to fulfil the order.

Thomas sank back into his chair, staring at the swirling pattern of the carpet beneath his boots. He hadn't the faintest idea what he intended to ask of Mr Anderson this time. But one thing was clear: he needed answers, and quickly.

He had no intention of letting Miss Weatherby slip from his life entirely—not until he was certain she was safe and happy.

If he couldn't have her for himself, the least he could do was secure her happiness in the arms of another.

But could he ever truly let her go?

That, he feared, was the question that would haunt him until the end of his days.

When Mary came over to the Weatherbys' the next morning, she was in high spirits, and Alice could almost deduce from her smile what had happened.

"Mr Carmichael has proposed!"

"How wonderful," Alice cried, and they hugged. "So, what did you answer?"

"Oh, stop it, silly person!" Mary gave Alice's arm a swat. "I said yes, of course!"

"I'm very happy for you," Alice said, holding both of Mary's hands.

"Now I'm only hoping that you soon will experience the same happiness. As you can understand, I will not attend the ball at Mrs Sophie's tomorrow. As an engaged woman, it would be inappropriate," she said, unable to conceal her pleasure at her new status. "But I'm sure that Mr Stockton will keep you well entertained."

"I do too. It's one of his many talents."

"And I'm sure he will soon do what is right and offer you the same happiness as I have been graced with. He would be mad not to secure you when he has the chance."

"And who says he has a chance?"

Mary blinked, showing a face of pure incomprehension.

"What?"

"I'm just joking with you, dear cousin. I fancy him well enough."

"Oh, glad to hear," Mary said, nipping her gloves off by the fingers. "So why even say a thing like that? Sometimes I don't understand you at all. Will you be arriving at the ball together?"

"Yes, that is what has been arranged."

For some reason, the image of the Duke of Hexam beside her, looking up at the fireworks, resurfaced. He had come to her in a strange mood, and his straightforwardness had not only rivalled but superseded her own. Why he had come to her with thoughts so personal was something to ponder. If one were to see it in a negative light, it was because she was of no greater importance to him, and he therefore felt he could speak to her about things not suitable for his more esteemed friends. A more positive way of looking at it was that he felt she could understand him—and she had understood him, even if she couldn't fully sympathise.

If he married Lady Emma, he would have maybe a few happy months before discovering her true personality, but that was a misfortune waiting to happen and could therefore not affect his happiness today. The overarching feeling from the previous night, however, was the surprising change in the duke. It was only because of that change they were able to speak to each other in such a manner.

She tried to picture having a similar conversation with Mr Stockton, and it almost brought a laugh out of her. No, that wouldn't do. Mr Stockton was a whirlwind of smiles and compliments, an easy and enjoyable man, much like a gentleman was supposed to be. But was he anything more than that? Was he her winning lottery ticket? Her sister, Lucinda, had said that a year of courtship was a year of theatre—no one showed their true self during that year.

But the duke had, and he had chosen to do so with her. She couldn't help being flattered by that.

It wasn't as hard as Thomas had feared, to sit in the carriage with Lady Emma and her father, travelling from London to Somerfield. He just smiled, nodded, and threw in some platitudes here and there. To his great astonishment, they seemed to settle for that. He couldn't help thinking how a conversation with Miss Weatherby would fare with that strategy. Not well. Not well at all. He was still somewhat embarrassed by how he had burdened her with his thoughts about freedom and happiness the last time they met, but there was just something about her that invited it. She had looked at him with her dark, attentive eyes while he talked, the corners of her mouth angled in something that could be the beginning of a smile. But that was his interpretation. Maybe those angles at the corner of her mouth were a result of her trying to subdue her awkwardness? He really didn't think so. It felt like he could talk to her about anything—except, of course, the most burning issue: that he had become increasingly certain his future happiness was closely tied to hers.

And see, he had been right about one thing at least. He was travelling away from London, away from her, but that damned woman was still in his head.

When they neared Somerfield Hall, Emma started complimenting the trees and the well-kept roads, and burst into a full-blown *oooh!* when Somerfield became visible on the other side of a shallow valley, resting behind a vast man-made lake.

"You haven't exaggerated the beauty of your estate, Thomas," Emma said, putting the tips of her gloved fingers to her bosom. "Such exquisite proportions. And the façade. It has such a wonderful honey tone."

"It's local sandstone," Thomas replied. "From the quarry at Fowl's Bend."

"Hmm, yes. Very impressive," Emmet said, leaning forward on his cane to see better.

"Wonderful!" Lady Carnbury exclaimed, and while going up the long road to the house, lined with century-old oaks, she complimented every detail, from the fields to the horse master's quarters.

"Pray, is the Dowager Duchess expecting us?" she asked Thomas.

She very much was. She had travelled to Somerfield two days in advance to prepare the house for noble guests. She knew what his invitation to the Fairchilds meant, and nothing, if she could help it, should fail to impress them during their stay at Somerfield.

When the carriage stopped in front of the house, the whole staff, from the butler to the kitchen maids, were lined up at the front of the stairs, hands clasped in front of them, ready to greet the guests.

"Oh, look at that," Lady Carnbury said. "They have all come out to greet us. Isn't that lovely?"

"Yes, very, Mother," Emma said. "I'm sure they did it wholly of their own accord."

"Do you really?" her mother asked.

They stepped out of the carriage, and the Dowager Duchess came forth with a bright smile and her hands stretched out. Lady Carnbury took them, cooing like a pigeon with pleasure, while gushing her praise about Somerfield Hall.

Emma gave Thomas a look and a shrug that seemed to say, *Mothers, right?*

He gave her a soft smile in return. Suddenly, what had felt easy in the carriage became hard. Was this what his life would amount to? To live inside the walls of Somerfield, his last retreat, with a woman he didn't like, smiling this insincere smile for years to come? Well, it was a bit late for thoughts like that. He had taken this too far to turn back now.

He didn't get to ponder the question for long, because his mother ushered them into the house for refreshments.

When the butler had taken the Fairchilds to see the house, the Dowager Duchess turned to Thomas.

"So, how are you planning this? I think it would be a good idea to talk to her father before the day is over, and tomorrow, crown the dinner by asking Emma for her hand."

"Maybe," Thomas said, a hand of dread gripping and twisting his stomach.

"Maybe? Isn't it better to handle this quickly and then enjoy the rest of the week together? It is, after all, why you invited them, isn't it?"

"It is."

"It's settled then. I suggest you talk to Lord Carnbury after dinner. I'll prepare the room with our best brandy."

After the tour of the house, the party continued outside to take a walk around the lake. Halfway around it, in a copse of birch trees, the Dowager Duchess had prepared a surprise: a picnic with servants standing ready with champagne, sandwiches, and chairs for herself and Lord and Lady Carnbury.

"What a marvellous surprise!" Lady Carnbury exclaimed, clapping her hands together. "It so very much reminds me of our first proper meeting with Thomas down at the Round Pond in Hyde Park. Most appropriate!"

"Yes, very nice indeed," Emmet said.

"Lovely," Emma added, giving Thomas a sideways glance.

Her fingers gently touched his.

"You've been awfully quiet today," she stated.

"Sorry, I didn't sleep all that well. Nothing a glass of champagne won't cure," he said with a smile.

She didn't smile back.

Blasted, it was all crumbling around him.

"Isn't this nice," Lady Carnbury said when all were seated, the young ones on the blanket. "To have two generations of two great families together on a day like this?"

"Yes, it certainly gives hope for the future," Emmet said, digging his teeth into a sandwich of light cornbread.

Another night of beauty, another ballroom. Alice was resting against the wall after the second dance with Mr Stockton, who had gone to fetch them refreshments. This night, though, was different in one distinct manner: she wasn't out of place. The ball at Mrs Sophie's was not for the lords and ladies. Around her she saw the sons and daughters of landowners and merchants. There were the usual beautiful gowns and well-dressed gentlemen but without that extra tint of extravagance that marked the members of the nobility.

Maybe this was a reason for her high spirits: that she wasn't regarded as someone who should be grateful to just be in the room? She very well thought it could be and decided, still panting after dancing her lively Scottish reel, that she would never again be tempted by the likes of Lord Merringer and his world. This was her world and her people, and even if her father wouldn't approve, she would never again be swayed to be the peculiarity on the dance floor. Her mother had retreated to the card room, where she rested her feet and gossiped with the other chaperones.

Mr Stockton returned with their drinks and a big, happy grin.

"You dance, Miss Weatherby, as if you've done nothing else."

"I thank you for your compliment, Mr Stockton, and may I offer in return that you're doing well to keep up with me."

"I certainly do my best."

They clinked their glasses and sipped the cold punch. It was impossible to imagine this night together with the duke, his serious face and distinguished manner; he would probably rather die than be seen dancing a reel. She smiled to herself.

"What kind of amusing things are you thinking about now, Miss Weatherby?"

"Oh, nothing," she said, waving her hand. "Silly things."

"As you might have noticed, I'm a silly person."

"That I have noticed, and I will bear that in mind if I ever decide to tell you."

"Am I part of those silly thoughts of yours?" he asked with a confident smile.

She shrugged.

"Could be."

"In that case, Miss Weatherby, could I maybe ask for the third dance as well?"

"You may."

Yes, the Duke of Hexam in the role of the cheerful charmer was quite unthinkable, just as the opposite was true. Or was it?

"But I think we need to rest a bit before continuing. You've done so well to keep up, Mr Stockton, and it would be unfortunate to see you stumble now."

"A lady's wish is my command, even if I think I could have managed both a third and fourth dance before the next glass of punch."

"Your confidence will be your downfall. No one outdances me."

"That certainly sounds like a challenge."

"Maybe it is?"

"I guess there's only one way to find out, after you've had your one dance of rest."

"Oh, you. Be careful that I don't force you to that third dance after all."

And so they continued until there came a rare pause in the conversation. They watched the line of dancers, and Alice asked:

"Mr Stockton, what is happiness to you?"

He smiled and stroked a strand of hair from his forehead.

"Dancing with a beautiful woman till the wee hours, thinking of nothing but the moment itself."

"A fine picture it is. But when your dancing days are behind you, what will give you happiness then?"

"The love of a fine woman, the sound of children's laughter, and a house in the country, preferably by a stream of water."

She nodded.

"Another appealing picture, I must say."

It was, and it echoed with her own longings, but didn't it sound a bit rehearsed? Suddenly she saw herself as the last in a long line of women who had heard the same words from his mouth. That was unfair. He had danced with women before her, and of course he had been asked this question before, and what kind of man would he be if he changed his answer every time someone asked him? That didn't mean his words were rehearsed.

After a brief pause, the lines of dancers once again formed on the floor. Mr Stockton emptied his glass and took hers, placing it on a table before grabbing both of her hands with a grin.

"No way to escape now, my dear. I accept your challenge."

Dinner was over, and everybody was leaning back in their chairs. The Dowager Duchess clapped her hands together with a smile.

"Now I think it's time for the women to retreat to the drawing room and leave the men to their business."

The women got to their feet, and Thomas saw Emma exchange a glance with her father, who in return gave her a quick smile, nothing more than a twitch at the corner of his mouth. When the women had left, Thomas and Emmet looked at each other, Emmet with an expectant smile.

"Shall we retreat to the inner room?" Thomas asked. "I've prepared it with our best brandy."

"Well, that sounds like an offer hard to turn down," Emmet said, rising from his chair.

As Thomas gestured towards the room, the duality of Emmet's words didn't escape him. Thomas's expected proposal had, during the Fairchilds' stay, been reduced to mere formality. If they had known what feelings he wrestled with, they would have been a lot less confident. He needed to have Emmet seated with his glass of brandy as soon as possible so he could get the proposal over and done with.

Blasted! Why was he such a coward? If he had any spine, he would just say that this had all been a big mistake, apologise for raising their expectations, and taking up their time. What was a moment of blackness compared to a lifetime in grey?

But, *Goddammit!* It wasn't just one moment of blackness. His mother would never again talk to him. The Fairchilds would slander his name. And to what gain? To eventually marry another woman like Emma, but less wealthy and prestigious?

The image of Miss Weatherby on the field, the wind moving her dress and making that strand of dark hair tremble over her forehead, returned. It was soon drowned out by Leana's tear-drenched face lighting up when he asked for her hand in marriage.

The treachery.

The bottomless black.

Emmet sat down with a sigh in the plush chair, close to the crackling fire that reflected in the heavy auburn of the glasses. Thomas sat down across from him, grabbing his glass and taking a deep gulp. Emmet eyed him with some caution.

"Everything alright, my dear boy?"

"Capital," Thomas answered, his heart hammering like it was trying to break out of his chest.

"You do understand that you have nothing to fear from this conversation of ours?"

"But maybe I do," Thomas said, closing his eyes in pure terror.

The words had escaped him before he had a chance to rein them in. The caution in Emmet's eyes deepened.

"What is that supposed to mean?"

He looked at Thomas over the rim of his glass. The boulder was already set in motion; there was nothing Thomas could do to stop its momentum now.

"I'm sorry, Emmet, but I can't marry your daughter."

Thomas didn't know what he had expected—a big outburst, screaming, and a face reddened with anger. Instead, he got a little chuckle.

"Of course you can, my dear boy. These feelings that you're now confronting are normal for every young man fond of their freedom, but they are passing feelings."

"I don't think they are, Emmet."

Emmet looked at him with expressionless eyes. Thomas continued:

"I don't love her. I'm not the man to bring her the happiness I'm sure every father wishes for their daughters."

"What I wish for," Emmet said in a slow, deliberate way, every ounce of warmth gone from his voice, "is for my daughter to be the Duchess of Hexham. What you want… my dear boy, is the funds such a connection will bring. I didn't contradict your false words when you said that your estate's finances had been sorted. I didn't contradict your foolish hopes of ever getting your father's war expenses compensated by the Crown. I decided to let you keep whatever pride you thought you were entitled to because of this conversation we're having now. But I'm not liking what I'm hearing."

"Lord Carnbury, I—"

"No," Emmet said and banged his glass down on the table. "Now it's *your* time to listen. I thought you a grown-up man, Thomas, but I see now that you're just a spoiled boy thinking of nothing but himself. It's your duty to unite our families, and I'm paying you richly to do so. If you're not to take reason, I'll talk to your mother and see that she does."

Emmet's words ignited a spark of anger inside Thomas, and he felt it threatening to engulf him in a roaring fire if he didn't keep it in check.

"I assure you, Lord Carnbury, that I'm a man of my word. No promise from me, regarding your daughter's hand, has ever been made, but listen to my words now—I will never marry your daughter, and I assure you, that decision is mine and mine alone."

Emmet's face went white. The fingers around his glass twitched. Then he reddened and banged his glass once more on the table, spilling expensive brandy over his clawed hand.

"Never in my life have I been thus insulted!" He bolted to his feet, starting to fiddle with his cravat, as if it were choking him. "You are certainly a man fond of assurances, Your Grace, but let me assure you that this is your biggest mistake, no matter how long you'll live and how many more mistakes you're going to make—and I have a feeling they'll be legion! But this day will stand out, and I assure you—yes, *assure* you—it will come back and haunt you!"

Thomas leaned back in his chair.

"I apologise for all of this, Lord Carnbury, and I will not keep you here at Somerfield any longer."

Lord Carnbury stood gaping for a moment, as if he had no idea what to do, except maybe burst at the seams, but then he stormed out of the room. Thomas listened to his hard steps moving towards the drawing room. Then there were loud voices and shouting, women crying, and something breaking.

Thomas looked at the opposite wall of the inner room, his face unchanged. He sat so for more than an hour before the silhouette of his mother loomed in the doorway.

"You bloody fool," she said in a thick voice. "You bloody, selfish fool."

Chapter 11

For two days and two nights, Somerfield Hall had been a place of anguish. A place where the servants walked like ghosts through the rooms, not even whispering to each other, as though something horrible would happen if the silence were to be broken. The Dowager Duchess had locked herself in her rooms, and the master of the house walked the gardens with his hands clasped behind his back, or sat in his library, brooding. The reason for all this consternation wasn't a secret to anyone. They had all heard Lord Carnbury's agitated speech, his daughter's crying and whimpering, her upset words to her father insisting that surely his grace hadn't meant what he said, and couldn't her father please talk to him again? But her father hadn't done that. He had taken his family and stormed out the door, leaving the manor as silent as a tomb behind him.

On the third day, Thomas once again knocked on his mother's door, but still, she refused to talk to him. He told her he would go back to London and write her a letter from there if she insisted on not speaking to him here. Before he left in the afternoon, one of his mother's chambermaids appeared at his door, telling him that the Dowager Duchess wouldn't join him in London but had nothing further to say.

Now he was at White's, with John cringing in the chair beside him.

"You actually said that? To Lord Carnbury?"

"I did."

John huffed through his nose, staring blankly across the dark-panelled room.

"I must say I'm impressed. Don't know why, but I am. But mostly I'm confused. Why? Was she really that appalling to you? She's rich and she's beautiful. That's usually enough for most men. Or haven't you yet come to terms with the truth that a gentleman's freedom is only on loan? Sooner or later, we all meet again, in the sheepfold."

"Really? And when will I see you there, my friend?"

"Maybe sooner than you think, considering that Emma Fairchild is back on the market. I think she likes me."

Thomas couldn't help laughing.

"Well, if you would ever have a chance, it would be now."

"Lend her my shoulder to cry on?"

"Something like that."

They drank their brandy in silence.

"On a different note, my spies have told me that Miss Weatherby and Mr Stockton were quite the success at Mrs Sophie's. They danced no fewer than four dances, and the day after, they were seen walking in Hyde Park. I can't help feeling she's slipping through my fingers. I need to take action to secure her for myself."

"What kind of action?"

"I'm thinking the theatre. *Artaxerxes* is playing, and the females are usually weak for it. And after, I might bring her back to the Vauxhall Gardens. I'm quite confident I can get her to take the Dark Walk with me. And in the darkness, far away from all judging eyes, I'm sure she will give me her affection."

John gave him a blink and a lecherous smile.

"She will be judged long before she enters the Dark Walk with you, which I'm certain she won't," Thomas mumbled.

"And I'm sure she will. Care to take a wager?"

John extended his hand.

"Certainly not."

"Don't be such a bore, brother," John said, collapsing back into his chair.

After finishing his drink, Thomas left White's and John to their own fate. When he was out on the sun-drenched street, he crossed to the other side. Lord Carnbury took his drinks at Boodle's, further up the street, and Thomas preferred not to meet the good lord while his blood most likely still ran hot.

He steered his steps northwards, towards Hyde Park.

It was still before luncheon, and most of the young women were out and about, walking. Miss Weatherby always walked in Hyde Park, and he didn't try to deceive himself about why he was going there. But if he saw her, he wouldn't approach her. He would admire her from a distance and hope she wouldn't see him.

While he walked, he thought about the night at Vauxhall Gardens, their talk, and how he had admired her in secret when the fireworks started. Even now, he could see her big eyes reflecting the fire in the sky.

Alice and Mary went out for their walk a bit later than usual. They had much to talk about. Alice and Mary thought it a splendid idea to have Mary's wedding reception at Longhall House, and after some reasoning with Mrs Weatherby, and with the promise that none of the expenses would fall on her, she had burst out that of *course* the wedding would be held at Longhall House! If that came with some expenses, so be it. It couldn't be her sister's fault that her husband had never bought a proper estate, could it? And to rent one just for the wedding? Preposterous! And to marry in the city? Couldn't come into question! With these affirmations, the two girls were content and left the house for their walk at Hyde Park. Mary was talking extensively about what tablecloths and curtains she envisioned for the reception, what would be on the menu, and how striking Mr

Carmichael would look in his marine tailcoat, being as tall as he was.

When walking in Hyde Park, they saw plenty of familiar faces. A big change from the first time they had walked here together, when Alice hadn't recognised a soul. Two of the faces she now recognised were those of the Peters, the elderly couple who had escorted her that misty morning when she had seen Mr Stockton thundering down Rotten Row. She smiled and nodded at them. Mr Peters tipped his hat and returned her smile, as did his wife. Alice, though, was looking for a special someone. Mr Stockton.

The ball at Mrs Sophie's had been a long and fun one, and with all Mary's talk about marriage, she felt the need for his easy manners. Her eye didn't find Mr Stockton. It found the Duke of Hexham, coming from a connecting path. He walked with his eyes far away, and for a moment, she didn't know if she wanted him to spot her or not. Then he did and smiled at her. Her smile in return came naturally, and she got the answer to her previous question.

"Miss Weatherby. Miss de Vries," he said and took a bow.

"Your Grace."

He had a strange look on his face, surprised, but at the same time happy and a bit… worried? If so, Alice shared his worry. Lady Emma's spies could be anywhere, and if they hadn't spotted her meeting with the duke at Vauxhall Gardens, they got another chance now. All those familiar faces she had seen during their walk belonged to people that knew her, and of course, if they knew who she was, they knew who Thomas Overton, the Duke of Hexham, was as well.

"May I walk with you?"

"Of course," Mary said when Alice hesitated.

And so, they walked, Alice with the duke by her side. He had retreated into himself, walking in silence. Had he reverted to the duke of before? The silent, awkward man for whom the company of others seemed more a burden than anything else?

She really hoped not.

She noticed that he kept looking at her from the corner of his eye. What was that about? Was her hair not in order?

Just when she thought she had him figured out, he surprised her with another unexpected twist in his personality. She knew she shouldn't comment on it—after all, as a duke, he had every right to behave however he pleased. Yet, deep down, she also knew she couldn't resist saying something.

"It's always a pleasure meeting you, Your Grace. One never knows who might turn up."

That made him laugh—a silent, almost tired laugh.

"I surprise myself in the same manner. I never know who I will be in your company."

What on earth did he mean by that?

"Maybe it's the weather?" she suggested. "Or the moon's placement in relation to the sun and the stars, as the mystics believe?"

"Oh, it could be all of those things, I'm sure," he said, and finally gave her a full smile. "All I know is that we're dealing with some powerful magic here."

"Magic, you say? Pray, do tell me more."

"I'd rather not, because another thing I've noticed is that I always speak out of character in your company. The source of this magic I'll keep to myself for the time being."

"How intriguing, Your Grace. Out of character, you say? Haven't we already stated that your personality is a fleeting and ever-changing thing?"

"It usually isn't," he said, and she felt that he was about to say more, but in the end, he didn't.

Instead, he moved over to less dangerous grounds.

"I hope I didn't intrude on your conversation?"

"Certainly not. We were just talking about Mr Carmichael, who has proposed to Miss de Vries, and how Longhall House would be a perfect place to host the wedding. I'm sure this is of no interest to you, so we will continue that conversation later."

"You are wrong, Miss Weatherby. It interests me greatly, and I do congratulate you, Miss de Vries. From what I've seen and heard of Mr Carmichael, he's very well respected and highly thought of."

"Thank you, Your Grace," Mary said, and was able to make a hasty curtsey while walking. "We're planning for an autumn wedding."

The thought of Lady Emma surfaced yet again, the duke's wife-to-be, if Lady Emma was to be trusted. Were they maybe already engaged? And as if her thoughts had some of that magic power the duke had been talking about, she saw a slender creature further up the road, in a splendid white silk dress and a French hat slightly askew, with a white parasol over her shoulder.

Alice's stomach froze to ice.

It was Lady Emma, out walking with two of her friends.

Thomas tensed beside her.

She could feel it without looking at him.

Lady Emma and her two friends stopped, Lady Emma gawking, her face pale and eyes red-rimmed. She wasn't her usual meticulous self. To be frank, she was kind of a mess.

"Oh, this is just capital," she heard Thomas mumble.

Capital indeed, Alice thought with a sinking feeling, thinking about her reputation being dragged in the mud, her father's hopes for acceptance into the higher circles shattered. Lady Emma's friends remained where they were, and Lady Emma approached them in singular majesty, looking from Thomas to Alice.

"Lady Emma," Thomas said and took a bow.

Lady Emma looked at him with her mouth half open. Her eyelids fluttered, like she was about to faint.

"Your Grace. I guess I shouldn't be surprised to see you here walking like it's just another day. I've seen much in you, Thomas, but I've never seen you callous before."

"Let's walk," he said, extending his hand to her.

"No!" She shrugged away from his hand, gripping her parasol like a drowning woman. "I don't care what you have to say because you can't hurt me more than you already have."

"I never intended to hurt you, Emma. I really didn't, and I'm sorry that I did. But I think we would have hurt each other even worse if we had carried on."

"Carried on?" Lady Emma snarled, her face turning ugly. "And now you plan to carry on with this… *person* instead?" she nodded at Alice. "To be discarded for such a lowly substitute. That hurts me more than anything else."

"I'm sorry, but for that particular hurt you will get no sympathy. I'm just walking with Miss Weatherby and Miss de Vries as an acquaintance."

"But of course, Your Grace," Lady Emma said, and made a deep ironic curtsey. "If you say so, it must be true. A man of your stature wouldn't lie." She turned to Alice, stabbing her finger at her. "I *warned* you. Didn't I? Now, when you've destroyed my happiness, I won't hold it beneath me to return the favour."

"Lady Emma, I—"

Lady Emma didn't listen. She turned where she stood and walked back to her friends, waving them before her like she couldn't leave Hyde Park soon enough.

Thomas looked after her with a sigh and tired eyes.

"What was that all about?" Alice asked, even though she had a pretty good idea.

"Lady Emma and her father—her whole family, actually—as well as mine, expected me to propose to her. I chose not to. She didn't take it well. I'm sorry you had to witness this. And in absence of an apology from Lady Emma, I'm sorry for how she spoke to you."

"I can live with it," Alice said, still a bit shaken by the sudden outburst of emotions.

"What did she mean by saying that you had been warned?"

Alice shrugged, not wanting to burden him with something that was out of his control.

"I have no idea, really, but I've been of the impression she doesn't like you talking to me."

Thomas nodded, a bit pale and looking more tired than ever.

"I see. And maybe it's in order for me to give a word of warning as well."

"Yes?"

"My friend… Lord Merringer. He's planning to take you to the theatre, and later to the Vauxhall Gardens and the Dark Walk. I love him as a brother, but he's not to be trusted."

"I thank you for your consideration, Your Grace, but I had Lord Merringer's true nature figured out long ago. I still haven't thanked you properly for saving me from a second dance with him at Blackwell's."

"It was my pleasure and maybe…"

"Yes?"

"Maybe you would allow me to save you again? The play Lord Merringer is planning to take you to is *Artaxerxes*. I've heard it's quite good."

"Are you… are you asking me to go to the theatre with you?"

"If you would like. Yes."

Alice heard Mary holding her breath in anticipation. For a fraction of a second, she didn't think ahead and instead followed her first impulse, because it was a strong one.

"I would like that very much, Your Grace."

She made a slight bow, and it was only now she started to realise what she had agreed to. What would people make of her arriving at the theatre with the duke? What did *he* make of it? And maybe most importantly, what would Mr Stockton make of it?

"Excellent," he said, and his smile washed some of her anxiety away. "I'll make the proper arrangements and I'll see you tonight then."

She tilted her head to him, her cheeks all of a sudden on fire. After Thomas took his leave, Mary started giggling, gripping Alice's arm.

"Oh, why did I accept?" Alice said. "Nothing good could ever come from it. He's such a peculiar man. He could've asked anyone and he decided to complicate my life by asking me."

"Sometimes, for being as smart as you are, you can be bloody daft! He's asking you because he's in love with you."

"Oh, stop it," Alice said and wriggled free. "After he insulted you and I corrected him, he felt the need to make amends. Now, his former fiancée, or whatever she was, has insulted me and he feels obliged to make amends, again."

Mary started laughing.

"Daft! Daft as daft can be! Do you even believe that yourself?"

"I do."

"Well, believe what you want. At least I can recognise a man in love; his mumbled words, his violent swings from exaltation to the deepest anguish. That magic he was talking about, that made him another before you. Haven't you figured out what it was, and why he didn't want to elaborate because he felt he was speaking out of character?"

"I do know what *you're* going to say, at least."

"And you're right. He's speaking about love. What else could make a man of strong character, with a person well-formed, become someone else?"

"I don't wish to talk anymore about this."

They walked on, Mary humming a happy tune while throwing anticipatory sideways glances at Alice.

"Well, he really is a most handsome man," Mary said. "And as tall as Mr Carmichael. And I would say his manners have improved greatly since the first time we met him."

"On that I agree," Alice answered in a mumble.

She was out, treading dangerous grounds. Was she as daft as Mary presumed, or did her words bring nothing new? In the poems, love was always as distinct and clear as a knife's edge and when experiencing it, one could never confuse it for anything else. In reality, it could be a lot more devious. Dislike had shifted into neutral feelings, to respect and… Why did that image of him at Vauxhall Gardens return to her? And why did it fill her with so much warmth? Why had it been so easy for her to smile at him when she met him today and feel a sudden pang of joy at the encounter, even though she knew what she risked by meeting with him?

Ohhh, she really had been bloody daft…

She had tried to force herself to feel for Mr Stockton. Had wished intensely to fall in love with him, because that had been the easiest way, the most proper way for her to go. To fall in love with a duke? That wasn't proper for a girl of her birth. But if the duke loved her? What avenues in her heart would that open? Avenues to disappointment and sorrow, of course. The duke maybe thought himself of a higher moral than his friend, Lord Merringer, but in the end, would he ever wait for her at the end of the aisle? She could not see that. He was lost in the maze of his feelings, but sooner rather than later his infatuation would pass, and he would beg his pardon and then look amongst his peers for a spouse.

She better remember that.

If she had had any sense, she would've declined his invitation. And, what kind of gentleman was he, asking her to join him at the theatre when he knew of Mr Stockton's interest in her?

She sighed.

It wasn't on him. It was on her. She wasn't engaged to Mr Stockton. The duke was in his right to ask. It had been up to her to decline, which she hadn't, encouraging him even further.

"Do you truly think he has those kinds of feelings for me?"

"Oh, I'm certain of it. I would say he's quite mad about you."

Unfortunate choice of words, Alice thought. It was madness alright, but a pleasant kind of madness that she knew she wouldn't be able to resist. It would be the easiest thing in the world to just send words to the duke that she had fallen ill and couldn't come to the theatre.

But she wouldn't.

She wanted this evening with him, despite the talk it would cause, despite what Mr Stockton would think of it. For one evening, at least, she wanted to walk by his side as if that was a natural place for her to be. Her feelings betrayed her. The walls came crashing down. She thought of his strong hands. His dark eyes looking at her, leaving her clueless of what thoughts were in his head. She thought of all the things she had noticed about him but stowed away in a dark corner of her mind.

The dangerous materials.

But tonight she would hold no borders. She would give her feelings free reign and tread the dangerous grounds.

Chapter 12

Alice was by her dressing table, watching Lovisa through the mirror, putting the last of the pins into her hair. Her father stopped at the door, watching her with a smile.

"You look quite spectacular, my dear. Well worthy of a duke."

Oh, so mother had told him.

"Thank you, Papa."

He sat down in the chair next to her.

"The Duke of Hexham I hear. Is it true?"

"It is."

"M*aaa*rvelous. Then all those expensive dresses weren't for nothing," he said with a grin.

"Papa."

"I beg your pardon, my dear. Of course, your charm and striking appearance had something to do with it as well." He turned to Alice's lady's maid. "Lovisa, leave us for a moment."

Lovisa nodded and made a small curtsey before leaving.

While putting in her pearl earrings, Alice said:

"You would do better to be a little less celebratory, Papa. I would've done better to decline his invitation."

"Done better!" Mr Weatherby blurted and gaped like a fish on land. "Nonsense! You can't do much better than a duke, can you?"

"That wasn't quite what I meant, and you know it."

"Of course I do. But the way I see it, dear child, to be seen in public with a duke can't be bad, anyway you choose to look at it. Mr Stockton will not be less inclined to marry you after tonight, rather the opposite; if he ever would ask the question."

"Maybe."

"Not maybe. It's a given. But why settle for Mr Stockton if you could have the Duke of Hexham?"

She gave him a look.

"Because he's a *duke*, Papa, and you're not. I refuse to be his distraction, his plaything, after his relationship with Lady Emma came to an end."

"Well, as young and knowledgeable as you are about all different matters, you may then also know that it's widely talked about that the duke refused Lady Emma because his heart was already otherwise engaged. There's a great deal of curiosity about who this mystery woman is. Most people have their bets down on Lady Sara. But the honourable Liza Everett has also been mentioned."

"There's bets down?"

"Oh, yes, certainly. You wouldn't know what's going on in the gentlemen's clubs, but there's bets down alright. So you can understand my surprise, and delight, when I hear that the woman the duke is taking to the theatre tonight is none other than my own daughter."

"Oh, my lord," Alice said and put her face into her palms. "Now I can't possibly go. Everybody will be staring, making assumptions."

"You're going, alright. And I'll be down at Boodle's to place a minor bet for tonight."

"Sometimes you're just horrible, Papa."

"Yes, but you don't get rich by being nice. But all the riches in the world can't give us what you can, together with some very expensive dresses. If you have ever sog slight a possibility to snare the duke, all the family expect you to at least try. Can you promise me that?"

"To *snare*, the duke?"

"Choose whatever word that is more to your liking, but promise me."

"I promise to do what my conscience allows me to."

"It's no time to be prude, darling. It's time to be practical. Would you like your sons and daughters to be mere Misters and Misses, or lords and ladies? To be the sons and daughters of a duke, or to be from a family of traders?"

"Why so much contempt for your own class?"

"It's not me that feels the contempt, but what you and I feel is of no significance, darling. We do not judge ourselves, that job is done by others and they have judged us hard. Do I have your promise?"

Alice looked down at her dressing table, feeling a bit dizzy. Her father's frankness on the matter more than bothered her.

He sighed.

"Tell me this then, at least. Do you like him?"

She nodded.

"Then all is well. Show it to him. Don't retreat into prudency. Act like you're his equal and then… you might just be."

And while Alice Weatherby spoke to her father, Thomas Overton had quite a different discussion with his friend John Merringer.

John was sitting in the chair by the corner, looking at Thomas while he tried out a new tailcoat by the mirror. Mr Gray took one step back and nodded approvingly at Thomas's appearance.

"You are taking Miss Weatherby to the theatre?"

"I am."

Thomas indicated at the door with the slightest movement of his head, and Mr Gray bowed and retreated through it.

Thomas turned to John.

"I am taking Miss Weatherby to the theatre and I'm fully in my right to do so."

"Even though you know I'm pursuing her?"

"Maybe that is the sole reason for me to do the same?"

John got out of the chair, looked at Thomas with a sly smile.

"I don't think it is."

"John, I'm sorry if this offends you, but—"

"Oh, not at all brother. I've been working very hard for it since your first encounter with Mrs Weatherby."

"Excuse me?"

"I can't say I wasn't tempted by Miss Weatherby, but your feelings for her were soon apparent and knowing you, I understood you needed some… encouragement to make an advance—like saving the fair maiden from a dastardly fellow like me."

Thomas just looked at him.

"Is this true? Not just a speech to save your pride?"

"It most certainly is true, my brother. I'm just surprised that it had to go as far as me threatening to take her to the Dark Walk before you came to your senses."

Thomas didn't know what to say in response. He saw in John's smiling, uncomplicated face that he actually did speak the truth. Thomas's inner was in turmoil. He had just accepted his feelings for what they were, and John had known all along? To be as deluded by oneself…

John grabbed him in a bearhug and gave him a little shake.

"Yes, people are going to talk. Yes, your dragon of a mother will hear all about it. Yes, the Fairchild's will be bonkers mad, but what is all that in the face of true love, brother!"

Thomas couldn't help laughing and gave John a little pat on the back to let him go.

"You conniving little…" he said and dried his eyes. "Was it that apparent, then?"

"It was to me, but less so to Miss Weatherby and yourself."

"What do you mean?"

"I've tried my best to be everything you aren't in my conduct with Miss Weatherby, to make her understand what she really wants and needs. Sparks flew on your first meeting. You're not used to people challenging your opinions in public. She? She couldn't care less. I spotted every single glance you stole of her that night. I've never seen you give a single woman that kind of attention before. But now I see the same kind of unfortunate behaviour with Miss Weatherby. She would like to turn her eyes to you, but for some reason she doesn't. She seems hellbent on destroying her future happiness with that lofty fellow, Mr Stockton."

Mr Stockton, yes, Thomas would be expecting Mr Anderson's back shortly, with a report on the "lofty" Mr Stockton. He really didn't know what he wanted the report to be.

With his spur-of-the-moment invitation to Alice, he had opened a door that couldn't be closed, and even if he longed for the night, it filled him with anguish.

Was this fair to Alice? To himself? And… the bottomless black hole opened—to Leana?

He had spurned her because of her birth, and choosing another woman that, in the eyes of the public, was beneath him—wouldn't that make the betrayal double? He had no hopes of ever being relieved of the memory of Leana's tear-drenched face, her hands clasping his while she repeated her *yes-yes-yes* to his proposal. He could never be free of that, but he had hoped that in time the memory would wane and be less painful. This night at the theatre, though, would make the wounds of the past bright and clear again.

It was insanity, he knew it, but couldn't any longer contain himself. He couldn't wait to be close to her again, feel the scent of her light perfume, to look into those lively eyes of hers.

What would become of them when evening shifted to morning and a new day began?

Would they be closer to each other, or the opposite?

And which of the scenarios did he prefer?

Damn you… Leana.

The ghosts of the past, interfering with the present. They would always do that. There was no way of escaping it.

"Are you still with me, brother?"

"Hmm?"

"You looked like you were a million miles away. I hope it was a pleasant place, but now we have to get ready for your chaise."

"He's here!" Wilma yelled from the window, standing on the sofa. "The tall handsome one!"

"Get away from there," Alice hissed. "Don't let him see you there, staring like a monkey in a cage."

Mrs Weatherby, the chaperon for the night, made a cooing sound of anticipation and started fiddling with the collar of her newly bought dress. Alice wore a silver satin dress and her hair set up with a series of extravagant pins with pearls that Lovisa had arranged in an intricate pattern. Mr Weatherby sat in a chair by the fire, his face not revealing any emotion. Wilma slid down on the sofa, looking malcontent with the response her discovery of the duke's chaise had received.

Soon the butler opened the doors to the drawing room and with a faint quiver to his voice announced the Duke of Hexham. The Weatherbys rose to their feet as one. The duke entered the room in an air of grace and confidence. The women curtsied and the men bowed. The duke shot Alice a glance and a short smile before addressing her father with all the necessary pleasantries—such a lovely home, nice to finally make your acquaintance, yes, city life is certainly something else than country life.

Alice stood silent, eagerly waiting for him to shift his gaze back to her. While waiting, she looked at him with a different eye, not the eye of an acquaintance, fogged by the many mishaps during their short time knowing each other. She looked at him with the eye of a lover, and now, unaffected by other feelings, she could see his graceful and pleasant ways. She knew this wasn't really him, but she liked that he made the effort for her father, a tradesman by birth.

He did it for her.

What had she ever done to be graced by his attention? Scolding him in public? Being an annoyance to him at every instance thereafter? Yes, but there had always been something more, in the background. She remembered the tug within her when she first laid eyes on him. It had been pure attraction then, nothing to build a future on, to use Lucinda's words. But the fact that that internal tug had become a strong pull, threatening to become a surge, that meant something.

She had never been in love before, not truly. She found now that the poets were wrong. Love wasn't an airy and light thing. It was something darker and stronger, almost animalistic. It made her heart pound harder, her belly knotting up, and she wanted nothing else than to be out of this house, with him by her side. She wanted to be in the darkness of his carriage, feeling him close, her lips against his and… oh, better reign those feelings. Nothing of the sort would happen. He was a duke and she a gentleman's daughter.

Her thoughts were improper, she knew it, but… she wondered how his dark hair would feel through her fingers, those strong hands on her waist, pulling her closer.

What was wrong with you! Get that nonsense out of your head!

He gave her a new glance, slowly nodding at something her father said. He smiled at her again. A thin, secret smile. For a second, she felt like he could see right into her, see all her improper thoughts—and she blushed.

Was this evening just a big mistake? She couldn't be sure of the duke's intention, but by placing himself in this position, introducing himself to her family, taking her to the theatre, he had started down a road that could have only one goal, lest there would be a minor scandal.

But would he?

It was far from unheard of that a man of his stature would marry beneath him, even more so when there was a great deal of money involved.

Was that it?

Was he aiming for her father's money?

Don't be daft, silly girl. Lady Emma's father was richer than hers. Mary had been right. She had been blind, but she did see now, and what she saw in his eyes was not the love of money. It was the love of… she could hardly even form the thought in her head. Why did she have such a hard time believing a man like the Duke of Hexam would marry her out of love? Because it was just too good to be true, and when it looked that way, it usually wasn't. If she started to wish for it, the illusion would break. Fate or whatever forces decided these matters would laugh her in the face and take it away.

You? Marrying a lord, out of love? Oh, *please.*

She wasn't prone to thinking ill of herself, and she wasn't going to start now, but some dreams just seemed too big.

The carriage ride down to the Royal Theatre at Covent Garden was nothing like in her runaway thoughts. Her mother talked incessantly the whole time—London by night really was one of the most beautiful things a person could ever hope to see—*ohhh*, look at those new gas lights, what an intense shine they have—there's Mrs Armiger, I met her over tea at the Wycombs the other day. Maybe she's going to the theatre as well? No, I don't think Mrs Armiger is of the disposition to be able to enjoy as intricate a piece of music as *Artexerxes*. Me, on the other hand, I'm a great lover of music. Pray, duke, have you seen the Italian original?

He had, in Verona as well as in Venice, but the English version of the opera really did measure up to the original, so they wouldn't miss out on anything of the experience. Between the bursts of words from Mrs Weatherby, Alice and Thomas shared a silent smile, Alice's a bit apologetic.

When they drove up to the theatre and one of the servants approached the carriage to open it, a blossom of nervousness swelled in Alice's chest. When they stepped out of the carriage, the talk would start. Would there be disapproving looks, words whispered before faces turned away? She knew there wouldn't. If words were whispered, it would be out of their sight. Maybe they didn't care about her, but they wouldn't want to displease the duke. No one turned their heads when they stepped out, other than to give a nod and a smile of greeting. Mrs Weatherby continued to marvel, this time over the theatre and its broad white façade in the classical style, with its line of Doric columns that took the mind to ancient Greece. They went inside, followed the portico through the flight of slow ascending stairs, draped in red to the second floor, so lavishly adorned it felt more like a palace of a maharaja than a theatre in London. It was a world of burnished gold and crimson red.

They sat down in the duke's private box in the second-floor balcony and placed their orders with the servant. Mrs Weatherby sat down beside her daughter, fanning herself like this experience was just too much for her.

"We're so high up. That man can construct buildings like this. One balks at the thought."

Then she whipped up her binoculars to see who was seated below her in the auditorium. From the orchestra ditch, there was a strange, swelling sound of instruments being played and tuned individually. Alice had always liked that sound, it was like a promise of what to come, because even in this disorganised manner, she thought the instruments sounded beautiful. This evening she didn't care for them though, her mother was occupied with her inspection of the less fortunate below, which gave Alice a moment of privacy with Thomas that she was eager to take advantage of, but all of a sudden something happened to her that had never happened before.

Her words failed her.

Whatever she was planning to say, she felt, would sound flat and forced as soon as they left her mouth.

"It's Sir Edmund Kean that's playing Artexerxes," Thomas said. "He's supposed to be really good in that role."

If she was fortunate, he cared about the opera as much as she did, but she latched on to his words.

"I guess he wasn't in the Italian original. How come you saw it in Verona?"

"I fell in love with the country during my grand tour and bought a country villa in Tuscany before Bonaparte started his wars."

A grand tour, casually buying an estate in a foreign country? The difference between them suddenly became more evident than ever.

"It sounds lovely."

"It is. Tuscany is like a soothing breeze through sunshine after a heavy rain and a storm."

And here, Alice thought, he would've invited me to come visit him at his Italian country estate, if he had been a Mr Stockton. But Thomas didn't. Instead, he silenced as if he felt the need to do just that, invite her, after gushing his praise over the Italian countryside, but for some reason just couldn't do it.

Then the instruments silenced. So did the chattering voices. The curtain was drawn and the opera started with a swell of tunes from the strings, brass blaring and Sir Edmund entered the stage in heavy, dramatic makeup and oriental clothes. Alice tried to enjoy it, but for some reason, the feeling of being out of place was stronger than ever.

Then she felt Thomas's hand touch hers in the darkness, his fingers just brushing hers in a brief caress. She answered the caress and felt tears sting her eyes when his hand folded over hers. Suddenly, she was exactly where she was supposed to be.

He leaned over to her. To her mother, the least attentive chaperone in the world, it probably looked like he was explaining the story of the opera to her or something, and Alice reinforced that by looking attentively out in the air. His words were not of the opera, though, they were of a different matter entirely.

"I can feel… hesitation from you, Miss Weatherby. I felt it when I invited you to the theatre. I felt it when I came to your home and was presented to your family, and I feel it now, even, despite your hand is resting in mine. I can understand that. I haven't done much to deserve your trust up to this point, but I'm not playing games, Miss Weatherby."

Finally, he talked to her straight. Her heart made an extra beat.

"So, what is this then, Your Grace? That question is the root of my hesitation. I'm no Lady Emma. I can't boast her connections or birth."

"You are right. You certainly aren't a Lady Emma, and that's why you're here tonight and not she. I don't know what this is, Miss Weatherby, but I want to find out."

He caressed the back of her hand with his thumb. She shouldn't settle for such a lofty declaration of intent, but his power over her was greater than she had realised, blasted man, and she could do nothing more than nod.

"I want that too. And there's another thing I wish for too."

"And that is?"

"That you rather call me Alice instead of Miss Weatherby. I think we're past that line of formality."

He gave her one of those smiles that warmed her to her core.

"If you would return that favour, yes. I'm tired of being *your grace* to you."

"In that case, I will oblige your wish, Thomas," she said and bowed her head in made-up servility.

That made him smile again. She yearned for him to kiss her but knew he couldn't. Instead, he squeezed her hand a little tighter.

Then her mother looked their way to comment on the fine quality of the painted décor, and the moment was over. Thomas retracted his hand and told Mrs Weatherby the name of the artist that was said to have worked on the décor for more than a year.

Then they sat in silence, listening to the opera. Alice didn't hear much of it, though. A warm fire was alight in her belly. What was happening here? Was it happening? She heard Mary's voice in her head again:

Sometimes, for being as smart as you are, you can be bloody daft.

For how long could she stay in sheltered disbelief, not daring to hope, just to risk disappointment?

Alice Overton, Duchess of Hexham.

She had never dreamt of it. Never strived for an elevation like that, and that it should fall upon her by nothing more than chance—she couldn't believe it. Would she feel the same for him if he had not been a duke? If he had instead been the son of a fisherman?

She stole a glance at him and felt that powerful surge when looking at his handsome face and the aura of strength that surrounded him. Her question wasn't one that could be answered, because he *was* a duke and the aura surrounding him was a result of it. Everything about him was the result of his predestined future of being the fourth Duke of Hexham. So how could she know if she would've loved a person that didn't even exist?

She became greedy. It wasn't enough to sit with him at the theatre. She wanted to sit across from him in a bed and caress his face, kiss every part of it and let her lips know what her eyes already did.

She looked at his hand resting on his knee. It was so close, but yet so far away. To let her hand travel the distance to meet his, that wasn't something she could allow herself to do.

When the final aria had been sung and they stood up to leave the balcony, Alice was a bit dazed. She felt exhausted, even though she had done nothing more than sit by his side.

"What a wonderful opera!" Mrs Weatherby said. "I enjoyed every minute of it. Every minute!"

"Yes, it's quite extraordinary," Thomas said, looking at Alice.

The carriage ride back home was a silent affair. There wasn't much Thomas and Alice could say to each other with Mrs Weatherby in the carriage. Mrs Weatherby had finally run out of words, looking out of the side window with slowly blinking eyes.

When the carriage stopped outside their house, Mrs Weatherby invited Thomas in, maybe for a glass of brandy with Mr Weatherby, but Thomas politely declined, saying he didn't want to impose at this late an hour. When he took his leave, he and Alice parted with great formality that was just a thin coating on what boiled beneath. Thomas gave her one more of those secret smiles before stepping back into his carriage.

When Alice and Mrs Weatherby turned to the door, Mrs Weatherby had gotten her words back.

"It was such a marvellous opera. I just wished his grace would've shown you, my dear, a bit more attention, and maybe had joined us for a brandy before leaving."

"I think he showed me the proper attention, Mama," Alice said, biting her lower lip.

"Yes, he was most courteous," her mother answered with a sigh.

Mr Weatherby ambushed them when they came into the house.

"Didn't you invite him for a drink?" he asked his wife with a thundering voice and raised eyebrows.

"I did! I did! But he declined."

"Declined?"

"Yes, he didn't want to impose on us this late."

"Impose? Impose on us this late?"

"Yes, that was what I said."

"Didn't you assure him that he wouldn't be imposing? That his company, in fact, would be most appreciated?"

"I did not. He seemed already set on the matter. And he didn't show our Alice the kind of attention one could've hoped for either."

"Highly troublesome," Mr Weatherby said, stroking his chin.

Since they didn't seem to need her view of the evening that had transpired, Alice bade her parents goodnight and retreated to her rooms, leaving them to their own worries.

Chapter 13

The day after the duke and Miss Weatherby had been seen at the theatre, a particular sinister piece of gossip was born, something about the fair Miss Weatherby and the Dark Walk of Vauxhall Pleasure Gardens. It was first mentioned over tea in a salon at Regent Street, by two of Lady Emma's close friends. The day after, it had spread to noble ladies not at all associated with Lady Emma, and since no one really knew the origin of the rumour, it gained in credibility.

The duke, it was said, was lured into a great disaster by a harlot that had already been tainted by Lord Merringer. Lord Merringer? Some said. I heard it was a certain Mr Stockton?

Maybe it was the both of them?

Maybe none?

Maybe a completely different gentleman?

Maybe not a gentleman at all?

Surely not.

Which gentleman would behave in such a disgraceful manner?

None. None at all.

Miss Weatherby, on the other hand… What reasons could there be for her fast elevation from obscurity to high society? From the countryside to the Royal Theatre with a man like the Duke of Hexham?

It was unheard of.

Women like her should better know the dividing lines of the world. Temptation to climb the ladder was understandable, but that didn't excuse the foul doings of Miss Weatherby, of which, everybody agreed, there were many.

Soon most of the city was aware of Alice's low morals and the great embarrassment that was awaiting the Duke of Hexham's future. The only ones oblivious to the rumours were the families mentioned in them.

Meanwhile, Alice and Mary met with Thomas at Hyde Park for a walk during the early hours. Alice did wonder why he hadn't come to her house and walked with her to the park, but on the other hand, she understood he might want to avoid her mother's choleric rants and praises. This was a more pleasant experience for both. It wasn't for her father, though.

Since the night of the theatre visit, he had been in a constant state of malcontent, grumbling and talking to himself. All he could think of was that the Duke of Hexham, his future son-in-law, seemed to have slipped through his fingers. He had asked Alice, numerous times, if they maybe soon could expect a visit from his grace? Alice didn't want to tell him what had happened at the theatre since she knew he would erupt in celebratory joy and set Mrs Weatherby to plan the wedding.

Instead, she said nothing more than the expected:

Yes, his grace had been very agreeable and behaved every bit as one could expect from a duke. Her father hadn't liked that more than half.

This morning, she didn't think of her father, though. She hastened her steps to reach the park, and Mary was getting short of breath beside her.

"Calm down, cousin. I'll assure you he will be there, as he's been every morning since last week."

He was. She saw him waiting at the oak tree in the mist, the silhouette of him with his walking cane as familiar to her as the backside of her own hand.

"See. I told you."

Thomas gave a slight nod and a smile to Mary.

"Miss de Vries."

And then he took Alice's hand and kissed the back of it.

"Miss Weatherby."

"What happened to Alice?"

"It takes time, Alice. But I'll get there," he said. "And I wouldn't want to upset your chaperon by being too forward."

"Oh, please don't mind me," Mary said, lifting her eyebrows. "Press her against the tree and kiss her till your heart's content. I won't tell."

"Mary!" Alice said, half laughing with surprise.

"No need to get upset. I can turn my back at you for five minutes or so. That's all I'm saying."

"A most refreshing view of the duties of a chaperon," Thomas said.

But of the offer itself, nothing more was said. They started walking. The gravel paths were deserted this time of the day. Alice enjoyed the silence of the surroundings, the mystery of the mist, enshrouding trees, and shrubberies. Mary was the one primarily talking, and she had big news to deliver.

"I've already told you about Mr Carmichael and Mr Stockton being in the same line of work. Now they have decided to merge their two businesses to be one of the bigger companies in overseas trading. Isn't it marvellous!"

"Very," Thomas said, but Alice noticed how he reacted to Mr Stockton's name.

Alice hadn't heard from Mr Stockton since the night of the Mrs Sophie's ball, where they had shared such a good time. But, in honesty, she hadn't given him much thought either. She had made no formal promises to him but still felt she needed a formal ending to their association, whatever it had been, but to seek him out to do it… it didn't feel it was up to her. She had expected his visit since last week, since he couldn't be unaware of Alice and Thomas showing up at the theatre together, but he hadn't come. Now she hoped to meet him by chance, maybe here today, like she had on a morning much like this one, up at Rotten Row. But she didn't. Instead, she met the old couple from that very morning, Mr and Mrs Peters.

She stopped, expecting them to do the same, but with sharp nods at Thomas, they continued without giving Alice as much as a look—their mouths tightly shut.

What strange behaviour.

"Do you know Mr and Mrs Peters?" Thomas asked.

"I thought I did," she mumbled as they continued their walk.

They reached a part of the park where the foliage was dense and the path long and straight. Much of the mist had cleared and the path was empty.

"Oh, look what pretty flowers," Mary exclaimed. "Will you two give me a couple of minutes? Maybe five?" she asked but walked off the path without waiting for their reply.

She was gone in the thickets. They could hear her rustle in there, sighing about twigs in her hair.

Thomas took Alice's hand and brought it to his lips, kissing it with closed eyes. She stepped in close to him, looking up. He embraced her and then his lips were on hers, and he kissed her with boyish eagerness. She answered the kiss, violently, pulling her hand through his hair. His cold cheek was against hers and he whispered in her ear:

"I love you, Alice Weatherby."

"And I you, Thomas Overton," she said, her eyes welling over.

He stroked one of the tears away with his thumb, and then he kissed her again.

"Blasted wilderness!" Mary said from the thicket. "It's tearing my hair out by its roots! I'm coming back out!"

And that she did, flapping her hands around her head like she was attacked by angry bees. Thomas stepped away from Alice, but still held her hands in his. Alice's heart was thumping, her chest heaving. He looked at her with eyes that were alight. Mary looked between them and nodded.

"Well, worth a trip into the savage woods, I guess. Shall we continue?"

And continue they did. Alice's head was buzzing. It had all happened so fast. They had met less than four weeks ago. She had discovered her feelings for him a mere week ago, and today, he had kissed her. Where did they go from here?

During their slow walk, which got slower the closer to the end of the trail they came, he discretely reached for her hand, and took it.

Later that day, at White's, drinking a glass of brandy with some friends, Thomas was still, mentally, in the park with Alice. After their walk, he had come to the unfortunate conclusion that he was an idiot. It takes a toll on a proud man to realise such a thing, but on the other hand, the evidence had been piling up these last weeks. His only intelligent decision regarding Alice Weatherby had been that he needed to stay away from her, since he couldn't trust himself with her. Had he done that? No. No he hadn't. Quite the opposite, actually. He had taken her to the theatre, he had kissed her and if that wasn't enough, he had declared his love for her. It was the truth, but a truth he had sworn to hold to himself. She had asked him at the theatre what his intentions were, and he had evaded the question. His intentions, if spoken without shame, were to be near her as much as possible without taking the final step. But he couldn't do that. He had taken this far beyond that point and… by the almighty lord… why was he to deprive himself of happiness because of a mistake—no, that was cowardly put—because of a moment of weakness that happened years ago?

Would Leana be more at peace if he never married? Was she reading the papers to see if the name Overton ever popped up in the wedding announcements? And if it did, would she run to the closest river and drown herself? He thought not.

He was standing amongst his friends, hearing them talk and laugh, but he wasn't there. Then a laugh and a loud handclap jerked him back to the real world. John Merringer walked up to them, smiling with his arms spread.

"Oh, just look at them, a pack of laughing hyenas. If I ever saw truer friends."

The gentlemen around Thomas suddenly looked uncomfortable, gulped brandy before excusing themselves. Thomas looked after them with a puzzled look.

"What was that about?" he asked John.

"I'll tell you, but I think I'd better do it in the inner room."

The inner room was a small room with a distinctly medieval feel, with two heavy leather chairs and a small table.

"What is this all about?" Thomas asked.

"In a moment. First, I want to know if you intend to do the honourable thing with Miss Weatherby. After your visit to the theatre, people have been seeing you walking daily with her in Hyde Park."

"I don't think it's for you to—"

"Thomas. Please. I'm asking as your friend."

"I see… I do want to do the right thing, but…"

"But…? Leana I guess?"

Thomas gave him a look.

"Yes."

John Merringer played the role of the lovable scoundrel who seemed not to have a care in the world. Thomas knew better. At times, like now, it was a touch unsettling to realise that John knew him just as well.

"How can I marry Alice when I humiliated Leana and scorned her for her low birth? It's an inconsistency that I..."

"Thomas, may I offer an outside perspective?"

"Please do."

"What pains you about Leana isn't that you didn't marry her. What pains you is the promise you made and then broke. I think you're terrified of making the same promise to Alice before you're absolutely certain there's nothing in the world that could stop you from keeping it. Am I right?"

Thomas wasn't surprised to find that he probably was.

"Maybe."

"Whatever you feel for Miss Weatherby, you need to reaffirm it for yourself—and quickly. Because there's a rumour circulating."

"Rumour? What rumour?"

"Rumours about Miss Weatherby. Apparently, she's of… low morals."

"What on earth are you talking about?"

"They're saying she's tricking you into marriage. That she's already been… tasted by both me and Mr Stockton. And, apparently, other unnamed men."

Thomas gave an indignant laugh.

"That's utterly preposterous!"

"I know. My guess? The architect of this vile tale is someone who once fancied herself in possession of your affections."

"I've no doubt it is! But what can be done about it?"

"Nothing, my friend. Absolutely nothing. You'd have more luck halting the flow of a river by stepping into it with arms spread wide.

When I heard this nonsense, I called it a foul lie, but my words won't carry nearly as far as the lie itself."

"That… woman," Thomas muttered, pressing his folded hands to his lips. "I actually heard her say it—that she'd ruin any chance of happiness for Miss Weatherby. And this is how she intends to do it?"

"Apparently."

"If Alice hears these whispers…"

"She will, eventually. So, if you intend to make promises to her, make sure you mean them. Your loyalty to her will be tested, and her reputation will always be under scrutiny."

"That's not fair."

"I never said it was. But it's how our little world operates."

Later, as Thomas walked home, he scrutinised every passer-by who nodded or touched the brim of their hat. Did they know? All of them? Surely there must be something he could do. Could he stand up and speak for Alice, vouch for her character and virtue? No, that's what a fool, blinded by infatuation, would do, right? He needed to think this through and devise a solution.

It was his indiscretion that had brought Lady Emma's wrath down upon Alice.

When he got home, Mr Morley told him that Mr Anderson was waiting for him in the drawing room. Thomas nodded. He had almost forgotten about Mr Anderson. He felt less enthused over the private investigator's report now, since he had a hard time thinking Mr Stockton was still a relevant factor in Alice's life. But since Mr Anderson had already concluded his investigation, and Thomas had paid for it, he could just as well hear what the man had to say.

"Good day, Mr Anderson," Thomas said when entering the drawing room.

Mr Anderson got up from the sofa and fingered his hat.

"Your Grace. A fine day it is."

"It sure is. Can I offer you something to drink?"

Mr Anderson eyed the glass decanter on the mahogany drink table.

"Help yourself to it," Thomas said and sat down on the sofa.

"Thank you, Your Grace."

He listened to Mr Anderson clinking with glass behind his back, slowly stroking his chin. What was Alice doing in this very moment? Had the foul words already reached her or did she remain in ignorant bliss?

Mr Anderson returned and sat down on the sofa across from Thomas.

"Mr Stockton Your Grace asked about, yes. And a good thing he did."

"What do you mean?"

"That Mr Stockton, shiny teeth and perfect hair, is a little bit less perfect when you look behind the curtain."

"Few people are."

"True, indeed, but Mr Stockton is a whole different kind of beast compared to the pedestrian sins of ordinary men."

"Meaning?"

"In short, he's a gambler. Most gentlemen are, I know, but not in such a destructive way as Mr Stockton. The one thing that is surprising with Mr Stockton is that he's managed to keep his staggering losses a private matter."

"He's a rich man. He can afford it."

"One would think, but no. I guess one of the reasons that have allowed Mr Stockton to keep his losses a secret is that his father, the older Mr Stockton, officially still is in charge of the family business and would've reacted to any excessive losses on the son's behalf. Problem is, the older Mr Stockton isn't among us anymore. Sure, he's here in body but not in spirit and certainly not in mind. He sits on the second floor of the family house on Exeter Street, looking out on the park, being spoon-fed by a nurse. The younger Mr Stockton has, in essence, been in charge of the family business for the past four years. During those four years, he has managed to turn a healthy profit into debt, and that debt is growing larger by the day. He's selling his ships now, using his father's forged signature, and I think you understand how much a trading company without ships is worth?"

"Not much," Thomas mumbled, feeling a chill in his body; hadn't Miss de Vries mentioned that Mr Carmichael, her fiancé, had merged his company with Stockton's? But how could he have?

What sort of falsified documents might Stockton have presented to convince Carmichael the merger was in his best interest? Or—and perhaps this was closer to the truth—had Mr Carmichael simply taken Stockton's word on the soundness of his company?

Mr Carmichael... he wasn't a fool, but he did have the unfortunate habit of thinking the best of people.

"I've heard of a merger between Stockton's company and…"

"Ah, quite right. There's a Mr Simon Carmichael who is now the happy co-owner of Mr Stockton's debts. I guess that is a great relief for Mr Stockton since his criminal incompetence and behaviour are soon to be unearthed. One of my colleagues has been employed by a Mr Wainwright, one of Mr Stockton's biggest creditors. We have exchanged information, and when he leaves his report about Mr Stockton, this will become public. All the creditors will come rushing in, demanding their money. Bankruptcy will surely follow, for both Mr Stockton and Mr Carmichael."

"I see," Thomas said, leaning back in the chair.

The damage was already done. Miss de Vries's fiancé was ruined, and with him, her happiness as well. That, in turn, would surely affect the happiness of someone far more precious to him than Miss de Vries or Mr Carmichael. But was he the one to deliver the bad news? He supposed he might have to be. Better it come from him than from the stark, black headlines of the newspapers. Perhaps something could be salvaged before the story became public. He doubted it, but that was for others to decide.

The real problem was that Miss de Vries would tell Alice where she'd got the information, and naturally, Alice would want to know why he had been investigating Mr Stockton. That would be a difficult question to answer. Worse still, these things had a way of unravelling. If Alice discovered that he had looked into her as well… he wasn't particularly fond of that prospect.

Still, something had to be done—and he thought he knew what.

Chapter 14

Alice wandered from room to room on the second floor, gazing out at Hyde Park and revelling in her lightness of heart. She wasn't looking for anything in particular; she simply couldn't bear to sit still, posing as the perfect flower in one of her mother's sofas.

She didn't need to close her eyes to relive the kiss with Thomas, nor to summon the memory of his scent or the warmth of his hand around her waist. It was all-consuming. Yet now, pacing the second floor of their London house, it felt almost unreal—like it had happened to someone else. She hadn't even entertained the possibility of such a moment, but when it came, she realised she had yearned for it. It was dreamlike, yet faintly unsettling. She was so accustomed to being her own master, but in that moment, she'd felt utterly at his mercy.

When they parted at the southern gate of Hyde Park, Mary had been a barrel of a million questions. Alice couldn't deny her; after all, it was Mary's doing that had made the moment with Thomas possible. But she couldn't share everything. The memory, though vivid, felt delicate, as if woven from air. Still, she'd given Mary enough to satisfy her curiosity—for Mary had congratulated herself on her ingenuity and Alice on her impending wedding.

Ah, that burning word that shaped futures.

Wedding.

Thomas hadn't said a word about it as they walked back. Alice, inexperienced in such matters, wondered if Thomas was now meeting with her father to declare his affections and seek Mr Weatherby's consent, which he would most gratefully get?

More questions than she wanted to ponder at this moment. She wanted nothing to bring her lightness of heart down.

A maid appeared, hurrying up the stairs. Alice turned to her.

"Miss de Vries is here."

"Miss de Vries?"

The maid nodded.

That was strange. Mary was more than an hour early for their walk. A sense of unease settled over Alice, and it was confirmed when she entered the drawing room to find Mary with puffy, red eyes and a trembling jaw.

"Oh, it's all lost, cousin," Mary gasped, collapsing onto the sofa. Her despair sent the footman at the door retreating into the hallway.

Alice held up a hand, signalling him to remain nearby, and then sat beside Mary.

"What is lost, sister?"

"*All*! *All* is lost!" Mary wailed, dabbing her eyes with a lace handkerchief. "Mr Stockton is filing for bankruptcy, and he's dragging Mr Carmichael down with him."

"What are you saying?"

"Exactly what I said! We had a visitor late last night—a private investigator named Anderson. He'd been looking into Mr Stockton's business for a client, and he didn't like what he found. He uncovered how Mr Carmichael was lured into this rotting ship of a venture that's now sinking."

"This cannot be true."

"It most certainly can! Stockton's a gambler, a heavy one, and he buys racehorses for sums that would shock even the Prince of Wales. He had no scruples about concealing his poor finances to trap my dear Mr Carmichael. Now Mr Carmichael will be indebted for life. The wedding must be postponed—if my father even still approves of him."

Mary threw herself back onto the sofa, sobbing uncontrollably. Alice stroked her back, numb from the dreadful news. Yet amidst the shock, something didn't sit right. Why would a private investigator go out of his way to deliver bad news to someone who hadn't paid a penny for it?

"Who was the private investigator's client? Did he mention that?"

"Who cares about his client? What difference does it make?" Mary snapped. "He can sit back with a smug smile, knowing his foresight saved him from the misery that now falls on Mr Carmichael and me. He's hardly the one who deserves pity!"

"Of course not," Alice murmured, though her thoughts were already spinning.

Alice accompanied Mary back home but declined her cousin's invitation to join her for tea. She knew Mary well enough to understand that what she truly needed now was rest and solace. Instead, Alice made her way to Hereford Square and knocked firmly on the door at number 25.

She had expected a butler to answer, but to her surprise, it was Mr Stockton himself. He appeared half-dressed, his hair dishevelled, and there was a broad, almost gleeful smile on his face. She realised instantly that he was drunk. An unpleasant odour wafted from him, and behind him, she spotted an empty brandy bottle lying on the floor and a chiffonier with one leg broken, leaning precariously against the wall.

"Miss Weatherby! What a delight to see you this fine morning!"

"Is it true?"

"What, my dear? You take me for a mind reader, which I assure you I'm not. There's so much this 'is it true' could refer to, and none of it is particularly pleasant. So, do indulge me—speak plainly."

"That you lured Mr Carmichael into a partnership, knowing full well you would be filing for bankruptcy this week?"

"So, it's out, then?" he muttered.

"It isn't yet, but it will be soon. How could you do this?"

"It wasn't my intention, I swear. One big win—that's all I needed to save both me and Mr Carmichael from this pickle. There was a fight in Dorset. One of the fighters was supposed to be paid off. A sure thing, they said. It wasn't."

"You disgust me."

"Well, at least now you feel *something* for me."

"More than you deserve. Was this your plan all along? To marry me so you could get your hands on Father's money?"

"The money wasn't unimportant, no."

"I see. I wish I could muster more outrage at your villainy, but my dear cousin's despair, caused entirely by you, has drained me of it. For you, personally, I feel only contempt and pity. But if you've any shred of decency left, salvage what remains of your soul and release Mr Carmichael from this prison you've built for him. At the very least, do that."

"I cannot. I don't discuss business with women who don't understand it. Mr Carmichael's business and mine are no longer separate—they're one and the same. As are the debts and the bleak future we now share. And for that, I am truly sorry, but the world is harsh, and one must dare to win. Sadly, I lost."

Alice had no more words for him. His slack expression and unapologetic eyes tempted her to abandon all decorum and strike him squarely on the nose. Instead, she turned on her heel and walked away.

"Send my regards to the duke!" he called after her, his voice thick with drunken slur.

Heads turned in her direction as she hurried away from the disgraceful scene, her cheeks burning with humiliation.

The lightness of her heart, entirely gone now.

Thomas had been sitting at the coffee house on George Street for more than two hours before he saw the gate at the other side of the street swing open. He straightened in his chair. Lady Emma and her friend, Lady Anchessa, walked out with umbrellas over their shoulders. Thomas threw a handful of coins on the table, put on his coat and hat, and left the coffee house. Lady Anchessa spotted him first, when he came crossing the street. She whispered to Lady Emma, who turned to him with a haughty smile.

"Your Grace? This isn't your usual place of walking?"

"It isn't. May I walk with you?"

"Oh, I don't think that's a good idea. Who knows what talk that could ignite?"

She smiled thinly.

"Yes, who knows," he answered. "Then, may I speak briefly to you regarding that very thing you just brought up, people talking? I would guess you have heard the rumours surrounding Miss Weatherby?"

"Oh, haven't we all?"

"And would I be mistaken to assume that you, in fact, are the creator of these rumours?"

"Yes, you would. If you are coming to me for solace, words to clear the reputation of that harlot you're seeing, you've come to the wrong place."

"Emma, I—"

"That is Lady Emma to you, duke. And have I understood you perfectly clear, you make an enemy out of me, wound me in a near fatal way, and now you're coming asking for favours?"

"I'm only asking for you to do what's right and honourable."

"That would be your speciality, acting in the honourable way."

"I know I hurt you, Emma, and I'm sorry for that, but it is I who did you wrong. Don't punish Miss Weatherby for my wrongdoings."

"I'm doing nothing of the sort. There's no smoke without a fire, my dear. Maybe your innocent flower isn't as pure as you would like to believe? Maybe you should ask her what she did alone on Hereford Square this morning, leaving Mr Stockton's house, the latter only half-dressed? If you don't believe me, ask someone you do trust. People saw them, you know. They don't even try to keep their association a secret. Once again, if you have come in hope of me releasing you of your doubts about this woman, I cannot help you. I'm not the fabricator of these rumours."

"So, you will do nothing? You have set the ship on fire and will see it go down without lifting a finger?"

"Such boisterous language. I've done nothing and I will do nothing. No need for me to get myself dirtied by your questionable affairs. If you want to build a future with that woman, go ahead. I will not stand in your way."

"I see that I made the right choice of angering your father. It was well worth it to escape lifelong imprisonment in your company, my dear. I wish you a healthy and long life."

Lady Emma's face whitened and her jaw fell open. Thomas bowed and took his leave.

When he walked back home, he did so in the way Alice had seen before, in his own world, brooding with eyes looking down on the road. He hadn't expected Lady Emma to admit what she had done, but he had hoped to appeal to her sense of decency, to plant a seed of shame that, in time, would make her do what was right—to say to those who needed to be told, that she had been mistaken about Miss Weatherby. He didn't know if that would make any difference when the rumour was already out there, but he had swallowed his pride and asked, because he couldn't very well do nothing.

Emma hadn't shown even a glimmer of remorse. What she had said about Alice didn't become him, except… there was one thing that left a little bit of discomfort—her words about Alice visiting Mr Stockton this very morning, the latter only half-clothed. Would she say such a thing if there weren't others to confirm it? Well, if Alice really had visited him this morning, she had a reason to, he supposed.

When he came home, the butler informed him he had a visitor, a Mr Weatherby. Thomas slowly handed his coat to the butler.

Mr Weatherby?

A pang of guilt hit him. Thomas had been seen courting his daughter for weeks now, but he hadn't yet spoken a word about it to Mr Weatherby. Still, he couldn't figure out why Mr Weatherby had come to visit him in his home.

Mr Weatherby was waiting by the window, looking out. When he heard the door open, he turned around, smiling broadly.

"Mr Weatherby," Thomas said.

"Your Grace, I hope I don't intrude on your privacy with this unannounced visit?"

That remains to be seen, Thomas thought but said:

"Of course not, Mr Weatherby. Please sit down. Can I offer you something to drink?"

He could, and the butler moved silently to the glass decanter and prepared two drinks of brandy. When he arrived with the tray and they lightened its burden, Thomas asked the butler to step out of the room. There was something in Mr Weatherby's tense demeanour that gave Thomas a feeling he had come on private matters. Of course, he had. The matter in hand could only be Alice.

The butler bowed and left the room.

"Much appreciated," Mr Weatherby said, nodding at the door. "That's the fine thing with a man of your stature, some things needn't be said, they are just understood."

"You flatter me."

"Certainly not. I meet the lords and the leading men of London on a daily basis as a member of Parliament, and I see this… sensibility time and time again. It's most remarkable. Me, a gentleman by birth but a tradesman by profession, can only learn."

"I see," Thomas said, not knowing how to respond to such praise, not only to him but his whole class.

"Therefore, it gave me great satisfaction to see your growing fondness for my daughter. She really is a fine young woman and I can assure you she didn't lack suitors back in Walston, and neither does she here in London. Oh yes, she's caught a great many eyes, I can tell you that."

"I'm glad to hear."

"I…" Mr Weatherby clasped his glass with both hands, looked down at the table with a furrowed brow, as if in serious pain. "I hope I don't offend you, Your Grace, but I can't help seeing that there would be a great benefit for both our families if they were to be united. To have a daughter married into a great family such as yours would be an unprecedented honour and I can assure you that even if we Weatherbys are short on reputation, we're not when it comes to wealth."

"What exactly are you saying, Mr Weatherby?"

"Once again. I don't mean to offend you, Your Grace, but I know that your finances are left a bit… wanting after your father's glorious victories abroad. A marriage with my daughter would alleviate that problem."

"Ahh, I see."

"I do understand that a man of your position is spoiled for choice on the marriage market. But—"

"Marriage… market?"

"I'm sorry. I didn't mean to sound blunt. But as we both know, the world is constituted in a certain way, and even a duke needs to be able to pay for his way of life. And—"

"Why are you coming to me with this offer at this precise moment, Mr Weatherby?"

Could it really be a coincidence that Alice's father came to his door, trying to force a marriage as if no time were to be wasted, at the same time when this talk about Alice leaving Mr Stockton's house in the early morning started to circulate? Alice would never do anything improper, Thomas knew that, but apparently her father didn't hold her above it?

And, the forbidden thought slipped through:

Who knows her better, I or her father?

"Well, to be truthful, I was hoping that your attachment to my daughter would've grown after your visit to the theatre, but we haven't seen you as a guest in our house since. I hold you to no obligation whatsoever, but I wouldn't be much of a father if I didn't try to do my part to secure my daughter's happiness."

"And exactly what is that, Mr Weatherby?"

"Once again, not meaning to be blunt, but I plan to leave my daughter with a very healthy dowry, and..." Mr Weatherby leaned forward as if to pass secret words. "I know this is a bit... unconventional, but whatever dowry I will bestow upon my daughter, I will pay twice as much straight to you."

Thomas stared at him.

"So, in fact, you're paying me to marry your daughter?"

Mr Weatherby must've heard the contempt in his voice, because his back straightened.

"Now, Your Grace, I think you're the one being overtly blunt. My daughter is very fond of you, and what wrong is there in me, as her father, trying to secure her happiness? Men of your stature can afford to marry out of love, but if love and fortune can be combined, where's the harm in that?"

"Oh, no harm at all. You have presented your offer. Now let me think it over in privacy." He turned to the door. "Morley!"

The butler appeared with a slow bow.

"Mr Weatherby was about to leave. Please escort him to the door."

Mr Weatherby made a stiff bow before taking his leave. In his absence, the full meaning of his words finally sank in. He had tried to sell off his daughter as if he were trading horses. Thomas had gotten Mr Weatherby all wrong. He had heard he had his own ways, that he always plotted the straightest line to his goal, a strategy that had served him well through the years, but the lengths he would go to…

He was a ruthless man. Thomas saw that now. Had Mr Weatherby talked his plans over with Alice? If he had, what had her reactions been? Very much like his, he hoped.

He had looked forward to tomorrow night when they were to appear at the ball at Lady Ender's together. Now that anticipation had been tampered with, knowing everyone would look at them and whisper. The rumour was out, and as soon as they stepped through the door, it would build upon them like a black cloud no one could miss.

Oh, if Alice hadn't visited with Mr Stockton this morning, fuelling the fire even more. What in earth's name had she been doing there? Unchaperoned and all? It wasn't a thing to ask a woman, but he knew he had to, because it would gnaw within him… until the itch became a bleeding wound.

Chapter 15

Her father had been in an odd mood all day. When he returned from his business meeting, he was positively fuming, and when he heard over dinner that she was attending Lady Ender's ball with the Duke of Hexham, he gave her a strange look.

"When did he invite you to this ball?"

"Last week."

He buttered a piece of bread, his mouth drawn tight and his jaw visibly clenched.

"That is… surprising."

"Not really," Alice replied, casting him an anxious glance as she spooned her soup. "Mary and I have been walking with him in Hyde Park every day this past week. He's very pleasant company."

"I'm sure he is," her father said, exhaling sharply through his nostrils.

"Is everything all right, Papa?"

"Yes, perfectly fine," he said, forcing a tired smile. "Although, if news of you and his grace had reached me sooner, things might have been… easier."

"I assumed it had, considering how much your friends in Parliament and Boodle's love to talk."

"Yes," he said, frowning. "That is strange."

Her brother, who had been uncharacteristically silent throughout the meal, suddenly set down his knife and fork.

"Father, I need to speak to you in private."

"Now? In the middle of dinner?"

"Yes, it can't wait."

Mrs Weatherby glanced nervously between them, her mouth slightly open.

"Oh dear, what misfortune awaits us now?"

Mr Weatherby rose from the table, and George followed, leaving the room—a scene so unprecedented that Alice felt deeply unsettled. Wilma leaned towards her.

"What's this about, sister?" she whispered loudly enough for the entire table to hear.

"I don't know, Wilma," Alice replied coolly. "They'll tell us when they feel we need to know."

Moments later, the door opened again, and her father reappeared. His cheeks were flushed, and his eyes burned like smouldering coals.

"Alice, join me in my study," he said.

Though phrased as a request, his tone left no room for refusal.

Her heart pounded as she rose from her chair. Ordinarily, when she found herself in trouble, she had some inkling as to the cause. This time, she was utterly clueless. Could it be about Mr Stockton's deception?

When her father shut the study door behind her, she saw George already there, slumped in a chair by the desk, looking thoroughly defeated.

"What is this about?" she asked, her voice trembling.

"It's about you," her father said grimly. "And Mr Stockton. And Lord Merringer."

She looked between them, but George avoided her gaze.

"I heard it down at Boodle's this afternoon," George murmured. "I walked in unnoticed, and they were laughing at the duke."

"At his grace?" Alice almost laughed. "What reason could they possibly have to laugh at a man like the duke?"

"They're saying he's about to be lured into marriage, his precious name tainted by scandal," her father said coldly. "Apparently, he's infatuated with a woman who has already shared beds with several men during her brief stay in London."

Alice paled.

"Are you talking about me?"

Her father's hard, relentless eyes bore into her.

"You tell me, Alice. Am I?"

"No!" she cried, sinking into a chair by the wall. "I've done no such thing. Please, Papa, you must believe me!"

He turned his back to her, staring at the etchings of ships that hung above his desk.

"It's not whether I believe you that matters. It's what everyone else believes."

"It matters to *me*!" she cried, leaping to her feet and trying to turn him towards her.

He shrugged off her hands, his gaze fixed on the etchings.

"They're saying you've been bedded by both Mr Stockton and Lord Merringer. That you're obsessed with Stockton and were seen leaving his house yesterday morning."

"It's not true, Father! Please, believe me!"

"Is it not true? It's not *true*?" her father said, finally turning to her. "People *saw* you, Alice."

"It's true I visited him, but implying I was leaving his house in the morning is vile slander. I went to plead with him, distraught over my cousin's future. I begged him to release Mr Carmichael from ruin. He was drunk—I stayed only as long as necessary."

"You foolish girl!" her father roared, raising his hands. "Going to his house alone at such a time! Did you not think anyone might notice? Especially with rumours already circulating about you and Stockton!"

"Rumours that have just now come to my attention," she said, her eyes welling over. "Papa, you've known me all my life. What does your heart tell you?"

She heard a scraping sound when her brother got off his chair, possibly to leave the room, to leave her to wallow in her own shame. Instead, he embraced her, hard. She clasped him like a drowning woman, sobbing at his shoulder.

"I believe you, sister. I too have known you for your whole life, and I know these accusations to be false."

Their father's stern face softened into a mask of resignation, his illusions and hopes crumbling before them.

"So, we're under attack," he muttered. "Someone wishes to bring misfortune and shame upon this family?"

Alice nodded, wiping her eyes.

"Yes, Papa, and I know exactly who—and why."

She explained Lady Emma's threat and recounted their encounter during her walk with Thomas.

"No fury like a woman scorned," George muttered, rubbing his chin.

"What can we do but bow our heads and wait for it to pass?"

"Bow our heads?" Mr Weatherby snapped. "Shall we grovel when this shame is based on lies?"

"It's all we can do."

"Pray these rumours haven't reached the duke," her father said. "If they have, all is lost. His marrying Alice is the only thing that can silence this slander."

"If he doesn't know, he must be told," Alice said. "If he proposes without knowing the risks to his reputation, our marriage will be based on a lie. I won't allow that."

"You'll do as you're told!" her father roared.

She didn't flinch. Her inner turmoil had solidified into a core of steel.

"No, Papa. If he doesn't know, I'll tell him. If he chooses not to marry me, then you'll have to place your hopes for family glory on Wilma instead."

Mr Weatherby clawed in the air in frustration, gasping.

"So you're determined to ruin everything?"

"Keeping it from him will ruin everything as well—just more slowly."

"But will you still attend the ball with him?" George asked.

"I will. Not going would be tantamount to admitting guilt. The only one who can defend my honour is Thomas. If he marries me despite the rumours, nothing could better vindicate me."

"But will he?" George asked softly.

Alice felt a faint flutter in her heart.

"That, dear brother, I do not know."

On the night of the ball, Alice was dressed entirely in white—the colour of innocence. Wilma, as usual, was the first to spot Thomas's carriage as it arrived. But unlike the last time he came to their house, she wasn't rewarded with the sight of him stepping out.

Mrs Weatherby gave Alice a puzzled look. She hadn't been told about the rumours; Mr Weatherby had decided to spare his wife the grief. Mr Weatherby himself sat by the fireplace, reading the newspaper for the second time that day.

As Alice and Mrs Weatherby rose to leave the drawing room, he spoke without looking up.

"Send my best wishes to the duke."

His tone was difficult to interpret, and Alice decided she wouldn't pass on her father's wishes to Thomas.

When they stepped outside, the servant seated beside the coachman climbed down, opened the carriage door, and helped them in.

Thomas was waiting inside, shrouded in gloom. He greeted them with the appropriate courtesies, complimented Alice's dress, and apologised for not coming into the house—insisting they couldn't risk being late to the ball.

From his first words, it was clear he had heard the rumours. Alice found it hard to meet his eyes.

Why? Didn't that make her appear even guiltier? Of course it did. But sitting in this confined space with him, with this tension hanging between them, was almost unbearable.

"Mr Weatherby sends his best wishes," Mrs Weatherby said, chirping like a delighted bird.

Alice closed her eyes and gave the faintest shake of her head. Thomas smiled, but it was a strained, hollow smile.

"Please convey my best wishes to Mr Weatherby at your earliest convenience," he replied.

The carriage ride to the ball was a quiet one. Even Mrs Weatherby, who was usually so full of cheerful observations, seemed to notice the tension and fell silent. Alice glanced at Thomas, but he didn't return her gaze. Instead, he stared out of the window, his expression sombre.

The last time they stepped out of a carriage together, Alice had worried about drawing the wrong kind of attention. That worry had proved unnecessary then. Now, however, one would have to be blind to miss the whispers, the averted eyes, and the false smiles.

Oh, Thomas, please stand by me now. Don't desert me.

Together, with their heads held high, they ascended the steps and entered Ender House.

"You're awfully quiet tonight, Thomas," Alice ventured.

"It's been a busy day, Miss Weatherby."

Back to Miss Weatherby it is? The formality stung. She didn't like it—not at all. Perhaps attending the ball had been a mistake. No, there was no perhaps about it. It *was* a mistake.

Thomas seemed like a different man entirely. He was suffering from this ordeal just as much as she was. So why were they putting themselves through this? Was it to show strength and defiance to those who slandered them?

If that was the intent, it had failed. They had only added fuel to the fire. No one could miss their discomfort, their distress.

When they entered the ballroom, the whispers and fleeting glances became unmistakable. Alice noticed lords and gentlemen whom she knew Thomas considered friends, but unlike at every other event, none of them approached to greet him.

"Would you like something to drink, Miss Weatherby?"

"Yes, please," she replied in a small voice that didn't sound like her own.

"I'll be right back," he said with the faintest shadow of a bow.

He left Alice and Mrs Weatherby standing by the wall. Mrs Weatherby immediately began commenting on the room, noting that it was lovely but hardly the most beautiful ballroom she'd ever seen. When Alice didn't respond, her mother fell silent with a sigh, muttering to herself, "Oh, the woes of youth…"

When Thomas returned—after more than a little while—he already smelled faintly of punch, even though he held a fresh glass for himself and another for Alice.

"Apologies for the delay," he said. "I ran into some friends who wanted a word."

Alice nodded and sipped her punch.

"Perhaps we should exchange a few words ourselves," she ventured.

"Aren't we doing so now?" he replied, giving her the same strained smile as before.

She didn't answer, only looked at him, and after a moment, his shoulders sagged.

"I don't recognise you tonight, Thomas," she said softly. "And I fear I might feel like a stranger to you as well. We both know what lies between us, and if we refuse to address it, it will destroy us."

"I don't put any weight on rumours. I…"

Alice turned to her mother.

"Mother, could you give us a moment? You can still keep an eye on me from the other side of the room."

"Of course, my dear," Mrs Weatherby replied, though her voice carried a faint note of hurt.

Once she had gone, Thomas sighed.

"I know you haven't done the things these rumours claim. I haven't known you long, Alice, but I *do* know you."

"Thank you for saying that," she replied, feeling tears prick her eyes.

"But I can't ignore the fact you were seen leaving Mr Stockton's house in the early hours. I have no reason to distrust you, but I do wonder—what was the purpose of your visit?"

She stared at him.

"Then you *do* distrust me. Why else would you ask?"

"Do you deny being at his house?"

"I do not."

"Then why were you there?"

"If you must know—and clearly, you must—I went on behalf of my cousin, or rather, Mr Carmichael, to see if I could spare him from the ruin Mr Stockton has arranged for himself."

Thomas drained half his punch in one swift gulp.

"I see," he said, nodding, though it wasn't a gesture of understanding. The thorn of doubt still festered. "I understand," he added, finishing the rest of his punch in a single draught.

"What do you understand?"

"That I need another of these," he said, setting his glass down on a table with a sharp clink.

Heads began to turn, and Alice's cheeks burned at the attention.

"Thomas, do you really?"

"I do, really," he said, and without another word, he strode off toward the punch room.

Alice followed him, her steps quick and purposeful.

"You say you trust me, that you understand, but nothing in your behaviour shows it," she said, her voice tight.

"Could you lower your voice?" he muttered, turning to face her.

"I will—if you stay and talk to me. You can't just turn your back on this and hope it disappears."

He met her words with silence, his eyes unreadable. And then something inside Alice seemed to fracture as she grasped the meaning behind his stare.

"You can," she whispered. "You *can* turn your back on me. Is that what you want, Thomas?"

She knew he was drunk—perhaps he'd already been so in the carriage—but if he was considering ending what he had started, she needed to hear it from him.

"No," he said, shaking his head, though the vacant look in his eyes remained. "I know what I feel, but sometimes feelings are a curse."

"What do you mean?"

"That every instinct tells me I should walk away from you, but my heart won't let me. As I said before, I don't know you, Alice, and when something—or someone—feels too good to be true, they usually are."

"You don't mean that."

"I think I do. Your father came to visit me the other day—was that at your urging?"

"What? I didn't even know he'd visited you!"

"Oh, he visited," Thomas said bitterly, scooping a large ladle of punch into his glass and downing it immediately. "He's a very enthusiastic advocate for our marriage. He offered to pay whatever I demanded to make it happen."

"What?"

"Yes," he said, filling his glass again. "But I try not to judge a daughter by her parents. Still, I can't ignore the timing—your father appeared at my door the very same day you were seen at Mr Stockton's."

"Please, Thomas," she said, her voice breaking. "Just stop."

"Ah, ah, you wanted to talk about this, so let's talk," Thomas said, his words sharp and slurred.

"You're drunk. I want to speak to *Thomas*, not this version of you," Alice replied, her voice trembling.

"Oh, really? Is that it? Then let me retort—what *character* are you playing, my dear? As I said, the daughter shouldn't be judged by her parents' actions, but how could she not be *aware* of them? And how could her father's lifelong ambitions and hopes for her not also become her own?"

Alice had tried to keep her emotions in check, but now her vision blurred with tears.

"Thomas, you say you know me, but that isn't true. If that's what you think of me, then you don't know me at all."

"For fuck's sake," he spat. "Your father goes door to door, offering you to the highest bidder. What kind of man does that? And what kind of family does a man like that raise?"

The sorrow that bloomed in her chest hardened into steel. Without thinking, Alice slapped him as hard as she could, her eyes blazing with fury.

"Thomas Overton! You are a despicable man, devoid of honour! You call yourself a noble, but your actions do not merit a title like that!"

She turned on her heel and strode away, but as the tears spilled down her cheeks, her walk became a run.

The ballroom fell silent. Out of the corner of her eye, she saw the acid stares of the onlookers, and her mother beginning to move toward her. The room felt impossibly vast, like a never-ending plain, but she reached the open double doors and stormed out.

She had arrived in Thomas's carriage, but she didn't stop to arrange for another. She didn't care—she just needed to get as far away from Ender House as possible.

Before she even realised it, she was out on the street, running blindly with tears blurring her vision. Behind her, she could hear her mother's voice, screaming for her to stop.

Chapter 16

Thomas woke up face down on his bed, still wearing his shirt and boots. He rolled onto his back, and the whole room spun with him. Nausea surged up his throat, and he swallowed hard, his diaphragm trembling like the skin of a drum. His heart thudded violently, making his head feel like a split tooth. He pressed the back of his hand to his forehead—it felt hot, as though he were running a fever.

He couldn't remember the last time he'd been this hungover. What on earth had he been doing the night before? What could possibly have made him spin out of control like this? Had he been out with John?

No...

A sudden wave of dread hit him.

He opened his eyes and stared at the ceiling.

He'd been at the ball. With Alice.

His mind fumbled to piece together the fragments of the evening. His memories felt like shards of a shattered mirror, each one reflecting back at him with an accusing glare. He had said something to her—something that had made her eyes glisten and her jaw tremble faintly. How could he remember such minute details but not the words themselves?

Then it came back to him, and he squeezed his eyes shut.

"Oh, you bloody fool… This time you've really done it."

Now he remembered. He saw Alice running across the ballroom floor, her mother chasing after her. And what had he done? Turned back to the punch bowl roaring to a staring gentleman to mind his own bloody business. He remembered Lady Emma's gleeful smile. And then—nothing.

Obviously, Mr Gray had tried to undress him for the night, but had given up. If Mr Gray had given up on a task like that, it meant Thomas had tried to fight him, or worse.

Oh, blasted.

He had a faint recollection of Lady Emma and her mother driving him home in their carriage. For a fleeting moment, he wondered if the situation could possibly be more humiliating, but the thought quickly dissolved. Nothing could be worse than hurting Alice as he had. He needed to put things right immediately.

Thomas swung his legs over the side of the bed, steadying himself with both hands as the room tilted alarmingly.

"Mr Gray!" he bellowed.

The man appeared shortly thereafter, his posture impeccable and his expression unreadable.

"I'm sorry if I was... difficult last night, Mr Gray."

"Oh, you were nothing of the sort, Your Grace," Mr Gray replied, his hands clasped neatly behind his back, his face giving away nothing.

"I very much doubt that, but I thank you for your discretion. I need to get to Victoria Street as quickly as possible. Can you arrange for my carriage? Actually, no—a walk might suit me better this morning."

"It's hardly morning any longer, Your Grace. May I suggest a bath before you leave?"

"There's no time, Mr Gray."

"I would strongly recommend it, Your Grace."

Thomas looked at him, then gave a reluctant nod.

"In that case, please see to it."

"I'll see to it that breakfast is arranged as well, so you can dash off on your adventures well-fed and with your locks in order."

"Much appreciated."

When Thomas left his house, there was little dash in his step. He hadn't managed to stomach much of his breakfast, and sweat was already breaking out across his back. The streets were alive with people, as they always were—his people. They looked at him and smiled, touching the brims of their hats as if it were just another ordinary day.

Perhaps the scandal he'd caused last night hadn't yet spread.

No, of course it had. Gossip like that travelled faster than wildfire.

He didn't care what they thought of him. He only cared about getting to the three-storey house at the end of Victoria Street as quickly as possible.

When he arrived, he pulled the chain and heard the bell echo on the other side of the door. The butler answered. Thomas introduced himself and requested to see Miss Weatherby. With a bow, the butler stepped aside to let him in.

Thomas waited in the dim vestibule, thumbing the brim of his hat while the butler went to inform Alice of his arrival. Time seemed to slow in the gloom, and dark thoughts crowded his mind. What if she refused to see him?

But she didn't.

The butler returned and opened the drawing room doors, announcing him with formality.

"His Grace, the Duke of Hexham."

Alice sat on the sofa to the right, wearing a simple cotton dress that somehow made her look more beautiful than any lavish creation from Bond Street could have. Her eyes were red-rimmed, her mouth tight. Across from her, Mrs Weatherby sat on another sofa, her expression severe.

"Mother, would you please leave us?" Alice asked, turning her head slightly towards her mother.

"But I—"

"I assure you, his grace will act in accordance with his station. My virtue is in no danger."

Alice's tone carried its usual hint of irony, but where there had once been a playful spark, there was now only a flat monotone.

"Well, I suppose…" Mrs Weatherby murmured, her sentence trailing off. Rising reluctantly, she left the room.

Alice didn't look at him, her gaze fixed on the window as though she were watching his carriage.

"Alice, I—"

"No," she said, shaking her head. "Don't call me that. It hurts too much."

He nodded, his fingers worrying the brim of his hat.

"Miss Weatherby," he began, "I'm here to say that even if my behaviour last night cannot be excused with words alone, I hope they can at least serve as a beginning. Please forgive me, Miss Weatherby. I hope we can forget this, turn the page, and continue as we were."

"The previous course," she said slowly, as though tasting the words. "I don't even know what that was anymore… I thought about this moment during the long hours of last night… How I would act if you came asking for forgiveness. I imagined staying civil, telling you that I forgave you. That way we cold part at least with the illusion of friendship. I had hoped to send you away with the memory of a strong, unmoved woman you might remember fondly and even admire."

"Part? We're not to part, Miss Weatherby. That's not why I'm here. Quite the opposite."

She ignored him, speaking as though he hadn't said a word.

"But now I find I don't have that strength in me. You gave me something precious, Your Grace, and then you took it away in the most brutal fashion. I'm sorry to say I'm not strong enough to face that with a pleasant smile."

"I understand that I hurt you, and for that I am so sorry, but I didn't mean what I said. I wasn't myself."

Her eyes met his for the first time, and he wished they hadn't. There was an awful hollowness in them, and he knew that hollow would soon fill with anger and resentment. Had he lost her for good?

"But you *were* yourself, Thomas," she said. "I had hoped you would be strong, that the love you claimed to feel for me would be stronger than the opinions of others. It wasn't. And for that, I can only mourn. But don't stand here and tell me you didn't mean those words, that your doubts about my character and your disdain for my family weren't real. Your drinking only let you say what you truly thought, and for that, I'm grateful. Marrying you, with those dark thoughts of yours... It would have been a disaster."

She turned back to the window.

"If it matters to you, Thomas, I forgive you. But those words no longer mean anything. Now, please leave. I don't want to see you again. If you don't respect that wish, I promise you our next meeting will be far less civil."

The monotone was gone. The hollow was filling. He heard a tremble of anger in it. This was a lost cause. The realization hit him like a ton of bricks.

He nodded and got to his feet. He searched for some words that could leave him a bridgehead back to her, but all the bridges were on fire. She would become a desolate island, forbidden ground. He was void of words, her hollow now becoming his.

"Then I bid you farewell," he said with a muffled voice, putting his hat on and turning for the door.

He stole one last glance at her when he turned for the entrance doors. She was still looking out of the window, unmoving like a statue with a single tear rolling down her cheek.

Before he reached the front door, footsteps approached behind him. It was Mr Weatherby. Thomas gave a mental sigh. Did this man never give up? Clearly, he had intercepted Thomas in hopes of patching up what was beyond repair, refusing to let go of his dream of making his daughter a Duchess.

The older man looked at him with mild contempt.

"I'm surprised you had the backbone to show your face here."

"Mr Weatherby—"

"No. Now is the time for you to listen, not to talk. For the longest time, I thought you a man of honour. I admit, you had me fooled with that title of yours, but you, Your Grace, are a walking masquerade. Masks and charades, that's all that you are. My daughter is far too precious to be wasted on a man like you. You are no longer welcome in this house."

Thomas nodded, staring down at the floor.

"That has already been made abundantly clear," he murmured, pushing open the door.

Alice didn't move until she saw his back vanish through the gate. Then she buried her face in her hands and wept, despising herself for her weakness. She had cried far too many tears for Thomas Overton.

No more.

She wiped her eyes and looked back out the window with her eyes puffed up. Thomas Overton had hurt her, Mr Stockton had disappointed her, and Lord Merringer had been a lost cause from the start. She had no time to dwell on the men who had brought her so much grief.

Her mother burst into the room, her eyes shiny with sympathy—sympathy Alice could not return.

"Oh, my dear girl! That odious man is nothing to cry over. Nothing!"

"I know," Alice said, forcing a faint smile. It was easier to be brave for her mother than it had been for Thomas. "But I'll retire to my rooms for the rest of the day," she added, her voice bleak.

Her mother followed her to the stairs, uttering all the usual phrases of sympathy and understanding. Alice climbed the stairs with heavy legs, and when she finally closed the door to her bedchamber, it was a melancholy relief. There was no need to put on a brave face anymore—though she found she didn't have to. She was out of tears.

She lay down on the bed, staring at the ceiling, her hands folded over her stomach. *Love.* She had come to London in pursuit of it, filled with romantic notions. But she hadn't been searching for anything real. Love wasn't like the poems or the plays. It was bleak and practical, and when practicality clashed with emotion, practicality always won.

What had she expected? That Thomas would defy his mother's will, the expectations of his class, and marry beneath him simply because she had briefly caught his eye? He was, like all men of his station, capable of having his head turned, satisfying his curiosity, and then carrying on as though nothing had happened. He was no different from John Merringer, just more discreet about it. How many women had cried over Thomas Overton? She didn't know and didn't care—she only knew she wouldn't be one of them any longer.

She would forget him—his smile, his understanding eyes. None of it had been real. It was just an act to play with her for a fleeting moment.

And yet… the hurt in his eyes when she sent him away. That had been real, hadn't it? After all, he had come to her house, asking for forgiveness. Perhaps he had truly felt something for her before reality swept in and crushed their fragile dream. Or perhaps he came only to satisfy his pride, to convince himself he had done his part and acted with honour. If that were true, he was worse than Merringer—at least Merringer was honest about his motives.

But the fact remained: there was nothing for her in this city. Her name was sullied, her presence unwanted, and she was no longer chasing love. If love existed, it wasn't to be found in the grand ballrooms of London.

The family dinner that evening was a sombre affair. Mrs Weatherby declared Thomas Overton to be the worst of men, vowing that his name would not be spoken within their walls. Mr Weatherby said little, eating with quiet concentration, only breaking his silence to ask his wife to pass the salt. George followed his father's example but occasionally glanced at Alice, who felt suffocated by the oppressive gloom at the table. Even Wilma, who always had something to say, remained silent.

After dinner, Alice walked with George in the small garden behind their house. Autumn had arrived, and there was a chill in the air. The leaves on the maples were tinged with red and yellow, rustling gently in the breeze. George knew her better than their parents did and understood that the best thing he could do was simply listen, avoiding any well-meaning but empty platitudes.

"I've never seen Father like this," Alice said. "So melancholy."

"Me neither," George replied. "But it's not him I'm thinking about. How are *you* doing, sister?"

"Oh," she said with a faint shrug. "I've been punched on the nose by destiny, teaching me not to chase dreams that aren't mine to have. It hurts, but like all things, it will pass."

George walked in silence for a moment before speaking.

"I don't know why you're calling it a dream not meant for you. It isn't like you to have such a low opinion of yourself. History is full of lords marrying women from other classes."

"It isn't about class, not really. In a way, it is, but it's more than that. The dream, I think, was to fall in love and be loved by a man like Thomas Overton—not the man he turned out to be, but the man I believed he was."

"You idealised him," George said thoughtfully, almost to himself. "You loved the dream of Thomas Overton."

"Maybe."

"People rarely live up to our expectations," he said. "They fall short. But *how* short is the critical question. Yes, his grace fell short, but not, I think, by the deadly margin you now claim."

"What do you mean?"

"I know the man. Not well—we're mere acquaintances—but people talk about men like his grace. I've never heard anyone question his character. He's not known for courting or conniving with young women. Whatever happened here, I believe he approached it with honourable intentions."

"Maybe. I'm more inclined to think he was too afraid to marry Lady Emma and allowed himself, briefly, to entertain the idea of a different future."

"Oh, don't think he ended things with Lady Emma lightly. People talk about the Duke of Hexam, yes, but they also talk about men like Lord Fairchild. I promise you, there will be no mending fences between them, not even if his grace takes Fairchild's daughter to the altar tomorrow. Fairchild was livid when the duke informed him of his decision, and from what I hear, he's livid still."

"Is that so?"

"It is."

They walked in silence for a while longer before George spoke again.

"So, what will you do now?"

"Going back to Walston. London has become such an ugly place to me. I need to breathe country air again, sit by the pond, and find myself. My time here in London has been a wild merry-go-round, and I feel… strewn all over the place. I need to collect myself."

Chapter 17

Thomas was back in the library at Bleaker House, seated in his reading chair, staring at the rows of books. He had sat here much the same way not long ago, thinking of Alice and a future that could never be theirs. He had resolved to stay away from her, convinced she was poison to him. Yet, he hadn't done so. At the first sight of her, he had folded, setting into motion the vicious spiral that had once again left him here, with everything in shambles.

He knew it had been a mistake to approach her, but he had done so anyway. Why, though, was it a mistake? He had come to believe he needed Alice in his life to survive. It was Lady Emma who was the real poison. She was death. Alice was life.

The mistake was his alone. He had assured Alice that he paid no heed to the rumours, but his drunken self had been less certain. And that drunken self was still him. Alice had been right, and he couldn't shy away from that. It had been him, at the ball, questioning her virtue. "I trust you," he had said, only to take it back with a cruel, unspoken doubt. It had been the worst kind of lie.

What had he hoped to achieve by visiting her earlier today? He had received everything he deserved, from both Alice and her father.

He sighed, rubbing his brow.

All the bridges ablaze... He had held onto the faint hope that new bridges might be built, but the look in her eyes during their last meeting had extinguished that hope. He had hurt her as deeply as he had hurt Leana. He hadn't thought such a thing possible, given what he had promised Leana and failed to deliver. He had believed that so long as he didn't make Alice the same promises, he couldn't hurt her. But now he realised a promise could be made without words ever being spoken.

A knock at the door drew his attention. Mr Morley entered and bowed slightly.

"Lady Emma Fairchild is here to see you, my lord."

Thomas sighed, his gaze drifting to the window.

"Very well. Tell her I'll be with her shortly."

When he entered the room, Lady Emma rose to greet him. She was as poised as ever, dressed in white muslin with a small hat perched askew on her head. Yet something was different—the hard, confident glint in her eyes was gone. He gestured for her to sit.

"Lady Emma, to what do I owe the pleasure of your visit?"

"Concern, dear Thomas. Last we met properly, we didn't part on the best of terms. Last night, you behaved as though a demon had taken hold of you. I wouldn't call myself the cleverest of women, but I understand the cause of your distress. I've come—perhaps in vain—to seek reconciliation. I know you didn't mean those harsh words, and perhaps I said some in return. It may never be as it was, but could we not at least be friends? Two families such as ours at odds... I can't see the benefit in it."

He regarded her for a moment. He ought to feel enraged—her vicious gossip had been the root of his torment—but he felt only emptiness. He was a burnt-out candle, weary of the fight.

"Yes… I agree."

She gave him a cautious smile.

"I'm glad. These have been trying times, painful for both of us. I won't mention *her* name, as I know it will upset you, but people agree you did the right thing by showing her the door."

"They do, do they?"

"Yes. They understand your honour demanded it."

So, he was back in favour? Drinking himself into a stupor and publicly humiliating a young woman was all it had taken to restore his standing?

"I'm glad to hear it," he said, his gaze drifting out of the window. "But I must admit I'm ashamed—of how I behaved towards her and how I presented myself."

Lady Emma folded her hands in her lap and offered him a soft smile.

"Such things happen. You're hardly the first gentleman to have had a glass too many, and you certainly won't be the last. It will be forgotten in a week or two."

"I seem to recall travelling home in your carriage that night?"

He didn't mention what he thought he remembered—lying on his back, boots propped against the window, his head in her lap, while she gently stroked his temple and he slurred drunken musings about life's many deceits.

Her cheeks coloured as she glanced at the floor. So, it had happened.

"Indeed you did, though you slept for most of the journey. Many offered to escort you home, but I insisted, given our history. They were kind enough to agree."

"And your mother?"

"The feud between our families is strictly a matter for the men. Mama wishes for reconciliation as much as I do."

"Capital," he muttered.

"If I might offer some advice?"

"By all means."

"It won't do to sit here brooding. You should return to society, show your peers you're in good spirits."

"And what would you suggest?"

"Lord Blackwell is hosting a shooting party at his estate this weekend. I know you have an open invitation to his gatherings. Sir Andrew is attending with Miss Chambers, and you know how well she and I get along."

Fresh air. Shooting pheasants. Perhaps he could bring John along. It might be just what he needed to clear his thoughts—or perhaps it wouldn't. Either way, he was done torturing himself with memories and regrets.

"That sounds delightful."

The clock in the corner went *tock-tock-tock*. Rain pattered against the windows of Longhall House. The world outside was cloaked in iron grey. Alice, seated on the sofa with her embroidery, sighed loud enough to draw Lucinda's gaze.

"Now, what was that?"

"Nothing, sister. Perhaps I should practise the pianoforte instead."

"Oh, please, do spare us."

Alice couldn't help but let out a soft laugh. Lucinda glanced at her with a mischievous smile. Alice had kept much of the reason for her return to Walston to herself, and Lucinda hadn't pressed her for details. Yet, if given the chance, Alice would have dearly liked a confidant to share her thoughts with—but Lucinda, despite her good intentions, wasn't that person.

If only Mary could come to visit. Alice was sure she would if asked, but Mary was ensnared in troubles as dire as Alice's own. Mr Carmichael faced ruin and disgrace, having bankrupted the company his great-grandfather had built. That Mary still intended to marry him, despite everything, was what made her the best of confidants. Mary wasn't pragmatic like Lucinda or a cold strategist like Father—she was foolish enough to let her heart guide her. Alice had tried the same, and look where it had brought her: straight back to the ancestral home, the clock ticking in the corner as it had for every second of her life in this house.

"By the way, Mr Evans is bringing his brother to dinner tonight. I don't expect much of you, sister, but perhaps you could make amends for your behaviour towards him the last time you met?"

Oh, the younger Mr Evans again. What a delight. The elder Mr Evans had received her a few days ago with a pompous air, as though he truly believed himself the lord of the manor in Father's absence. She had half-expected him to show her to her room, but thankfully his delusion hadn't gone that far. Even so, he had seated himself at the head of the table, occupying Father's chair, and attempted to impose his silent authority on the women around him. He was still waiting to move into the parsonage across the river, but Alice suspected he had developed a taste for his borrowed life at Longhall House.

"You will be pleased with me, sister," Alice replied, though something in her tone made Lucinda raise an eyebrow.

"I hope so. I trust your stay in London has helped you realise the world outside Walston isn't some bright fairy tale and that you now have a greater appreciation for the attentions shown to you here."

"Sometimes you sound more like Mama than Mama herself."

"It doesn't matter who says the words, as long as they're true. And since Mama isn't here, someone must say them."

So there was a new Mistress of the House. Alice hid her irritation as Lucinda squinted towards the window.

"It looks as though it might clear up. Wouldn't it be nice to take a walk before dinner?"

"When can we expect your husband and his brother?"

"Within the hour, I'd say."

Lucinda was right on both counts. The rain ceased not thirty minutes later, and soon two riders appeared on the oak-lined road. One was tall and hawkish; the other was plump and sat poorly in the saddle, bouncing with each stride.

"Looks like they're here," Alice muttered.

The younger Mr Evans slid off his horse and strode to the front door, craning his neck like an owl to spot her through the window. When he entered with his brother, without waiting for the butler to announce them, his face shone with anticipation. Alice rose reluctantly as the younger Mr Evans stepped forward, hat in hand. He smoothed his damp hair back in a theatrical manner and approached her.

"Miss Weatherby, so very nice to see you again."

He took her hand and kissed the back of it. Alice fought the urge to recoil. Lord Merringer had done the same when they first met, but it hadn't felt like this. There was a world of difference between Merringer's flamboyant charm and Mr Evans's clammy, wet lips pressing against her skin.

"Thank you. I trust you've been well since we last met?"

"Oh, indeed! I rarely have cause for complaint, but my existence is, of course, further elevated when you are part of it."

Further elevated? My lord…

He smiled smugly, clearly pleased with his effort. Alice wondered how long he'd rehearsed that line.

"We've all missed your presence at Longhall and are delighted to have you returned to your rightful place," the elder Mr Evans declared.

"Indeed," Lucinda agreed.

"How was your stay in London?" the younger Mr Evans inquired.

"It was… an experience."

"Of course it was," the elder Mr Evans interjected. "One must see what's out there to truly appreciate what one has at home. The razzle-dazzle of the city is enticing to young hearts—yours more than most, Alice. But the life in London appalled me. Sin at every corner. High lords behaving no better than farmhands, drinking and gambling away their legacies. Life in the country may be slower, less dazzling, but it holds real worth. We are closer to God here."

"Indeed," the younger Mr Evans chimed in. "One can see His presence in every aspect of nature. You won't find it in bricks and mortar, I assure you."

Lucinda cut in. "I was thinking we might go for a walk while Mrs Rose prepares dinner."

The Evans brothers eagerly agreed.

As Alice pulled on her boots and draped a wool scarf over her shoulders, something inside her gave way. She hadn't fully realised it until now—she had been brought back to where she had started. In London, she had looked back at Mr Evans as something she had escaped, an almost-destiny she had eluded, and laughed in relief. But destiny didn't take kindly to mockery, and here she was again, courted by the younger Mr Evans with no other options.

They had all told her what London had been like, but none of them were right. It hadn't appalled her. She had experienced sin, yes, but also beauty. She had met a man who was everything the Evans brothers were not. Even if he had been a lie, she cherished the memory of him.

Yet Lucinda had been right in one respect: London had held nothing for her. Deceit and betrayal had greeted her there, and whatever future she would build had to be built here in Hertfordshire. Surely there were better options than the younger

Mr Evans? Perhaps she could persuade Papa to let her attend the assemblies at Royston?

Yes, perhaps.

But she didn't want to. She didn't want to meet any men. She wanted to wander alone through the meadows and oak forests around Longhall House, hearing nothing but the wind in the trees. She felt wounded, perhaps fatally, and only the forest's silence could mend her.

Lucinda, ever-practical Lucinda, wouldn't understand such a need. Her baby sister would be fine once she was married and properly settled. There would be no debate about it.

As they left the yard, following the path along the west field into the woods, Lucinda and the elder Mr Evans led the way, leaving Alice with the younger one. Lucinda glanced back with a satisfied smile, clearly pleased with herself.

The younger Mr Evans breathed in the damp country air and exhaled with a smile. "I love the smell of nature after a good rain. It smells like… life!"

Alice nodded absently.

She, too, loved the smell of the countryside after rain, but today it brought an ache to her chest. The vibrant colours, the glistening leaves, the steaming earth—it was all too much. Tears pricked her eyes. What was wrong with her? How could such a beautiful day make her feel this way?

But she was done crying. She was not a weak, snivelling girl to be tossed about by men's whims.

She refused to be.

"The sun," the younger Mr Evans murmured reverently, "the life-giver. The eye of the Lord Himself."

Alice hummed in agreement, though she couldn't summon a proper reply. The last time she had walked with a man, it had been in Hyde Park, when Cousin Mary had taken her battle with the thorn bushes to give her and Thomas a moment of privacy. And how they had used that moment. Despite the despair that followed, the memory brought a faint smile to her lips.

"There," the younger Mr Evans said with a grin. "I was beginning to think my company bored you."

"Oh, not at all. I appreciate your… unique reflections on the world. They are certainly thought-provoking."

"Oh, I wouldn't say that. They're just thoughts. They come to me unbidden, often when I least expect them—while studying the Good Book, placing wood in the fireplace, or, as now, walking with a woman of quality."

"I thank you."

"Please don't. I'm happy to share. What is an insight worth if it isn't shared?"

"That is true."

He smiled at her, and they walked in silence for a time. Alice noticed Lucinda subtly tilting her head, as though trying to catch their conversation. Alice knew she ought to contribute more but found herself utterly devoid of anything she wanted to say to Mr Evans. He seemed perfectly content to fill the silence himself, but to make the walk less of a wasted effort, she decided to keep her promise to Lucinda.

"I apologise if I offended you the last time we met, Mr Evans. I had no right to speak to you as I did. Mama made certain I was thoroughly scolded for it."

Lucinda, perhaps unknowingly, gave the slightest nod of satisfaction at Alice's words.

The younger Mr Evans waved dismissively, grinning broadly. "I hardly remember it. Water under the bridge, my dear."

My dear? Alice thought, noting how emboldened he had become.

"I must say," he continued, "your time in London has done you good. Your demeanour is much improved."

She nodded curtly. "I'm glad to hear it."

They walked on—he strutting with a confident smile, she blinking away tears that threatened to overwhelm her.

Dinner that evening was lit by half the usual number of candles, Mr Evans declaring that enough light was when one could just about see each other across the table. He buttered a slice of bread, glancing from face to face with satisfaction, seemingly revelling in the silence.

Alice focused on her green pea soup, making an effort not to meet his eyes. If she did, she might say something foolish that would shatter the younger Mr Evans's favourable opinion of her.

What a loss that would be.

The situation was painfully familiar. It reminded her of June, just before her father had burst through the door, declaring they must pack and prepare to move to London. That evening had been a whirlwind of joy and anticipation. Tonight, there would be no such rescue.

For a fleeting moment, her imagination carried her away. The door slammed open, and there stood Thomas on the threshold, determination in his eyes.

She quickly reined herself in, scolding herself for such foolishness. She had released him from any obligation to her, and for that, she was glad. Truly glad. It allowed her to part with some semblance of pride intact.

Men liked to think pride was their exclusive domain, but Alice believed it mattered just as much to women. They simply didn't speak of it so often. No, Thomas would not appear on her doorstep, and for that, she was—yes—glad.

"Ben," the elder Mr Evans addressed his brother, "I hear you're close to securing a rectory for yourself?"

The younger Mr Evans nodded, dabbing his mouth with a linen napkin before replying. "That's true. It's in the parish of Badger's Warf, about ten miles north. Not as grand, perhaps, as the rectory awaiting you, brother, but a lovely limestone house by a stream, surrounded by willows. Quite the sight, really."

"That does sound lovely," Lucinda said, pressing a hand to her chest. "Don't you think so, Alice?"

"It sounds like paradise," Lucinda continued before Alice could answer.

"I wouldn't say paradise," the younger Mr Evans replied with a modest smile, "but it's a piece of God's green earth that I'll be happy to call my own."

The dinner dragged on, and by the time it ended, it was too late for the younger Mr Evans to leave. He spent the evening with the others by the fire, a glass of sherry in hand, listening to his brother read from Scripture in a stern, solemn voice.

The next morning, before his departure, he approached Alice for a private word. To her surprise, he asked if he might visit her again. Alice, who hadn't realised he was at Longhall House *exclusively* to see her, felt compelled to give a positive response.

The glow of anticipation returned to his cheeks as he grasped her hand in both of his, declaring how much he looked forward to being in her company once more.

Chapter 18

Bang! The sound of the blast rolled over the hills and echoed back.

"Splendid shot, dear boy," John Merringer said, as the hound, yelping with excitement, bounded off after the pheasant, still spiralling to the ground, its shredded feathers scattering in the breeze.

Thomas handed his smoking shotgun to thc footman and accepted a freshly loaded one in return.

"Thank you."

"But you look far from jubilant, I must say."

"If you must."

"Thomas... this charade has gone on long enough. I was surprised to see you arrive with Emma, but I'm not anymore. You're really not here at all, are you?"

A volley of bangs erupted as three gentlemen fired at the same bird.

"It's that obvious, then?"

"Of course it is."

Another series of bangs. Thomas's shoulders twitched.

"Shall we take a walk? Away from all this?"

"Certainly."

John signalled to the footman to take Thomas's shotgun. They turned their backs on the shooting party and strolled away from the open field, into the cool, shaded woods.

"You pride yourself on knowing me so well."

"I think I do," John said.

Thomas nodded, walking in silence, his eyes fixed on the footpath.

"I behaved in the worst possible way towards her. What I did to her is, in some ways, worse than what I did to Leana."

"I tend to agree. By shaming her publicly, you essentially confirmed the rumours about her. It was unforgivable. She left London the very same day you visited her," John said.

Thomas gave him a sidelong glance. "I thought you were on my side here?"

"There are no sides, my friend. If you're looking for someone to pamper you or feed you comforting lies, you've come to the wrong person. What you need is the truth. Only when you see this for what it is can you begin to address it."

"But what can I do? You didn't see the look she gave me when she sent me to the door. If you had, you'd understand—whatever we had is beyond repair."

"*Whatever we had?*" John repeated, frowning in disgust. "Can you hear yourself? Are you truly afraid to name it, even now, when you claim it's lost?"

Thomas glanced at him again, then looked back at the ground. "Now more than ever."

"For as long as I've known you—and that is a long time, mind you—you've never been one to wallow in self-pity. No, I didn't see the look she gave you, but I can imagine it was chilling. Even so, there's always something you can do. If you try and she still rejects you, at least you'll know you gave it your all. To do nothing is to accept failure in advance. That's not you, Thomas. This almost crippling sense of loss you feel should be all the motivation you need—it tells you that what you've lost is worth fighting for."

"But how?" Thomas stopped on the path, turning to face him. "If she demanded I conquer Arabia or swim the Atlantic, I'd try. But no herculean feat in the world will win her back for me."

"Maybe she doesn't want a herculean feat. Maybe all she needs is to feel… for want of a better word, safe with you."

"How do I achieve that?"

"I don't pretend to know the answer, my brother. And I certainly can't claim to know Miss Weatherby well enough to say. That's something you must figure out for yourself. But if you don't, I promise you I'll be there to scoop her up. She's quite catching, you know."

Thomas gave him a grim smile. "So I've noticed."

That evening, the gentlemen dined on pheasant in rich gravy at Woodsworth Manor, Lord Blackwell's ancestral home. Thomas sat beside the hostess, Lady Marianne Blackwell, a thin woman with delicate features, shallow blue eyes, and a perpetually surprised expression. Lady Emma, seated at the opposite end with Lord Blackwell, smiled at Thomas, her gaze travelling the length of the table with deliberate intent.

"She's such a lovely woman," Lady Marianne said, her tone tinged with envy. "You should count yourself lucky to have her."

"I wouldn't say *have* is the right word, Lady Marianne. We're friends, and nothing more."

"Oh, yes, of course," she replied with a knowing look that dismissed his attempt at denial. "But that smile she just gave you was very… friendly, wasn't it? There's no need to conceal what everyone already knows. And now that the matter with that ghastly woman is behind you, there's nothing to stand in the way of your happiness."

Thomas froze, his glass halfway to his lips. "What ghastly woman are you referring to?"

Lady Marianne hesitated, then said cautiously, "Well, the Weatherby girl, obviously."

"I see," Thomas replied, setting his glass back down. "I can assure you, Lady Marianne, there is nothing ghastly about her. Quite the contrary. Of all the women I've met—whether of my class or another—none embody the qualities we hold in highest regard better than Miss Weatherby."

His words were loud enough to draw the attention of nearby guests, silencing their conversations.

"What I've heard about her doesn't suggest quality," Lady Marianne said, her voice tight with indignation.

There were murmurs of agreement around the table.

"Well," Thomas said, his voice firm, "perhaps those who spread such rumours should consider their source and question the motives behind them. The accusations against Miss Weatherby are false—slander of the blackest kind, born of envy and wounded pride."

Lady Marianne, clearly displeased, asked, "If you truly believe that, why aren't you here with her tonight?"

"If only I could," he murmured.

He looked at Lady Marianne, then around the table at the others watching him intently.

"You all know me. You know my character. I have never been one to bare my private thoughts in public, but tonight is an exception. I begged Miss Weatherby to forgive me and take me back, but she refused. I was weak—so weak that in a drunken stupor, I doubted the virtue of someone whose character is beyond reproach. She punished me for it, and rightly so."

He sighed, pushing his glass away. "And I am weak still, sitting here at a table with the very person who fabricated those vile rumours about her. I can no longer abide it."

He stood, tossing his napkin onto the table. "I bid you all a pleasant evening."

"You can't just leave in the middle of dinner!" Lady Marianne exclaimed.

As he walked away, he heard John call out from the table, "Let the man go, dear."

Moments later, the sharp clatter of heels echoed behind him.

"Thomas, what are you doing?" Lady Emma demanded.

"It was a mistake coming here."

"Perhaps," she said with a forced smile, "but how do you think it looks to leave in the middle of dinner? We can discuss whatever it is—just come back to the table and act civilised."

"No," he said, shaking his head. "I will never go anywhere with you. If you go one way, I'll go the other. I despise you, Emma Fairchild, and from this moment on, I will have nothing more to do with you."

Her cheeks flamed. "Oh, we're back to this, are we? Grow up, Thomas. Leave this romantic nonsense where it belongs. People like us marry for duty, to maintain standards. That's how we keep our bloodlines pure."

"Then I'd rather see my bloodline die than continue it with you. I'd rather die old, alone, and miserable than die miserable with you. Do you understand me?"

Her lips thinned to bloodless lines, her cheeks and neck burning crimson.

"I do. And I know you'll come crawling back once you've regained your senses—or after a word with your mother. But I won't be here waiting. There are only so many insults I can bear."

"Oh, I hope there's more for you to endure," he said. "And when you return to that table, you'll find the tide has turned. They'll know what you've done. It may take time, but when it sinks in, they'll tear you down, just as they raised you up."

"And you truly believe that?"

"I do. Time will prove me right."

"Go to hell, Thomas Overton."

"After you, my dear."

Chapter 19

He left Woodsworth Manor under the cover of darkness, riding west by the light of the full moon. The moonlit road provided enough illumination for both him and his horse, and he spared no thought for the possibility of highway robbers. All he wanted was to be away—away from the grand manor, away from Lady Emma, and as far as possible from the weight of his burning bridges.

At first, he had no clear destination, but before long, he realised he was heading home to Somerfield Hall. He wouldn't complete the journey in a single night, and when dawn broke, he stopped at the first inn he encountered. There, he slept for a few hours and enjoyed a late, leisurely breakfast, allowing his horse time to rest and feed as well.

Close to noon, he resumed his journey and reached the oak-lined avenue leading to Somerfield just as the sun began to set. As he led his weary horse to the stables, a young stable boy hurried forward to take the reins, followed by the butler, who approached in haste.

"Your Grace! We weren't expecting you back today—nothing is prepared."

"Nothing needs to be. Whatever Mrs Ivers can manage for dinner will suffice. Is my mother at home?"

"Yes, Your Grace. The Dowager Duchess is present."

"Then we'll dine together," Thomas said, though he wasn't entirely certain she would join him. They hadn't spoken since his departure after what he privately called *the great Fairchild Eruption.*

While waiting for dinner, Thomas bathed, leaning his head against the edge of the tub. His body ached from the long ride, but inwardly he felt only numbness—a numbness that had gripped him ever since Alice had given him that look which told him everything was lost.

For two days, he had sat in his library, unable to form a single coherent thought. It had taken John's intervention at the shooting party to spur him into action, though even now, the numbness persisted. In truth, he dreaded its release. To feel the full force of his loss might shatter him.

To soften the blow, he tried convincing himself there would be other women in his life, that Alice would fade into a distant memory. But the idea was laughable. He had never felt for anyone what he felt for Alice—not even for Leana—and he doubted he ever would again.

The loss was vast, immeasurable, and utterly beyond his grasp.

When his valet, Mr Gray, arrived to inform him that his dinner garments were ready, Thomas understood his mother would indeed join him. He wasn't sure if that brought him relief or unease.

Dressed and composed, he descended the staircase to the dining room, where his mother was already seated. She nodded at him, giving him a sideways glance as she sipped from a tall glass of white wine.

"Mother."

"Thomas."

The footman pulled out his chair, and he sat down, snapping the napkin open across his lap.

"You look well, Mother."

"Looks can be deceiving."

"Are they, in this case?"

She gave a small shrug, prim and deliberate, before taking another sip of wine.

"The roars of Emmet Fairchild still reverberate in these halls, and as long as they do, I'll never be at ease. He haunts me like a ghost."

"I'm sorry to hear that."

"I'm sure you are."

The servants brought in white soup with chicken—his mother's favourite. They ate in silence for a while, the only sound the clinking of spoons against porcelain.

"Lady Hurley visited me yesterday," his mother eventually said. "She was eager to offer her sympathies regarding recent events in London… concerning you."

"Oh? Whatever could she mean?"

"Don't be clever with me. Is it true?"

"Some of it."

"Such as?"

Thomas dipped his spoon into the soup but paused, meeting his mother's unyielding gaze.

"It's true I was courting Miss Weatherby. What isn't true are the rumours about her virtue. But you needn't worry, Mother—I'm courting her no longer."

She pursed her lips, her expression softening just slightly.

"At least you've retained some sense, then," she muttered, finishing her wine. A footman immediately stepped forward to refill her glass.

"It had nothing to do with my senses," Thomas said. "She simply wouldn't have me."

His mother frowned, clearly puzzled by his words. She dismissed them as an odd attempt at humour and pressed on.

"Well, perhaps now we can move forward. If Lady Emma doesn't suit, there are plenty of other suitable young women. Your reputation has been tarnished by dalliances with low breeds, but a wife of impeccable background would restore it."

"Perhaps. But that's a matter for tomorrow."

"Then perhaps you'll occupy yourself with the estate in the meantime? We're losing tenants; the fields are overgrown. Your bailiff comes weekly asking for funds to make repairs, but as you know, we have none."

"What of our claims to the Crown?"

"What of them? Nothing has come of it. The war chest must remain full, and no one will divert funds for our sake. I pray that little Frenchman gets himself shot or hangs, but neither seems likely."

"I'll look into it."

His mother sighed, giving him a weary look before returning to her meal.

Later that night, Thomas lay in his four-poster bed, staring at the moonlit sky. A strange melancholy settled over him. It seemed as though nothing truly mattered—whether the Frenchman won or lost, whether Alice returned to him, or whether Somerfield Hall fell into ruin. The hollow ruin already existed.

It was him.

Is this what it feels like to give up?

The numbness finally released its grip, and it felt as though he had been stabbed in the chest, cold waves of despair radiating outward. He pressed the back of his hand against his eyes, jaw tight, breathing out through his nose.

Then, as his upbringing dictated, he forced the feelings down.

In time, this too shall pass.

Turning his back to the moon, he pulled the blankets up and tried to will himself to sleep. But sleep did not come, and as dawn broke, he rose from bed, unrested and hollow.

Thomas was back on his horse, riding slowly with the sun at his back. His breakfast had been a robust glass of brandy. For a brief moment, he had considered emptying the entire bottle and going for a reckless gallop through the thick woods, but in the end, he refrained. Now, he swayed lazily in the saddle, riding with no particular destination other than to avoid another conversation with his mother about *low breeds* and *perfect women.* He had endured it the previous evening; he wouldn't today. If he tried, his roar would echo through the halls of Somerfield alongside Emmet Fairchild's.

It wasn't until the sun was high in the sky that he realised he hadn't been riding aimlessly after all. His disconnected mind had stitched together a purpose without his conscious knowledge.

To his left, the deep beech forest stretched endlessly; to his right, a slow-moving river meandered through green fields.

What force had brought me here? he wondered. *What part of my fractured mind had led me to this place?*

Perhaps he had simply followed familiar paths, unaware. But he doubted it. He had thought of coming back here many times, balancing on the knife's edge between fear and longing, yet never daring to. Now, as he found himself at the threshold of the past, he couldn't turn back.

He guided his horse down a narrow path through high grass and a thicket until he reached the riverbank. Following the river for half a mile, he glimpsed the top of the mill through the trees beyond the next bend. He hesitated, then turned back into the woods, dismounted, and continued on foot. Careful not to be seen from the opposite side, he approached quietly until the watermill came into view—a quaint house of rounded stones and mortar with a chicken coop beside it.

On the green expanse before the house, two children played: a girl, slightly older, and a boy who busied himself with a small wooden boat. Thomas's eyes lingered on the girl. *What could she be—five? Maybe six?* She had dark hair, like him.

The cottage door opened, and a woman with chestnut hair neatly pinned in a bun emerged, carrying a bucket. Thomas's breath caught in his throat. He would recognise her anywhere, even after all these years.

It was Leana.

She stepped into the chicken coop and disappeared for a moment before re-emerging, still holding the bucket. She called out to the children, and the boy immediately ran to her, grinning as she spoke. She smiled back at him.

Thomas clutched the branch he was hiding behind, his heart pounding. Leana turned her back to him, returned to the cottage with the boy, and a moment later, the girl followed.

When they were gone, Thomas sank to the ground, resting his head in his hands. He sat like that for some time before finally rising, retracing his steps to his horse. His head swam, and his stomach churned. Perhaps it was the shock of seeing Leana again—or the girl who was almost certainly his daughter—or perhaps it was simply hunger.

Knowing Leana was at the mill and occupied with chores, he dared to venture into the village in search of an inn.

The Swan was dim and empty, its low, uneven ceiling supported by exposed beams. The dining hall to the right was slightly brighter, with windows overlooking the road. From the kitchen, he could hear a man speaking and a woman replying sharply.

He approached the counter and rapped it with his knuckles.

"I'll be there shortly!" the man bellowed, followed by more muffled bickering.

Thomas sighed and knocked again.

"Don't get your knickers in a knot! I said I'll be there!"

The man emerged from the kitchen, still shouting over his shoulder, but froze when he turned and saw Thomas. His angry frown vanished, replaced by wide-eyed deference, clearly recognising Thomas's fine clothes and the class they implied.

"I-I'm so sorry to have kept you waiting, sir. Just a little… discussion with the missus."

"It's quite alright," Thomas replied, refraining from correcting the man's use of *sir* instead of *your grace*, wishing to keep a low profile. "I'd like to eat."

"Of course, sir! Immediately, sir. Please, take a seat in the salon. Today we've rabbit and potato stew, but if you'd prefer something else, I'll see to it personally."

"Rabbit will do fine. Bring me an ale as well."

"Of course, sir. Right away."

The ale arrived quickly, and Thomas drained it before his food came, ordering a second when it finally did. He knew he shouldn't drink—not after the debacle at the Ender's Ball—but what harm could it do in a village far removed from prying eyes? After the past few days, he needed the release.

When the innkeeper came to clear his plate, Thomas enquired about a room. There were vacancies, and he requested a brandy, asking the man to see to his horse as well.

The next thing he remembered was being helped up the stairs by the innkeeper and his wife.

When Thomas awoke, the sunlight streaming through the curtains made his head throb. He raised a hand to shield his eyes and saw a large man sitting by the door, his rough hands folded and his expression grim.

"Who are you?" Thomas asked, too hungover and miserable to muster fear.

"I'm more interested in who you are."

"I'm sure you are. Here to rob me? That'd be a waste—I don't carry much."

"That's not why I'm here. You'd be Thomas Overton, the Duke of Hexham?"

Thomas blinked, then let his head fall back onto the pillow.

"You presume correctly. And may I trouble you for a name in return?"

"Robert Levin. Husband to Leana Levin."

Thomas stared at the ceiling, his heart sinking.

"Is that so?"

"It is."

"What can I do for you, Mr Levin?"

"You tell me, Your Grace. When I heard about a gentleman drinking himself senseless at the Swan, I had a pretty good idea who it was. And why you're here."

"Did you, now?" Thomas muttered, forcing himself into a seated position. "You'll have to excuse me—I'm not at my best."

"That's plain enough. But even at your best, I wouldn't consider you my better. Knowing what you've done, I couldn't."

"And I wouldn't consider you beneath me," Thomas murmured.

"So, we're equals, then?"

"At the very least."

"Good. Then allow me to speak plainly."

"By all means."

"The day I married Leana was the happiest of my life. It wasn't easy—she was hurt, thanks to you—but I've been there for her ever since. She trusts me. She's forgotten you. Seeing you here… it doesn't sit well with me."

"You've no need to worry. I'll be leaving soon and won't return."

"Hollow words," Levin said, looking away. "You didn't come here just to drink and chat."

"True. But I assure you, I have no desire to disrupt your life."

"You already have. Leana knows you're here. She wants to speak with you."

Thomas's heart stuttered. "Why?"

"I don't know. But she won't be persuaded otherwise."

"Perhaps you could convey my apologies and explain I'm unable to see her?"

"That'd be difficult—she's waiting downstairs."

Bloody hell. The day of reckoning.

"I'll get her," Levin said, standing. He turned to Thomas. "Make it short. If you upset her, you'll regret it—duke or no duke. Understand?"

"Perfectly."

Levin left the door ajar, his heavy boots clunking down the stairs. Thomas barely had time to rake his fingers through his dishevelled hair before he heard lighter footsteps ascending. His heart pounded, his chest heaving.

The door opened.

It was her, Leana, and she looked exactly as he remembered her, but her face wasn't scrunched up by sorrow and no tears wetted her cheeks.

"Thomas?"

"Leana… It's been a while."

What a foolish thing to say. Yet, she didn't seem to mind. She closed the door behind her and sat down on the chair her husband had vacated.

"Yes, it has." Her gaze swept the room before settling on him. "You look… well."

He nodded, unsure how to respond to such an obvious lie.

"You do as well," he replied, almost adding *my dear* but stopping himself just in time.

Five years had passed, yet the words felt so natural, so close. The words he *needed*, however, were nowhere to be found. He had played this meeting out in his mind countless times. Would he fall to his knees, begging her forgiveness? Would his long-buried love for her erupt violently, compelling him to promise her marriage and a life at Somerfield Hall once more?

But now, faced with her presence, neither scenario rang true.

He felt guilt, shame—nothing more. His heart was occupied by another now, fully and irreversibly.

"Why are you here, Thomas?"

"I wish I knew," he admitted, though he knew that wouldn't suffice. He had intruded on her life yet again. "You've haunted my memory since the day I last saw you. I didn't come here to intrude, and I hadn't planned to seek you out. But I've often rehearsed what I might say if we ever met again."

"And?"

"And now the words are gone. All I can offer you are hollow apologies. I shouldn't have promised you what I did—marriage—and failed to honour that promise. And I certainly should have been man enough to tell you myself, rather than leaving it to my mother."

She nodded, her expression calm but firm.

"That you should. That was what hurt most—not your broken promise, but the way you had your mother deliver the news to my father, turning it into a disgraceful negotiation. I ran upstairs and cried, cursing your name. It took time, but I eventually forgot you and your betrayal. And now, I'm glad I did."

"Glad?"

She nodded again.

"We were so young, Thomas. What did we know about the world? Perhaps we would have been happy together, but I doubt it. We're not alike—something I didn't realise during our brief, intense affair. I've never dreamt of being the mistress of a grand house, with servants and formal dinners. If I'd stayed in love with you, I would have endured it for your sake, but I'd never have liked it. You're a man of the world. I'm far more grounded."

The only words that truly reached him were: *If I had stayed in love with you.*

"Why do you think you wouldn't have stayed in love with me?"

"Oh, Thomas… We were young. You were the most handsome man I'd ever seen. You swept into my life and dazzled me. I thought it must be love, but it wasn't. It was infatuation.

"Robert, though—he's always been in my life. My earliest memories are of us playing by the stream, tossing twigs in the water and running to the other side of the bridge to see whose would arrive first. From the day he understood what love was, he gave all his to me. When you left, he was there. I told him I was already pregnant, that he couldn't possibly want me, but he did. He said he didn't care, that he would raise the child as his own. And he has.

"I didn't know what love was until Robert showed me. So yes, I'm glad for what happened. I'm glad to hear your actions tormented you—you certainly deserved it—but torment yourself no longer. From your perspective, the mayor's daughter marrying a miller might seem a great misfortune. But it isn't. I'm happy. Happier than I would have been as your duchess—or even the wife of the Prince Regent. I don't envy you, Thomas, living in a world where marriage is an agreement, not an act of love."

"So, you forgive me?"

She let out a soft, tired laugh.

"If those words mean anything to you, then yes—I forgive you. More than that, I thank you. I wouldn't undo our time together because it gave me the most precious little girl in the world."

Thomas nodded, looking away.

"What's her name?"

"Olivia."

He nodded again, his throat tightening.

"Could I—"

"No," she interrupted sharply. "You will never be part of her life, Thomas. Robert is her father, and if you ever do or say anything to make her doubt that, you'll discover what true torment is."

"I understand. But I want to help—financially, at least. I want Olivia, and you, to have a secure and comfortable life."

"My life will never be *comfortable*, Thomas, and I don't want it to be. I'm not suited to grand parlours. But I will accept your money, as security against the hard years that will surely come—droughts, poor harvests, and the like."

"Then it's agreed. I'll make the arrangements."

She nodded, rising and smoothing her dress.

"For that, I thank you. And please, Thomas, do not seek me out again. Rest assured, I'm happy. Olivia is happy."

"I promise," he said softly, watching her turn for the door.

She didn't look back. There was no smile of reconciliation, no parting glance. She simply left, shutting the door quietly behind her.

He listened to her footsteps descending the stairs, and then she was gone.

The ghost from years past had vanished.

Chapter 20

The warmth of summer had gone. When Alice took her morning walks, there was a rawness in the air that left no doubt about the season. This morning, she followed the path along the fields at the edge of the woods. A fine drizzle fell, and fog hung low over the stubbled fields like a collapsed cloud. It was October. Nearly three months had passed since the ordeal in London, and every childish hope she had clung to—hopes for miracles to bring happiness back into her life—had withered, turning as bleak as the mist around her.

Alice rarely spoke of her time in London, but those who knew her well could see she was still hurting. At Lucinda's insistence, she had confided why she seemed "so gloomy" all the time. Lucinda had sighed, rolled her eyes, and told Alice not to be such a goose for thinking a duke would look at her twice—at least not with honest intent.

"Why bother with childish dreams when you hold the heart of the younger Mr Evans in your hands? It's time to grow up,"

Lucinda had said. "Haven't you heard that our brother George is courting a girl in London? A daughter of a member of Parliament, no less. It's serious—he'll surely marry soon. Do you really want to be at Longhall when George inherits it, being a burden to everyone? I certainly don't. I'll make Mr Evans's rectory the most wonderful of homes and return to Longhall only as a most appreciated guest. Granted, his rectory won't be as fine as his brother's, but with some care and improvements, it'll do well enough. Be reasonable, sister. I don't see suitors lining up to offer for your hand."

Lucinda was right, of course. George would have no trouble securing a wife of good standing, and Longhall couldn't be Alice's home forever. Yet what she hadn't told Lucinda—what she admitted only to herself—was that she would rather live alone in a cabin in the woods than spend her life with Ben Evans.

At least the reign of Lucinda and Mr Evans had ended with Mrs Weatherby's return from London. At dinner that evening, Mrs Weatherby took her rightful place at the foot of the table, shooting Mr Evans a sharp look when he tried to sit at the head. Blushing, he retreated to the chair on Mrs Weatherby's right, relinquishing his imaginary power.

The efforts to secure the rectory resumed, and according to Lucinda, they would move in before Christmas.

Jolly.

Later that evening, Alice's mother handed her a letter from London, smiling ambiguously. Alice's heart swelled with hope—it was from Thomas.

It wasn't. Of course it wasn't. It was from Mary.

Alice read it by the fire in the drawing room.

Dearest Cousin,

A great blessing has been bestowed upon us! Simon is no longer in danger of bankruptcy. Mr Stockton appears to be missing vital documents regarding the merger, including one bearing Simon's signature. I'm ashamed to admit it, but the very day we heard of this, we burned Simon's copies in the fireplace. Perhaps we needn't have, as there's evidence the board of Mr Stockton's company never approved the merger. Apparently, Mr Stockton forged his father's signature—his father being the chairman of the board!

I'm sorry if this explanation seems muddled; I don't fully understand the workings of business. But everything is now as it should be, and I thank the good Lord for this miracle. Simon, bless him, initially believed Mr Stockton had come to his senses and done the honourable thing. However, a visit to the man himself quickly dispelled that notion.

Mr Stockton ranted about stolen documents, claiming someone had forced open his desk and that he'd seen a man in a tattered bowler hat fleeing down the street. He even threatened to send Simon to prison! But now that the forgery has been uncovered, it's Mr Stockton who may face jail, not Simon.

I've wanted to write for weeks but waited until the matter was resolved. Now that it is, Simon and I can proceed with our wedding! We still hope to marry at Walston Church and host the reception at Longhall. If this would weigh on you, dear cousin, considering all that has happened, I understand. Please tell Mrs Weatherby that my father will cover all the costs.

Looking forward to your reply, dearest Alice.

Yours lovingly,

Mary de Vries

P.S. Soon I'll sign my letters as Mrs Mary Carmichael! Doesn't it have a lovely ring to it?

Alice set the letter down in her lap, laughing incredulously. What magnificent news! Miracles *did* happen. She folded the letter and sprang up, filled with more life than she'd felt in months.

"Mama!" she cried, hurrying to the salon to share the good news.

Throughout the autumn, the correspondence between Hertfordshire and London grew frequent. Mr and Mrs Weatherby approved the plans for hosting the wedding reception, and in late November, Lucinda and Mr Evans moved into the much-discussed rectory. Alice felt a pang seeing the shimmer of tears in Lucinda's eyes as she left Longhall for the first time. They returned for

Christmas, joined by Mr Weatherby, home from Parliament during its recess.

He brought rumours of Mr Stockton, who had apparently fled London and his creditors. Some claimed he'd gone to the colonies; others whispered he was hiding in Bath with an uncle. Alice no longer cared about Mr Stockton's fate. What she secretly hoped for was news of Thomas—was he engaged? Married? But Mr Weatherby seemed as indifferent to the duke as Alice was to Mr Stockton. Not a single word about him was mentioned. Instead, Mr Weatherby spoke at length about Napoleon's imminent downfall.

"The esteemed Duke of Wellington sent the French running at the Nive, chasing them along the riverbank under English cannon fire. Mark my words: this war will end before spring."

"Could it truly be?" Mrs Weatherby asked. "After more than a decade of war?"

"Time has little to do with it, my dear. Wars end, and this one is nearly over."

Winter gave way to spring. Napoleon lost his war, abdicated, and was exiled to Elba. The world seemed reborn.

And, almost as important, Mary and Mr Carmichael arrived at Longhall, filling the house with laughter and joy. The younger Mr Evans, anticipating the wedding, seemed hopeful it would inspire Alice to want one of her own.

She, however, was unmoved.

This morning, while eating breakfast with Mary and Mr Carmichael, the butler informed her that Mr Ben Evans had come, asking to talk to her.

Mary shot Alice a glance over the table, knowing the only possible reason for Mr Evans's unannounced visit this early in the morning.

"Oh, dear," Mary said, putting down her fork.

"Oh, dear indeed," Alice answered.

"Oh, dear what?" Mr Carmichael asked.

"It seems that Mr Evans has come, animated by spring and his strong affections, to ask for Alice's hand in marriage."

Mr Carmichael looked between them.

"And that's not a good thing, I presume?"

"Oh, how blind you can be sometimes," Mary replied, exasperated.

"So, you are not going to accept him, then?" Mr Carmichael asked.

Alice hesitated. Even for a suitor as unwanted as Mr Evans, it felt wrong to share her answer with anyone before giving it to him directly.

"I need to hear what he has to say," she said, rising from the table.

"What could he possibly say that would change your mind?" Mary said, baffled.

"I'm not spoiled for choice, Mary. And both Mama and Papa see him as a good match. That means I owe it to them—and to myself—to hear him out."

"A *good match*?" Mary said with some acid in her voice. "Why don't they let you attend proper assemblies? At least then you'd have *some* choice."

Alice couldn't explain that it had been *her* decision to avoid assemblies. Even now, more than six months later, the loss she had suffered in London still loomed too large for her to enjoy herself at a ball. She had known love and was certain she would never find it again. That left her with two options: settle for someone who could offer her a secure, respectable life, or remain alone. She had long leaned towards the latter, though the thought of never having children tugged her in the opposite direction.

But then came the question: what sort of children would she have with Ben Evans? Complacent, self-satisfied children with no curiosity about the world, content with four walls, a roof, and a fireplace?

Sighing, she went to the vestibule, where Mr Evans stood waiting in his finest tailcoat and black boots polished to a mirror shine. His chin was raised, his expression severe, his cheeks flushed. To someone unfamiliar with him, he might have appeared angry. But Alice recognised this as his most animated and self-conscious state.

"Mr Evans," she said.

"Miss Weatherby," he replied, bowing low. "I beg your pardon for this early visit, but I can wait no longer."

"Mr Evans, I really think—"

He stepped closer, taking her hands in his and pressing them to his chest.

"No, Alice. Now it's my turn to speak. I believe you cannot have misunderstood my admiration for you, my sweet child, and I believe those feelings are reciprocated. My heart can no longer hold me back. Alice Weatherby, I—"

"Mr Evans, I—"

He put his finger over her lips, shaking his head with a smile.

"Compose yourself, my love. All in due time. Alice Weatherby, you are the woman to make me happy, to complete my home. Will you do me the immense honour of becoming my wife?"

Alice stared at him. His words were no surprise—she had known they were coming. Yet hearing them aloud made the moment starkly real. A flood of thoughts and images rushed through her mind, memories of the past—a man watching fireworks with an ambiguous smile—and a vision of her future. Answering him felt like a physical effort.

"Well?" Mr Evans prompted, his smile faltering.

"Have you asked my father?"

"Of course I have. I'm not a savage, my dear."

My dear? Was she now *his dear*? One word from her, and she would be forever.

"I thank you for your offer, Mr Evans. You do me great honour, but I need time to think about it."

"Time to think? What is there to think about?"

"As I said, it's a great honour. But what you're asking is a significant decision—the most significant of my life—and I need time."

"You behave as though my proposal is some great shock, but surely—"

"No, Mr Evans. It's no shock. But thoughts and plans are one thing; words and action are another."

"You can't mean," he said, his face paling, "that you're still waiting for that lord of yours to sweep you away on his white steed? You *cannot* mean that."

"I said no such thing!"

How did he know about that? There was only one explanation—Lucinda must have told him. Told him not to worry, that Alice would come around after her heart had healed. A heart broken by a ruthless lord who cared only for his own amusement.

"Well," he said, a thin smile on his lips, "as you yourself stated, thoughts and plans differ from words and action."

"I think you've said quite enough for one morning, Mr Evans," Alice replied, struggling to maintain her composure.

"Perhaps I have," he said, jamming his hat onto his head. "I will expect your answer by the end of the week."

He turned and left, closing the door hard behind him.

Alice stood alone in the dim vestibule, staring at the closed door. Was *this* the man she was meant to spend her life with? A man who could turn a proposal into a quarrel?

The door behind her opened, and a hand touched her shoulder.

"Please, dear Alice, don't marry that man."

She turned to see Mary and fell into her arms, tears spilling freely.

"But what am I to do?" Alice sobbed.

"Set up your own home in London," Mary said, holding her tightly. "Be near Simon and me. Become an eccentric, if you must—but don't tie yourself to that man. You're too different. He'll bring you nothing but misery."

The rest of the week dragged on, the shadow of Saturday's wedding looming ever closer. Since his proposal, Mr Evans's visits had grown less frequent, though the unspoken disapproval of her family lingered heavily. Over dinner, her parents treated her with civil, but subtly barbed, words, and Lucinda's voice had gained a distinct chill. Alice was the difficult one—the spoiled younger child throwing a tantrum because no suitor could meet her impossible expectations.

On Friday evening, Alice sat on her bed with Mary, smiling as her cousin chattered nervously. Laughter and conversation rose faintly from the drawing room below, where Mrs Weatherby's sister and her husband had arrived.

"I don't know how I'll sleep tonight," Mary said, her eyes sparkling. "Tomorrow, I'll be Mrs Carmichael."

"I'm so happy for you," Alice said, squeezing her hand.

Mary and Mr Carmichael would marry in the morning and leave for a honeymoon in the Lake District. Alice would miss her terribly—miss her confidant, miss her warmth. The house would feel colder in her absence.

And Mr Evans would expect an answer tomorrow.

When Mary broached the subject, Alice could only sigh.

"I don't know. Logic tells me it's a good solution, but my heart—and my sanity—tell me it's a terrible idea."

Mary shook her head.

"Sometimes you are blind, my dear. Thomas still holds your heart—that much is as clear as day. But that's no reason to throw yourself away on an obnoxious, self-centred buffoon. Answer me this: if you are determined to marry, why, oh why, don't you attend the assemblies and find a better option than Mr Evans?"

Alice sighed again.

"I just... can't..."

"Why not? If you can bring yourself to marry Mr Evans, surely you can manage *that*?"

"He's here. He's proposed. All I need to do is say yes, and the matter will be settled. If I attend the assemblies, I'll have to endure the courting game all over again—dancing, smiling. I've no more dances left in me, no more smiles to give. I can't force myself to do it."

"I see. Then let *me* help."

"What do you mean?"

"There are plenty of eligible young men of good birth in London, and I happen to know them. Once I'm married, you won't need a chaperone. Stay with me for a couple of months, meet them in less formal settings. If you like one, talk to him. If not, leave it to me."

"Maybe."

"Oh, don't be such a ninnyhammer. It's either yes or no. Surely it can't be harder than accepting Mr Evans tomorrow?"

"I suppose not."

"I won't press you further, dear cousin, but I also won't let the matter drop. Once I return from the Lake District, you'll come and stay with me and Mr Carmichael. We'll see what happens."

Mary spoke with the tone of finality that allowed no argument, and Alice didn't offer one.

The wedding was everything expected of a bright, joyful affair. Mary kissed Alice's cheek as she and Mr Carmichael exited the church, then climbed into their carriage. Mary waved from the window as they departed, leaving a cheering crowd behind. Among the well-wishers was Ben Evans, who smiled pleasantly at Alice.

Later, at the reception—where Mrs Weatherby had outdone herself with a dozen varieties of cake alongside tea and coffee—he approached her.

"What a lovely ceremony," he remarked, piling cognac cake and butter cookies onto his plate.

"Indeed."

"They looked so very happy."

"They did."

He gave her a sideways glance.

"Must I ask again? Surely you know the anxious anticipation I've felt, waiting for this day. Please don't torture me with your silence any longer."

He spoke as if they were alone, though they clearly were not. Alice noticed the subtle slowing of other guests at the cake table, their ears pricking as Mr Evans's words became the most intriguing offering of the day.

"This isn't the time, Mr Evans," Alice said firmly. "We'll speak after the reception, in private."

He nodded stiffly, pushing his lower lip out as he added another butter cookie to his plate.

It was near noon when the last guests departed. Mrs Weatherby sank into a sofa with a satisfied smile, clearly pleased with how well the reception had gone. Meanwhile, Mr Evans lingered.

After seeing to the final farewells, Alice asked him to join her in the garden. He agreed, bowing deeply and declaring himself "most obliged."

They strolled along the back of the house, down towards the pond and the pavilion.

"So," he said, an edge of impatience creeping into his tone, "what is your answer?"

Alice had intended to take him to the pavilion, to sit and speak with him properly before giving her decision. Yet the hurried tone in his voice—that sullen impatience so characteristic of him—made her decision clear. She stopped on the path and turned to face him.

"If you're so eager for my answer, I'll make you wait no longer. I'm grateful for your offer, Mr Evans, but I'm afraid I cannot accept."

His eyes fixed on her, unmoving.

"What?"

"I'm sorry, but we are too different. I don't believe we could make each other happy."

"I see it differently," he said, his lips tightening. "I cannot understand how you can dismiss me so lightly, considering your *limited* options. But know this: my determination is as great as my admiration. I will pursue you, Miss Weatherby, in every proper way, to prove my love is real and that I can indeed make you happy."

“I would rather you didn’t,” Alice replied, striving to keep her composure. “I have not dismissed you lightly, Mr Evans. I’ve given the matter great thought, and my decision is final.”

“You say ‘final,’ yet your words imply uncertainty. That, Miss Weatherby, is all the encouragement I need to continue my pursuit of your affection. For now, however, I bid you good day.”

He bowed stiffly, his anger evident in the rigidity of his movements, then turned and walked away.

Alice watched him go, releasing a long sigh—one she believed to be a sigh of relief.

Chapter 21

It was some weeks later, in June, when a most remarkable event occurred. For the rest of the world, the remarkable thing was that Napoleon Bonaparte, who had made an unlikely comeback, was finally defeated at Waterloo. For the Weatherbys, however, the remarkable event was a letter received by Mr Weatherby.

He carried it into the drawing room, his face slack, shoulders slumped. Alice rose from the sofa, thinking he must have received the most dreadful news. Mrs Weatherby paused her handiwork and looked up at him.

"What's the matter, dear?"

Mr Weatherby held up the letter, sealed with blue wax. "It's the seal of the Lord Chancellor himself," he mumbled.

Mrs Weatherby gasped, her hand flying to her mouth. "Then open it, for heaven's sake!"

Mr Weatherby sank heavily into his favourite chair and stared at the letter. At last, he broke the seal and unfolded the thick paper, which began to tremble in his unsteady hands.

"It seems," he said, his voice steadier than his hands, "that in the wake of this atrocious war, my financial and ongoing contributions to the war effort have been recognised. I hold in my hand a writ of summons reinstating my grandfather's baronetcy."

Mrs Weatherby let out an unabashed shriek of delight and pressed her clenched fists to her mouth. She sprang to her feet, and Mr Weatherby stood to meet her in a firm embrace. Warmth filled Alice. She knew how much this meant to her father, and seeing him achieve his lifelong goal brought tears to her eyes.

Mrs Weatherby immediately ordered Mrs Darrow to prepare the finest dinner the household could muster. Alice was in such high spirits that even the fact that a footman had been sent to summon Ben Evans for the occasion couldn't dampen her mood.

He arrived two hours before dinner, shook hands with her father, and bowed, promptly addressing him as Sir Walter and her mother as Lady Weatherby, despite their titles not being official for another month, when the baronetcy would be formally entered into the Roll of Baronetage.

Ben Evans seated himself close to Alice on the sofa, waiting for dinner to be announced, and said loudly enough for Mrs Weatherby to hear:

"What a great honour has been bestowed on your much-deserving parents."

"Indeed," Alice replied.

This was not her first encounter with Ben Evans since she had refused his suit. She had expected him to be sulky or high-strung, but instead, his demeanour was unchanged. It was as though their conversation in the garden had never happened. He had promised—or threatened, depending on one's perspective—to continue pursuing her in every proper way. Was this his method? To behave as though her rejection had never occurred? To hope his persistence would wear her down over time?

God forbid.

Lucinda and the elder Mr Evans arrived shortly after, Lucinda gushing in high, tremulous tones as she praised Sir Walter and kissed Lady Weatherby on both cheeks.

During dinner, Ben Evans seized the opportunity to rise and propose a toast to Sir Walter and Lady Weatherby. Alice knew her father didn't care for Ben's exuberant mannerisms, but that evening, he couldn't help smiling as he raised his glass in reply.

It struck Alice, not with malice but with resignation, how everything seemed to work out for those around her. Mr Carmichael had escaped financial ruin, Mary had had her wedding, and her father, after a lifetime of striving, had finally gained the title and prestige he so deeply desired. Yet her own prospects remained as bleak as ever.

Mary had been insistent that Alice should visit her for a month or two. Alice had hesitated, even more so now that the London season had begun. No matter how much Mary promised otherwise, Alice knew she would slip her invitations to balls and dinner parties.

She had no desire to attend such events. Any invitations extended to her would be mere courtesies to the Carmichaels. Her tarnished reputation would guarantee she'd be ogled and whispered about, left to stand alone by the wall, cheeks burning, wishing to be anywhere else. And the mere thought of encountering Thomas Overton at one of those balls...

But now, amidst the family's jubilant celebrations, the prospect of Mary's pleasant company seemed more inviting. That night, Alice wrote to her sister, sharing the good news and asking if the invitation still stood. Mary replied promptly, with congratulations and a line underlined twice:

Of course, dear sister! I wish for nothing else. Come as soon as you can!

A week later, accompanied by her brother George, Alice returned to London.

Mary had moved into Mr Carmichael's home, a three-storey house of honey-coloured sandstone on Park Street. She came out through the wrought-iron gate as soon as she saw Alice's carriage pull up. They embraced warmly as the coachman unloaded Alice's trunk. Mr Carmichael appeared shortly after, smiling with a mix of confusion and exhilaration at all the joy and commotion.

While two footmen carried Alice's trunk inside, Mary gave her a tour of the house. It was light-filled, with high ceilings and elegant furnishings. Alice found her trunk already in a spacious room on the second floor, where three large windows overlooked the street.

"Will it do?" Mary asked.

"It will most certainly do," Alice said, taking in the sunlit room.

"For what it's worth, I think I could stuff you into a cellar and you'd still say it was perfectly acceptable."

Alice laughed.

"Perhaps not a cellar, but I truly am glad to be here. The room is lovely, I promise."

"In that case, I'll take your word for it. I thought we might have a light lunch and then take a walk in Hyde Park, as we used to?"

Alice felt a chill at the mention of Hyde Park. She had walked there often with Mary, yes, but also with Thomas. The risk of running into him there seemed greater than anywhere else in London.

"That sounds delightful," she said, masking her unease.

Over lunch, Alice asked Mary and Mr Carmichael about their trip to the Lake District, but they were far more interested in hearing about Mr Weatherby's unexpected elevation.

"To be created a baronet isn't something that happens on a whim. Many are deserving, and to even be in contention, one must drum up considerable support for one's cause, demonstrating good standing and an impeccable reputation. Your father must have very important friends."

"I suppose he must," Alice replied, frowning slightly.

She had never heard her father speak of the possibility of being created a baronet. She knew, however, that if he saw even the slightest chance, he would pursue it relentlessly. Had he done so without her knowledge? It wasn't as though he shared all his plans with the family. Besides, he spent most of his time in London, and what he did there was largely a mystery to her.

When she entered Hyde Park with Mary, it felt as though no time at all had passed since she had last been there with Thomas. The memory of him kissing her, the fierce passion of that moment, filled her with a warmth she could not deny, even if she tried. It had been summer then. A long autumn and a harsh winter had since come and gone, and now here she was again, a gentle breeze brushing her face.

"I haven't heard much about him, if you were wondering," Mary said.

"Who?" Alice asked, though the answer was obvious.

"Oh, please."

They walked in silence for a while, Alice staring at the ground.

"The last I heard, he left London and returned to Somerfield Hall. No one has heard from him since."

"Oh," Alice murmured, uncertain what to make of the information.

Further along the path, she caught sight of familiar figures—Mr and Mrs Peters, the elderly couple who had walked with her one early morning when she had wandered into Hyde Park alone. Back then, they had been concerned for her reputation, seeing it as their duty as her elders to protect it. But the last time they met, they had looked away, refusing to acknowledge her greeting. She hadn't understood why at the time, but she did now.

Seeing them again, she hesitated, unsure how to conduct herself. In the end, she decided to act courteously. If they chose otherwise, that was on them.

As they came closer, Mrs Peters' face lit up with delight, as did her husband's.

"Miss Weatherby! How very nice to see you again. We've missed your fair face on our walks," Mr Peters said warmly. "Have you been out of town?"

"I have," Alice replied, startled by the shift in their demeanour. "I've been at the family estate in Walston."

"Ah, I see," Mrs Peters said, nodding knowingly. "A new season begins. The countryside is no place for a woman of quality."

A woman of quality? Alice thought. The last time they met, they might as well have regarded her as a succubus.

Before the Peters continued their walk, Mr Peters touched the brim of his hat and gave her a courteous nod.

As Mary and Alice walked in the opposite direction, Alice glanced at her cousin.

"Wasn't that a strange encounter?"

"Was it? Perhaps it was," Mary replied nonchalantly.

"Yes. The last time I met them, you were with me, and they wouldn't even look my way."

Mary waved a dismissive hand. "People find other things to gossip about. Perhaps they don't even remember what was said about you. Or maybe they've misremembered and think it was someone else entirely. They're old, you know."

"Yes, perhaps," Alice said, though she doubted it. The Peters might be old, but their minds were sharp.

Was it just the Peters, or had her reputation been restored in the eyes of society? The rest of their walk confirmed it was the latter. In turn, she encountered Miss Danbury, Miss Ashton, and Mrs Revere, all of whom greeted her warmly, as if the cold disdain of the past had never existed.

Her heart felt lighter, and she knew her father would be no less pleased by this shift in the Londoners' attitudes. Yet she couldn't help wondering what had brought it about.

Mary wasted no time in arranging the evening's activities. That night, they dined with a guest—Mr Andrews, a business associate of Mr Carmichael. However, it was clear his purpose that evening was something other than business. His attention to Alice brought a pleased smile to Mary's lips and courteous replies from Alice. Outwardly, she appeared every inch the young lady politely discouraging a suitor's advances to maintain the thrill of the chase. Inwardly, however, she was a bundle of nerves. She cursed Mary for putting her in this position, despite her explicit wishes to the contrary.

Yet, from Mary's perspective, how could this be anything but a kindness? Mr Andrews was far superior to Mr Evans in both appearance and manner. Why, then, did Alice feel such a strong urge to leave the table? It made no sense, but the feeling persisted. She needed time. Time to forget Thomas Overton. Time to find her footing again before she could leap into new adventures.

Time?

It had been a year. How much more time would she need? She couldn't say.

Just... more.

"...Wouldn't you agree, Miss Weatherby?"

She blinked, realising Mr Andrews was speaking to her. His pleasant smile and well-groomed appearance were a picture of refinement.

"Pardon?"

"I was congratulating you on your father's elevation. It is, by all accounts, well deserved."

"Oh. Thank you. We're all very pleased about the news." She paused. "You said 'by all accounts'? Is it much talked about?"

"Oh, indeed. A friend of mine, a member of White's, mentioned it. He heard someone say that certain lords, including Lord Blackwell, had championed your father's cause. If Lord Blackwell supports it, it must be deserved."

"Lord Blackwell," Alice repeated, looking down at her plate.

Did her father know Lord Blackwell? She had never heard him mention it. Knowing him, he would boast about such an ally. Lord Blackwell was, after all, a friend of Thomas Overton. Could this possibly be Thomas's doing? But why? Why would he help?

Her mind drifted to Mr Carmichael's miraculous escape from ruin. A man in a black bowler hat, Mary had said in her letter. Mr Stockton had been livid, claiming important documents were stolen by a man fitting that description.

"I see—" Mr Andrews began, but Alice interrupted him abruptly.

"Mary. When that private investigator came to tell you about Mr Stockton's business, what did he look like?"

Mary blinked at the sudden change of topic. "An older fellow. Scruffy, with a threadbare coat and a dusty old bowler hat that looked like he'd sat on it. He kept fiddling with it the whole time. Why?"

Alice's breath quickened.

"I need to visit Lord Blackwell," she said.

"What?" Mary gasped. "Why on earth would you do that? You can't just barge into a lord's home uninvited!"

"It can't be helped. I must."

"Good evening. My name is Alice Weatherby, and I'm an acquaintance of Lord Blackwell. I know this is uncommon, but I need to speak to Lord Blackwell on an urgent matter."

"Uncommon is the word," the butler replied in a slow drawl. "Acquainted how?"

"We have a shared friend in the Duke of Hexham."

"Oh," the butler said, raising his eyebrows slightly. "Miss Weatherby, was it?"

"Yes."

"You may wait in the vestibule," he said, stepping aside.

Alice waited in the dimly lit vestibule, her eyes straining against the gloom. She could see a thin crack of light beneath the double doors leading to the Blackwells' drawing room. The piano had stopped playing, and the chatter and laughter from within had fallen silent. Faintly, she could hear the butler's slow, deliberate tone as he spoke. Moments later, footsteps approached the door. The vestibule was suddenly flooded with light as the doors opened briefly, then closed again.

"Miss Weatherby?"

Her eyes, not yet adjusted to the gloom, recognised the voice before the figure.

"Yes, thank you so much for receiving me, Lord Blackwell. I know it's—"

"Yes, yes, how can I help you?" he interrupted, his voice gruff but not unkind.

Now she could see him clearly, the candlelight above casting a warm glow over the room.

"I have come to understand that you are responsible for reinstating my father's honour as a baronet. If you deny it, I will leave at once and trouble you no further."

"Who told you this?" he asked, his tone sharp but curious.

Alice's heart sank. *Oh, please let this not be just something Mr Andrews said to impress me. How foolish it sounds now—lords uniting in secret to support my father's cause. Stupid girl.*

"A friend," she admitted hesitantly.

"Ah, I see. And this friend heard it from another friend, who heard it from someone else, and so on?"

"Yes, quite possibly."

"And that was enough for you to immediately step into a carriage and arrive here, unannounced?"

"Apparently."

He studied her with a stern expression, his gaze unflinching. Then, to her surprise, the corner of his mouth twitched upward before his entire face broke into a smile.

"Yeees. It was me, and a few friends of mine. We put your father's name forward. Don't know the man in the slightest, but he seems decent enough."

The ground beneath Alice seemed to shift.

"But... why?"

"Why? That's a fair question, since I've never met the man. I did it for a friend, of course."

"Oh, please. What friend are you referring to?"

His expression softened, his eyes losing their sharpness.

"You don't need to ask that, Alice. There could only be one. And seeing you now, I'm glad I lent my name to further your father's cause. According to Thomas, he's worthy of the honour bestowed upon him."

Thomas. There it was, laid bare at last. She felt a wave of dizziness, her breath hitching as Lord Blackwell steadied her with a firm hand on her shoulder. She closed her eyes briefly, battling the surge of emotions—gratitude, relief, confusion, and a deep ache she thought she had buried.

"Alice? Are you quite alright?"

She opened her eyes, nodded, and managed a smile.

"Yes, very much so. I thank you dearly for this information, my lord, and I will trouble you no further."

"You've not troubled me in the slightest. In fact, this has been a rather uplifting visit. But," he added, his tone turning pointed, "considering I've done this favour for you, perhaps you could return the gesture."

"Whatever you wish, my lord."

"I want my friend back," he said simply. "Go and talk to him. Whatever needs sorting, sort it. That's all."

Chapter 22

Alice couldn't keep still. She moved from room to room, with Mary following close behind, her expression a mixture of confusion and concern.

"What do you mean, Alice? Are you saying it was the duke who resolved Simon's troubles with Mr Stockton? And the duke who ensured your father received his title?"

"Yes," Alice replied, spinning around, tears streaking her cheeks even as she smiled. "He did all of that. I must see him—to thank him for what he's done."

"Yes, I suppose you must," Mary said hesitantly. "Oh, dear. I just hope he didn't light this flame only to snuff it out."

"What do you mean?"

Mary waved a hand vaguely. "Oh, I don't know. It's just... seeing you like this—I'd do anything to make your happiness last, Alice, but who knows what men think? I just don't want you to be disappointed."

"You once told me, Mary, that I didn't see clearly what was between Thomas and me. *Daft,* I believe, was the word you used. Now I think it's you who are being daft. What other reason could he have for doing this for me, except—"

She faltered. Even now, she couldn't bring herself to say it. How pitiful.

"Yes, daft I may be," Mary replied, "but I beg you, temper your hopes. The way you two parted... it could have tarnished his sense of honour, the way he sees himself. It's possible he did all this for his own sake, not for yours."

"Then I need to ask him. I can't live with this uncertainty."

"You're talking about going to Somerfield? To his family estate?" Mary asked, her eyes widening.

"Yes, I am."

"Oh, please don't. If he truly did this for you, Alice, wouldn't he come to you?"

"There's nothing you can say, Mary, to dissuade me. This back-and-forth dance must end. I will go to him, and if he tells me he owes me nothing, then at least I'll know. I'll no longer torment myself with what could have been. I'll leave it behind for good."

More words were exchanged that evening, but none that mattered. When dawn broke, Alice found herself once more in a carriage, travelling north to Hertfordshire with Mary beside her.

"This is madness," Mary said, her lips pinched. "Madness, I say."

"Perhaps," Alice replied, staring out of the window at the rolling green hills. "But it must be done."

Her head was a whirlwind of thoughts, colliding and fracturing into more thoughts, leading her down endless alleys of hope and despair. She had barely slept, and only Mary's sharp words had kept her from leaving for Somerfield the previous night. Her head felt light, and when she closed her eyes, it was as if she were floating. She knew this wasn't how she wanted to present herself to Thomas, but it no longer mattered. She had no excuses left, no escape routes to take. Forward was the only direction, and she intended to see it through.

They would arrive at Somerfield late in the afternoon. Alice didn't argue when Mary suggested they stop at an inn for a meal. It felt like wasted time, but Mary was right—they needed to eat. Alice, however, couldn't manage more than a few bites. She had skipped breakfast entirely, and her stomach churned too violently with nerves to accommodate lunch. Mary chattered throughout the stop, her hands gesturing animatedly, but Alice heard none of it. Her thoughts crowded her mind, leaving no room for anything else. Eventually, even Mary fell silent.

When they were on their way again, the sun had begun its descent, casting long shadows across the landscape. They turned off the main road and entered the private drive leading to Somerfield Hall. The path wound through a serene beech forest, its floor blanketed with the brittle leaves of many autumns, resembling the vast hall of a cathedral. The forest gave way to farmland, where green fields stretched to the horizon.

The road dipped through another copse of trees, and when they emerged once more into sunlight, Alice saw the manor house in the distance. It stood by a lake, framed by an oak-lined gravel road. Its façade glowed softly in the light of the setting sun. Its proportions were so perfectly balanced that it wasn't until they drew closer that Alice realised how enormous the house truly was.

"Oh, would you look at that," Mary said, leaning closer to the window. "Isn't it the most magnificent house you've ever seen?"

Alice nodded absently, her thoughts no longer on the manor. Instead, she was picturing herself climbing those broad steps, knocking on the grand doors, and facing yet another butler's cold, disdainful gaze.

The carriage wheels grated to a stop, leaving behind a silence so heavy it was almost deafening.

Mary looked at Alice. "Well, we're here."

Alice nodded, placing a trembling hand on the door handle. Her heart raced as she exhaled deeply. She felt Mary's hand on her shoulder.

"Soon you'll have your answer."

Alice nodded again, then pushed the carriage door open. Stepping down onto the gravel, she looked up at the imposing manor that seemed to loom over her. She ascended the broad steps and stood before the massive double doors, each twice her height.

If she hesitated, she knew she might never find the courage to proceed. Seizing the gilded stag's head knocker, she struck it against the door.

The hollow sound echoed ominously. The seconds that followed stretched into what felt like an eternity. Just as she began to think no one was home, the door creaked open.

A tall, young butler stood before her, his expression neutral but his raised eyebrow hinting at disdain.

"Good evening," Alice began. "My name is Alice Weatherby. I'm here to speak with his grace, and—"

"Highly inappropriate, Miss Weatherby," the butler interrupted crisply. "One does not simply arrive at Somerfield Hall as if it were a common inn. This is the ancestral home of the Overton family. If the duke is to be disturbed, it is only by his peers, and at proper visiting hours, accompanied by a suitable chaperone—a male relative, for example—who can speak for you."

Alice blinked, momentarily stunned. "I—"

"Is that understood?" the butler pressed. "It's a simple yes or no question."

Before she could answer, a woman's voice floated out from the hall, causing the butler to straighten to attention.

"Declan, who is it?"

"A young lady, Duchess," the butler replied over his shoulder. "Wishing to speak with his grace."

"A young lady, you say?"

A slender hand rested briefly on the butler's shoulder, prompting him to step aside. Into the doorway stepped a tall woman with iron-grey hair and a wasp-like waist, dressed in a severe yet elegant gown. Her beauty was cold and imperious, her features regal and timeless. She regarded Alice with a thin smile, her gaze sweeping her from head to toe.

"He told me you would come."

Alice's breath caught. "He did?"

The woman raised an eyebrow, her thin smile deepening. "*He did?* Is that truly how you intend to greet me?"

Alice flushed. "I beg your pardon. Lady Overton, I presume?" She curtsied awkwardly. "My name is Alice Weatherby."

"Close enough, my dear. But if we are to be precise, it is the Dowager Duchess of Hexham. Though I see no need to be pedantic about it." She waved a dismissive hand. "Yes, Thomas told me you would come, and he asked me to deliver you a message: enough is enough."

Alice blinked, her mind reeling.

"Oh, don't look so dejected, child," the dowager continued. "This is what men do. They play their little games, like overgrown boys, acting on whims and impulses. Quite unlike us women, who shoulder our responsibilities with grace and fortitude." Her voice was smooth but laced with condescension.

Alice opened her mouth to reply, but the Dowager Duchess raised a hand to forestall her.

"Let us not pretend, Miss Weatherby. You have been richly compensated for any discomfort you may have endured. My son does not lend his good name lightly, and that he did so on behalf of your father is no small matter. Surely, you cannot ask for more than that?"

Alice barely heard her words, the dowager's cold dismissal washing over her like a numbing wave. "Maybe I can't," she murmured, more to herself than to the woman before her.

"You most certainly cannot," the Dowager Duchess said firmly. "There will be no further intrusions into our lives, Miss Weatherby. You have received your due—and then some. Now, I bid you good evening."

With that, she stepped back and closed the door.

Alice stood motionless, swaying slightly, her eyes shut as the enormity of the moment crushed down upon her. Slowly, she turned and descended the steps, her legs feeling as though they might give way beneath her. She returned to the carriage, where Mary sat waiting, her face a mixture of apprehension and sympathy.

"Alice?" Mary began gently.

Alice didn't reply. She climbed into the carriage and sat down, her movements mechanical, as though her spirit had been stripped from her body.

Mary reached for her hand, squeezing it tightly. "I'm so sorry, Alice. I truly am.

Chapter 23

Alice sat in the drawing room at Longhall House, the relentless ticking of the clock in the corner marking the passage of time. Outside, the sun shone brightly in an unblemished blue sky, and butterflies flitted lazily from flower to flower. But Alice noticed none of it.

She stabbed her needle through the cloth of her embroidery, piercing her finger. The pain was distant and dull, not even eliciting a flinch. Across from her, Lady Weatherby and Lucinda exchanged another of their many concerned glances.

At first, they had been perplexed by Alice's abrupt change in demeanour. When she had left for Mary's, she had seemed to be on the mend, but upon her return from London, she was worse than ever. It was as though she had become a fortress—a sad, locked castle with its drawbridge raised and its gates firmly bolted.

She answered questions politely, even smiled occasionally, but her expressions were tired and hollow, her voice distant. Lady Weatherby and Lucinda were deeply troubled. Then Mary's letter arrived, detailing what Alice—the foolish girl—had done, and everything became clear.

Though Alice's impulsive journey to Somerfield Hall warranted a scolding, neither Lady Weatherby nor Lucinda had the heart to deliver it. Instead, they spoke in private.

"I expected better of my little sister," Lucinda had said. "I thought she had more sense than to chase dukes like a naive fourteen-year-old who's read her first romantic novel. Will she ever grow up, Mother?"

"She might," Lady Weatherby had replied, "in time. Perhaps this was the harsh lesson she needed. It may yet ground her once and for all."

But there was another question that lingered between them—would Alice ever be herself again? For over a week, she remained withdrawn, the drawbridge to her emotions firmly raised. The thought that they might never again hear her laugh or see her face light up with joy cast a shadow over the household.

Even Wilma, sensing the gloom, avoided spending time with the women. She played by herself and declared that they were "no fun at all."

Not even Ben Evans, despite seeing an opportunity to resume his courtship of Alice, could endure the stifling silence at Longhall House. His visits became increasingly rare.

By the second week of Alice's return, July had given way to August, and another summer was drawing to a close. One afternoon, a rider appeared on the road leading to Longhall House. Lady Weatherby was the first to notice.

"Oh, who might that be?" she said, stretching her neck as if it might help her see the figure more clearly. "It looks like a gentleman."

Alice turned her head to the window, and it was as though fireworks exploded inside her mind. She would recognise that figure anywhere. It was Thomas. Her breath caught, and she lowered her embroidery to her lap, holding it as if it might steady her.

"It's him," Lucinda mumbled. "the Duke of Hexham. Why, I—"

Both women turned to Alice.

"Do you know what this is about, Alice?" Lady Weatherby asked.

Alice shook her head, breathing deeply through her nose. She watched as Thomas reined in his horse and dismounted. Rising abruptly from the sofa, she ran upstairs to the library.

Once there, she paced back and forth, her arms wrapped around herself. She felt as if she might be sick. She heard the knock at the door, followed by the low murmur of her father's voice. Then Thomas's voice, familiar yet jarring in its immediacy, confirmed his presence downstairs.

She froze, listening to the cadence of his words. The floorboard beneath her creaked as she resumed pacing, the noise eventually drawing her father out of his study.

"What is going on?" he demanded, his face a mixture of irritation and concern.

"I'm sorry, Papa," Alice said quickly.

"Not that I'm unhappy to see you up and moving, but what is all this pacing about?"

"It's him, Papa. He's downstairs."

"Him?"

She nodded, her face pale.

Her father's features darkened. "In my house?"

"Oh, Papa, please don't be cross with him. I didn't tell you, but he's the reason you got your grandfather's title back."

He stared at her. "What?"

In a breathless rush, she recounted everything she had learned in London and her meeting with Lord Blackwell. As she spoke, her father's severe expression softened.

"I see," he said at last, looking away, his face stunned. "I don't understand why he would… considering the things I said to him the last time we met. What is his angle?"

Before Alice could answer, there was the sound of rapid footsteps on the stairs. Lucinda joined them, her face bewildered.

"It's the Duke of Hexham, Papa. He wants to talk to Alice."

"He does, does he?" her father said, his tone firm with new resolve. "Well, he'll talk to me first."

He descended the stairs, each creak of the wood amplifying Alice's anxiety. She strained to hear the conversation below but could only make out muffled tones. Finally, a door shut, and all was silence.

She resumed pacing, her nerves taut as a bowstring.

Half an hour passed before her father returned. His face revealed nothing.

"I think you need to speak to him, Alice."

She nodded, taking a moment to collect herself before descending the stairs, her father's heavy steps following close behind.

At the bottom of the stairs, there he was—Thomas—standing in a wedge of sunlight from the window. His face bore an expression that flickered between sorrow and hope, and she felt a strange sense of strength at the sight of it. At least he wasn't indifferent to her.

"Miss Weatherby," he said, bowing slightly. "I apologise for arriving unannounced."

"Don't apologise," she replied, her voice unsteady. "It's a habit of mine as well."

The corner of his mouth twitched, almost forming a smile. "So I've heard. Will you walk with me? Just in the garden? I know you told me you wanted nothing more to do with me, but I ask you—please oblige me."

She nodded, her breath catching. "Yes. I will."

They stepped into the garden together, the gravel crunching softly beneath their feet. The late afternoon sun cast long shadows across the manicured lawns, and the scent of roses hung heavy in the air. Alice was acutely aware of her mother and sister's watchful eyes from the drawing room window, but she ignored them, focusing on Thomas instead.

"Once again, Miss Weatherby," Thomas began, his voice low and steady, "I apologise for arriving unannounced. I promised not to trouble you again, and I am a man who values his word. However, when I heard you had come to Somerfield wishing to speak to me, I realised the situation had changed. It seemed only fair to grant you the opportunity to say whatever it was you intended."

"I see," Alice said softly.

They walked in silence for a few moments, the gentle rustle of leaves and the distant chirping of birds filling the void.

"I'm sorry," Thomas said suddenly, breaking the quiet. "That sounded formal—too formal. I seem to lose my way entirely in your company."

"Ah, the fleeting character again," Alice said, attempting a smile.

"Yes," he said, his lips twitching upward briefly.

Alice took a deep breath, trying to steady the chaos of her thoughts. For one burning moment, she couldn't even remember why she had gone to Somerfield. All she could recall was the desperate hope that had propelled her there—the hope that he felt for her what she could no longer deny she felt for him. But then there was the memory of his mother, icy and implacable, extinguishing that hope.

"Yes, it's true. I came to Somerfield to speak with you, but you weren't there. It was a foolish thing to do, I know, and there's no need to scold me for it." She hesitated, then added, "I only wanted to thank you, Your Grace, for what you did for my father. And perhaps also for my cousin Mary and Mr Carmichael."

"You needn't thank me," Thomas said gently. "I was glad to do it."

"How did you manage it?" she asked, her voice barely above a whisper.

Thomas hesitated, as though considering how much to reveal. "The Prince Regent and I… well, we have something of a history. The crown owes my family a substantial sum from the war. Helping me in this matter—granting your father the recognition he deserved—was a small favour to restore good relations between us. It cost the Prince nothing but gained him much in my regard."

"You put my father's name forward to the Prince of Wales?"

"I did," Thomas admitted, "and I asked a few friends to spread word of your father's merits. He will find that his name is held in high regard when he next returns to London."

Alice felt her eyes fill with tears. "I'm most grateful, my lord. To think that you—"

"Please," Thomas interrupted gently, his voice softening. "Stop calling me that. If my efforts on your father's behalf have earned me any favour with you, let it be this: call me Thomas again."

"As you wish," she said, her voice breaking slightly. She dipped into a curtsy, and when she straightened, she saw him smile—a genuine, warm smile that seemed to thaw something deep within her.

"And as for why I did it," Thomas continued, his expression growing serious, "you know the reason, Alice. I needn't declare my love for you again, for it has never wavered. In every way I can, I will prove my devotion to you, until you have no reason to doubt my sincerity or the depth of my feelings."

"I—" she began, but her words were cut off by the sound of approaching hooves.

Both turned towards the house just as two riders entered the yard. It was the Evans brothers.

Alice's stomach dropped. *Oh, for the love of God…*

The Evans brothers dismounted near the stables, their curious gazes locking on Alice and Thomas as they walked towards the garden.

"You were expecting company?" Thomas asked, his tone carefully neutral.

Alice shook her head, flustered. "Oh, it's… It's the Evans brothers. The elder one is married to my sister, and the younger…" She trailed off, her discomfort evident.

"I see," Thomas said curtly, his jaw tightening. "It seems I've made a mistake in coming here unannounced. I shouldn't have put you in this position. I beg your pardon."

He turned as if to leave, but Alice instinctively reached out and grabbed his hand.

"No, Thomas. Don't go. The position you've put me in—I don't mind it in the slightest. In fact, it's everything I've wished for."

"It is?"

"It is. I'm so very glad you came. I know your mother doesn't approve, so I'm grateful you defied her to be here."

"My mother," Thomas said with a sigh. "Whatever she said to you, I apologise."

"You don't know?"

He shook his head. "She didn't mention your visit. I only heard about it from a stable boy recently. When I confronted her, she admitted it but refused to say why you had come."

"I didn't tell her. She made it clear from the start that I was unwelcome."

Thomas's expression darkened. "I can imagine. But I assure you, if you ever visit Somerfield again, she will receive you as though you were the Queen herself."

Alice's lips parted in surprise. She couldn't fathom such a change in the Dowager Duchess. But the idea that Thomas had fought such a battle for her stirred something profound within her.

"Much has happened since we last met, Alice. It's difficult to see clearly when your mind is fogged by past sorrows. It's like carrying a pack that grows heavier with each step. At some point, you'll buckle and fall to your knees. I've been there. I've reached my lowest point—when I shamed you so terribly at the ball. I wallowed in self-contempt, and the only way forward was to face my past. You see, you're not the first woman I've hurt, and my history stood in the way of what could have been between us."

He spoke of Leana then, recounting the guilt and shame that had eroded him over the years, like water dripping steadily onto stone, corroding his thoughts and making him bitter. He explained how he had sought her out, how she had forgiven him, and how that forgiveness had set him on the path to redemption.

"It doesn't erase the shame," he admitted, "but it lightens the burden of guilt. It's given me a narrow path to walk—a path back to the man I could have been, had I been stronger. I'm walking that path now."

Alice's heart was heavy with his words, but before she could respond, the gravel crunched underfoot, heralding the arrival of the Evans brothers. She had no choice but to make the introductions.

"Mr and Mr Evans, may I present Thomas Overton, the Duke of Hexham."

The elder Mr Evans paled, sweeping off his hat and bowing deeply.

"Your Grace! A most distinguished honour."

The younger Mr Evans stood frozen, staring at Alice with his mouth half-open. She turned away, unable to bear the sight of his awkwardness—standing there like a fish gasping for air. His brother, sensing the moment's impropriety, grabbed his arm.

"We'll intrude no further," he said hastily, and the two retreated towards the house.

Alice turned back to Thomas, aware that they were once again being watched from the drawing-room window.

"What I'm trying to say, Alice," Thomas continued, his voice steady, "is that I've spent my time away from you clearing every obstacle that might stand between us. I've worked tirelessly to secure our estates in the north—they are now financially sound. I need not marry you for money, and I trust your father's hunger for honour has been somewhat appeased by his new title. If I marry you, it will only be for love."

"You're talking about… marriage?"

"I am." He took her hands, his thumbs brushing gently across the backs of them. "I don't know if I've done enough to change your opinion of me, but I love you, Alice Weatherby. I cannot live without you. With you, everything is light and full of promise; without you, only darkness remains. Will you do me the honour of becoming my wife?"

Tears blurred her vision as she placed a trembling hand over her mouth and nodded.

"Yes," she whispered. "I would like that very much."

He pulled her closer, and she rose onto her toes as their lips met in a tender kiss. Alice's heart swelled, and in that moment, it felt as if all the jagged edges in her life had smoothed, and every tangled thread had straightened.

"They're watching us," she said with a smile as they reluctantly parted.

"Let them," Thomas replied with a grin. "I've already spoken to your father and secured his blessing. There's no escaping me now, Miss Weatherby."

When they returned to the drawing room, Alice felt as though she were floating. Her emotions teetered between laughter and tears, so she allowed herself both. She dried her eyes, took Thomas's hand, and walked inside.

Lady Weatherby leapt up from the sofa, her hands flapping as she cried out in joy.

"Oh, I always knew it! You were destined for each other from the very moment I first saw you together!" She embraced Alice tightly, then seized Thomas's hand in both of hers, shaking it fervently. "Welcome to the family, Your Grace!"

"I think you can call me Thomas now, Lady Weatherby."

"I will! I will!" she gushed.

Sir Walter approached next, his handshake firm but measured.

"It was a winding path, my boy, but we've reached the destination. No more needs to be said, except to echo my wife—welcome to the family. I trust Alice will be equally well-received into yours."

"She will be, Sir Walter. You have my word."

Lucinda, looking utterly bewildered by the turn of events, managed a curtsy. Thomas took her hand, bowing slightly.

"No more formality," he said warmly. "You are my beloved sister now."

Her lips curved into a small smile, and she inclined her head in appreciation.

In contrast, Ben Evans sat stiffly, his face a study in barely concealed conflict. Alice recognised the struggle—the disappointment of a rejected suitor battling the temptation to curry favour with a duke. Unsurprisingly, the latter won out. Rising from his seat, he made a deep bow, as though presenting himself at court.

Thomas returned the gesture with a polite nod, and Alice suppressed a laugh.

Chapter 24

The wedding at Walston Church was a grand affair, with esteemed guests arriving from far and wide. They marvelled at the radiant bride and the evident devotion of the groom. The only oddity was the absence of the groom's mother, but it wasn't a topic that lingered in conversation.

After the vows were exchanged and the couple emerged from the church, smiling and waving, a hearty cheer erupted from the crowd. They stepped into their carriage, bound for a three-month honeymoon in Italy.

Their time in Italy felt like a dream to Alice, filled with sun-drenched days, breathtaking sights, and the villa Thomas had once called his sanctuary. But all dreams must end, and by late September, they returned to England, heading for Somerfield Hall.

The golden leaves on the trees glowed in the warm autumn sunlight, though Alice couldn't shake the apprehension that tightened her chest.

"Will your mother be there?" she asked.

"I believe so," Thomas replied. "Even her pride has its limits. She no longer lives at Somerfield but in a smaller house nearby. I suspect she has realised she still wants to be part of this family. But make no mistake, Alice—you are the mistress of Somerfield Hall now."

As the carriage approached Somerfield Hall, the grandeur of the estate came into view. The manor's stately facade glowed in the soft light of the late afternoon sun, its windows glinting like jewels. Alice clutched Thomas's hand tightly, her apprehension palpable.

In the courtyard, a line of servants awaited their arrival, their aprons and caps fluttering in the gentle breeze. At the head of the group stood the Dowager Duchess, her back straight, her head held high, and her expression as unreadable as ever. Not a hair was out of place.

Thomas helped Alice down from the carriage, keeping her hand in his as they approached his mother. The dowager's eyes flicked to Alice, her mouth tensing.

"Your Grace," she said, inclining her head. "It's good to see you looking well, Duchess. I shan't stay long, but I wanted to personally hand over the keys to Somerfield Hall."

She extended a keyring, the weight of it clear in her stiff arm. Alice hesitated before taking it, lowering her head slightly in acknowledgment.

"Don't bow to her," Thomas said, his tone firm but quiet. "You outrank her now, my love."

The dowager's lips thinned, though she managed a faint smile. "Ah, always so particular about rank and formality, my son. You have every right to be disappointed in me, but I hope that in time, you can put the past behind you."

"I already am," Thomas replied evenly.

The dowager's composure faltered for a moment. She dipped her head, and when she spoke again, her voice was softer. "I rarely apologise, but I must do so now. I regret not attending your wedding. I allowed my pride and stubbornness to rule me, and for that, I am truly sorry. I hope you'll accept my well wishes for your future happiness."

"I accept your wishes, Mother," Thomas said, though his tone remained guarded.

Alice, sensing the tension between them, reached out and took the dowager's hand in hers. Smiling warmly, she said, "Thank you, Your Grace. I too regret your absence at the wedding, but I hope you'll make amends by becoming a frequent visitor here."

A tremor ran through the dowager's jaw, and her eyes glistened momentarily before she blinked the moisture away. "I would wish for nothing more," she said quietly.

"Perhaps tomorrow, you could join me to review the running of the household?" Alice suggested, her voice kind.

The dowager glanced at Thomas, who gave her a small nod. "If you would come, we would both be glad," he said.

Finally, mother and son embraced, the dowager clinging to Thomas as though she feared he might slip away. Watching them, Alice felt a warmth in her chest. Whatever battles they had fought, it seemed a truce was finally at hand.

After the dowager departed in her carriage, Alice and Thomas turned their attention to the line of waiting servants. Alice greeted each one personally, her smile genuine as she exchanged kind words. But when she reached the butler—Declan—she paused. He stood stiffly, staring straight ahead, a bead of sweat trailing down his temple. The memory of his cold dismissal when she had first arrived at Somerfield flashed through her mind.

Alice said nothing to him, moving on without acknowledgment. Thomas noticed her slight hesitation but didn't comment. When they were alone later, she would explain her decision: she wouldn't wield her authority lightly, but Declan's presence in her home was untenable. She would see him replaced with someone kinder and more suited to the role.

Inside Somerfield Hall, Alice marvelled at the grand interiors as they ascended to the third floor. They stopped at a window overlooking the terraced gardens, where rows of hedges framed hidden fountains and stone benches. Alice leaned her head against Thomas's shoulder, taking in the beauty of the scene.

"So," Thomas said, a smile in his voice, "when are we going to tell my mother about the baby?"

Alice turned to him, her cheeks flushing as she placed a hand on her belly. "One step at a time, darling. One step at a time."

Printed in Great Britain
by Amazon

59615414R00205